WEDDING PRESENT

Whitney's room in Keith and Becca's house resembled Garrett's office, but the perpetrator for this crime had used a knife instead of a blunt object. Everything was slashed. Whitney's black luggage, the pillows, and the curtains had jagged rips running down their lengths. It had been decorated like a shiny peach bordello turned into a set for a slasher film. The downy apricot bedspread spewed feathers from a wide gash in the middle, as if a flock of geese had duked it out in this room.

But the worst of it was reserved for her wedding dress. The garment bag that had carefully preserved the gown she was to be married in was ripped diagonally from one shoulder to the ground, leaving the bag and the gown within it in tatters. I couldn't touch the gown, but I could see it hanging open in front, a strip torn through the middle, right where Whitney's stomach would have been had she been wearing it. The delicate stark white sheath, covered in silver beads and seed pearls, was beyond repair. And sticking out above the dress, where the wearer's head would be, was a note cleaved to the door by a butcher's knife. It was printed with the message:

GO BACK TO BALTIMORE

Books by Stephanie Blackmoore

ENGAGED IN DEATH

MURDER WEARS WHITE

Published by Kensington Publishing Corporation

Murder Wears White

Stephanie Blackmoore

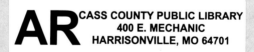

KENSINGTON PUBLISHING CORP.
http://www.kensingtonbooks.com

KENSINGTON BOOKS are published by

Kensington Publishing Corp.
119 West 40th Street
New York, NY 10018

All Kensington Titles, Imprints, and Distributed Lines are available at special quantity discounts for bulk purchases for sales promotions, premiums, fund-raising, and educational or institutional use. Special book excerpts or customized printings can also be created to fit specific needs. For details, write or phone the office of the Kensington special sales manager: Kensington Publishing Corp., 119 West 40th Street, New York, NY 10018, attn: Special Sales Department, Phone: 1-800-221-2647.

Kensington and the K logo Reg. U.S. Pat & TM Off.

ISBN-13: 978-1-4967-0480-1
ISBN-10: 1-4967-0480-0
First Kensington Mass Market Edition: February 2017

eISBN-13: 978-1-4967-0481-8
eISBN-10: 1-4967-0481-9
First Kensington Electronic Edition: February 2017

10 9 8 7 6 5 4 3 2 1

Printed in the United States of America

For Jon

Chapter One

"So you'll do it?" Whitney Scanlon stared at me with beseeching brown eyes and blinked back a fresh batch of tears. "He only has a couple months left."

Could I do it? Could I move her wedding up eight months and finish renovating my mess of a mansion in time to host her wedding? I looked away from her penetrating gaze and glanced around the room. The furniture in the parlor, including the couch we sat on, was covered with grimy drop cloths. Cans of paint and piles of lumber littered the room. The hum of a buzz saw filled the air, and enough sawdust coated the floor to transform it into a sandy beach. My lead contractor, Jesse Flowers, had promised he'd finish the job by the end of October, and I'd taken his word on it.

I drew in a deep breath, coughed on some dust, and plunged in.

"Of course!"

Whitney enveloped me in a swift and fierce hug. "I knew it, I just knew it! My dad will be so happy to walk me down the aisle." Her tears came freely, and I smiled as I returned her embrace.

Jesse ducked under the arched doorway and stuck his head in the room. He gave me an incredulous stare and mouthed, "You're killing me."

I stuck out my tongue over Whitney's shoulder. "We'll make sure your dad sees you get married." But my assurance faltered when I saw the disorder. It was one thing to promise the B and B would be ready in four weeks. Quite another thing to deliver. At least the weather would cooperate for Whitney. It was a picture-perfect October in Port Quincy, Pennsylvania. Leaves from ginkgo trees fluttered to the ground like golden fortune cookies, and each day the sun hung like a medallion in a brilliant cornflower-blue sky. Mellow smoke from wood-burning fireplaces perfumed the air, and geese practiced for their long flights south. Evenings were crisp and cool and clear, and if I could pull this wedding off, the grounds would be a gorgeous backdrop for a cozy and elegant party. *If* I could pull it off.

And I would pull it off. Whitney's father was dying. His last wish was to walk his daughter down the aisle, and he wouldn't be around for her original wedding date in June. Hers would be the first wedding held at my work-in-progress B and B, the official launch of my wedding-planning business.

What would have been the first wedding in December was for an exacting bridezilla who was already running me ragged. Just like when I was an attorney, I couldn't cherry-pick my clients. I was delighted to kick off my new career working with a bride like Whitney. No matter that I'd broken out in a cold sweat when she called this morning. I had nowhere acceptable to meet her. In the end, I'd shaken some dust off the couch in the parlor and decided Whitney should know what she was getting into.

I felt dumpy in the makeshift outfit I'd thrown on for my impromptu meeting. I'd shed my dingy overalls and slipped into a wrinkled turquoise sheath dress mere minutes before Whitney's arrival. I'd gained back all of the weight I'd lost for my canceled wedding, and then some, and the dress didn't quite fit.

"I've never seen you in a dress," Jesse had mused as I descended the stairs to meet Whitney. His lined face twisted into an amused smile, as if he'd caught me playing dress-up. The other workers stared at me like I was an alien as I twirled my curly sandy ponytail into a messy bun and jammed my feet into kitten heels. I'd worked alongside them since late summer, and they'd never seen me in anything but cargo pants or filthy denim, with my hair protected under a bandana or baseball cap. I smoothed out some wrinkles in the cotton fabric and vowed to look more presentable for clients.

"Thanks for coming through for me." Whitney beamed, seemingly impervious to the chaos. She dabbed at her mascara with a tissue she'd extracted from her tiny plum purse. Everything about her was diminutive. She was my height, five foot nothing, but much tinier and bird-like. She had delicate features and loose, strawberry-blond curls. She radiated strength, despite her apparent fragility.

"Excuse me, Mallory?" Jesse loomed over me and shattered my reverie. "There's a problem with the bathroom in the green bedroom. I thought you'd like to know. *Right now.*" He must want to grill me for promising this place would be wedding-ready in four weeks.

I shrugged in apology to Whitney.

"It's okay. I'd better get going. I'm so thrilled you can move up the wedding. It means the world to me that my father will be there. You're a lifesaver, Mallory." She rose to her feet and carefully navigated her way around the flotsam and jetsam of hardware in her path to the front hall.

"Let's meet later next week. We'll have a lot to do to plan your wedding in such a short amount of time." I crossed my fingers behind my back and made a wish to magically fix up a professional space amid the mess for meeting with her next time.

Whitney turned back to look at me. Her eyes sparkled, immune to the reality of renovation hell. She turned to leave as the massive front door swung open ahead of her. It was Garrett Davies, the delectable man I'd been seeing. His face brightened when he saw me over Whitney's shoulder, and his warm hazel eyes crinkled at the corners. He held a large brown bag bursting with lunch for me and the contractors. The gentle autumn sun backlit his tall frame, creating a pleasing silhouette. I was about to introduce him to Whitney, but she froze. Then she took a panicked step back and faltered on her high heels. She collided with me, and Garrett dropped the bag, moving forward to steady her. Sandwiches and soup spilled onto the floor. A pumpkin pie wobbled, flipped, and landed with a resounding splat.

"Ouch!" Whitney yelped as a splash of hot liquid marred her suede boots. She stifled a cry and scrambled away from Garrett. "You! What are you doing here?" Her voice was brittle and shrill and threatened to smash into a thousand pieces. She blanched as if she'd seen a ghost and blinked at Garrett in disbelief.

My breath caught in my chest as I saw her initial look of fear turn to pure, white-hot contempt. All of her effervescent happiness was gone, replaced with a deep look of dismay.

Whitney murmured an apology and slipped out the door. Once she'd put some distance between her and Garrett, she seemed to recover enough to feign politeness and call over her shoulder, "Thanks again, Mallory! We'll talk soon." She nearly ran down the drive to her Jetta and didn't look back.

The unfinished B and B hadn't rattled her, but seeing my new beau nearly drove her apoplectic.

"I don't blame her." Garrett tried to salvage what was left of lunch. He crouched down in the hallway in his three-piece suit and mopped up steaming, fragrant puddles of potato and chive soup.

He was one of the few people who could manage to look sexy cleaning up remnants of lunch, and I would've enjoyed the view if I hadn't been so rattled by Whitney's reaction. I wiped the wax-paper-wrapped sandwiches and distributed them to the contractors. My stomach growled as I mourned the loss of half of lunch. Garrett and I settled on the top step of the front porch to dig in. It was a cool day, but the sun warmed our faces and the wind was still.

I couldn't enjoy the weather, remembering Whitney's bizarre behavior. "She nearly fainted when she saw you. I wasn't sure if she was going to deck you or run away."

Garrett put down his turkey on rye and turned to face me. "Ten years ago I defended the man convicted of murdering Whitney's mother." He winced at the word "convicted," no doubt wishing, even now, that there had been a different outcome. Ever the defense attorney, he didn't say the man who *murdered* Whitney's mother.

"It was my very first homicide case. If I could go back in time, I'd do it all differently. But I knew then, and I know now, that Eugene Newton is innocent. Someone else killed Vanessa Scanlon, and they're probably still at large." He shivered.

"If you believe your client is innocent, then he is." I gently laid my hand on his arm and winced at the toll my attempts at construction had taken. My left thumb was blackened by an ill-aimed hammer, and the skin was rough and raw. I was clumsy, and many hours of working on the house hadn't made me more handy. Mine were hardly the hands of a professional wedding planner.

"But I understand Whit's reaction."

Garrett was still beating himself up about the trial from years ago. Not for the first time, I wished we could spend more time together. I had been busy with the renovation, and Garrett had his own commitments to his cases and his young daughter, Summer. We had yet to go out on an official date, and I doubted we'd spend much time together now that I'd promised to deliver a wedding to Whitney in mere weeks.

Garrett took my hand and shook his head. "That poor girl insisted on attending the whole trial. She was fifteen. Her mother's murder was particularly brutal, and she heard every detail. I couldn't imagine if Summer had to go through something like that. I'll never forget Whitney's face, and I bet she'll never forget mine."

My heart ached for Whitney. But I was still having trouble processing her reaction to Garrett. Did everyone in Port Quincy know about Whitney's mother?

"I don't really know much about this town, do I?" I blurted out. *Just once I'd like to know what's going on.*

"Give it time. Most people remember Vanessa Scanlon's murder. She disappeared when Whitney was five. Half the town thought she'd run off. The other half thought her husband had killed her and had hidden the body. She wasn't found until ten years later. But there's no way you could've known about it. And maybe Whitney prefers it that way, working with you. It couldn't have been easy growing up here, with everyone thinking her mother had abandoned her, then knowing she was kidnapped and murdered."

"Maybe that's why she lives in Baltimore." I wouldn't have guessed such a sad history for the strong, solid woman I'd met with.

"I hope she'll come back." Garrett resumed his lunch with a frown. "I'd hate to scuttle your first wedding."

"Of course she will! Won't she?" *Selfish, selfish, selfish!* I mentally chastised myself for thinking of the bottom line instead of Whitney's feelings. But creeping concerns about money eddied through my brain. Fixing up the old ruined mansion had blown my budget out of the water, despite Jesse's skill and frugality. I had a business to run. I needed this wedding. I could host it if the stars aligned and the B and B was finished in time.

"That's not even the biggest problem." I stirred half-and-half into my coffee. "I applied to the Planning Commission to have this property rezoned as commercial from residential, and I haven't heard back yet."

"The Planning Commission?" Garrett rubbed his forehead. "Most people give them several months to get their act together."

I raised my eyebrows. "Their website said they respond to requests in a month."

Garrett shook his head, his eyes incredulous. "That's not how they operate. I'm sure Jesse will back me up on this."

I recalled Jesse's displeasure back in the parlor. "Have you seen Jesse?"

He hadn't viewed the lunch cleanup perform-ance, and I wondered why he'd shaken his head at me.

As if summoned by my thoughts, Jesse burst onto the porch. His six-foot, eight-inch frame would have intimidated me if he wasn't such a softie.

"What were you thinking, Mallory? Are you nuts? There's no way this place will be finished in four weeks!" He took off his Pittsburgh Penguins hat and rolled the brim between his hands. His voice was a surprisingly high tenor for such a bear of a man.

I shimmied around on the top step to face him calmly. "That's not what you said last week. We're right on schedule. Aren't we?" I was used to Jesse's hyper-bolic way of speaking. Everything was an emergency, but they were crises that could be fixed immediately.

He defied the stereotype of a contractor, and so far, he'd finished everything on schedule. He had an uncanny knack for anticipating problems and coming up with creative, cost-effective solutions to fix them. I'd been able to hire him after his big fall project had fallen through. I was lucky to have him.

I counted down in my head, *three, two, one* . . . like clockwork, a motorized scooter rolled out the front door and glided up behind the contractor. A tiny woman dressed in a paisley-patterned brown peasant blouse and too-tight tan polyester pants, and wearing large gold hoop earrings, perched imperiously on the scooter's plush red-velvet seat. She sniffed with disapproval.

"You should've checked with Jesse first, before you made that promise." She squinted at me through the bifocals on the tip of her nose. "I knew today would be trouble, I drew the tower card." She sat back with a *humph*.

"Mother, stay out of it." Jesse rolled his eyes and stuck his large hands into his jeans pockets, instantly transformed from a lumberjack into a sheepish little boy.

I stifled a smile. I'd done a double take when Jesse brought his mother to our initial meeting. I'd wrongly assumed it was a one-time thing. The woman accompanied him everywhere and had spent the last month and a half riding around the house, calling out suggestions and getting underfoot. She fancied herself a fortune teller and read tarot cards for the contractors all day long, in return for them carrying her and her scooter up and down the stairs. She had a cackle like a bag of broken glass, she terrorized my cats, and she made eerie pronouncements that I'd learned to ignore. My sister had come up with an affectionate moniker for Delilah Flowers: the Witch on Wheels.

"I told you to not take on this job. I had a bad feeling about this, but you never listen!" Delilah crooked her finger with its heavy onyx ring and jabbed it at her son. She couldn't be more than ninety pounds soaking wet, and I wondered, not for the first time, how she had produced giant Jesse. But they had the same wiry gray hair, close-set amber eyes, and aquiline nose. She paused and scrutinized me from head to toe. "You should wear dresses more often, Mallory."

"Thanks, Delilah." I tried to be polite. I didn't want to encourage her. I had my own mother to razz me about dressing too much like a tomboy.

Delilah scooted off in a huff and left me to giggle in her patchouli-infused wake.

Jesse's broad shoulders relaxed, and he turned back to me. He'd stopped apologizing for her weeks ago. "Things were on track before I found the rotting subfloor this morning in your apartment while you met with the bride. She must be crazy or desperate to want to get married here in four weeks."

The latest gulp of hot coffee went down the wrong pipe, and I sputtered and set the cup aside. The floor had always felt a little squishy.

"The third-story floor will add another week, easy. Your brand-new water heater doesn't work, and it'll be days before they send a replacement. The existing radiators are too small to heat the bedrooms, just as I suspected, so we'll need to convert the wood-burning fireplaces to direct-vent gas ones or electric inserts. The three muralists I contacted about the parlor ceiling? None of them are free until spring. I can finish the basics in time for the December wedding, but for this new one? No way."

I became light-headed and steadied myself against a railing.

"But I thought we were running ahead!" I motioned around me. "And Whitney's wedding takes priority over the third floor." Renovations to the outside of the house were finished weeks ago. Jesse had restored the house to its original, heavy-cream parchment color. There was enough gingerbread trim to outfit a Bavarian bakery, and Jesse had the intricate swirls and curlicues painted verdigris, butter yellow, and slate blue, changing the wrought iron and wood into delicate, colorful lace. The place was transformed from a peeling dump into a warm, inviting house that looked like a wrapped present. And Jesse was a genius, designing on the fly, in addition to making the place shipshape and up to code. He'd surprised me with a thistle weathervane atop the widow's walk on the tallest mansard tower, a nod to the house's official name, Thistle Park. He'd added smaller weathervanes to the greenhouse and carriage house, and those structures, together with the mansion, reminded me of the *Nina, Pinta,* and *Santa Maria* majestically floating atop the wide green lawn. He'd said the place would be finished within the month, and I'd believed him.

"You can't plan for the unexpected, Mallory. And this house . . ." He scratched his scalp, where his hair had worn away. "It's full of surprises."

"Like what?"

Jesse dropped his voice and looked over his shoulder for his mother. "Sometimes I feel something funny's going on. We've had our share of little accidents, things we can't quite explain, like power tools going on after they've been shut off. Not to mention all the missing equipment. Things keep breaking, and I know my guys. They wouldn't sabotage a job."

"Oh, c'mon. What are you saying? The place is haunted?" Garrett laughed, but his mirth died.

I was glad Delilah had scooted off. She was obsessed with the occult and would seize on Jesse's pronouncement that there might be spirits hanging around Thistle Park.

"Not exactly. It's hard to explain." Jesse blushed, and his face began to match the loud red Hawaiian shirt he wore. "Forget I said anything. I can probably hire an extra crew of guys, and we'll try to finish by the end of October. There's more than one way to skin a potato."

I smothered a grin at one of Jesse's malaprops.

"You're my hero." I flashed my most grateful look at the contractor.

"I thought *I* was your hero," Garrett teased, looking fake put-out.

"You're both my heroes."

"It's going to cost you, though." Jesse showed all his teeth when he smiled, like the big bad wolf.

Cash register sounds clanged in my head as I pictured my bank account further drained. My inheritance from the artwork I'd found in the house was quickly evaporating.

From inside the doorway, Delilah called out with her spookiest affectation, "The four of coins! This renovation is going to be more costly than anything you've imagined, and I don't mean money."

"That's the story of my life." I picked up my sandwich. What did she mean?

A piercing scream ripped through the air.

Ohmigod, Rachel.

Garrett, Jesse, and I raced inside, our sandwiches forgotten. My sister stood at the top of the stairs, on the precipice of the balcony. She held onto the carved bannister, which wobbled and swayed over the hallway a good twenty feet below.

"Don't jump!" Delilah scooted into the room, and Jesse stopped her from going any farther. Ezra, Jesse's right-hand man, hovered under Rachel, as if to catch her. His face had turned a scary shade of split-pea-soup green, and he looked like he was going to lose his lunch.

"I'm not jumping, you old bat!"

Rachel swung backward and landed in a pile at the top of the stairs, with her limbs all akimbo, not a moment too soon. The gleaming cherry bannister, installed that morning, teetered, rocked, and finally fell free, clipping the edge of the antique crystal chandelier. The bannister crashed to the floor and became a shiny pile of kindling. The chandelier swung once, twice—

"Oh *no*—"

—and crashed to the ground, where it smashed into thousands of glittery slivers, destroyed in a deafening crunch. I tore my hands from my face, where they'd flown of their own accord to protect my eyes from the raining chips of crystal. Tiny shards nicked my hands and calves. The broken prisms sparkled and winked, even in the low light, like the aftermath of a biblical plague of hail.

"See what I mean?" Jesse let out a shaky breath and headed up the stairs to console my sister.

Chapter Two

That night Rachel and I moved our essentials from our third-floor aerie perch of an apartment to bedrooms on the second floor. The rotting attic floor threatened to crash down through the second-floor ceiling, and work was to begin immediately.

"I can't believe we have to relocate." My sister pulled two voluminous zebra-print suitcases down the stairs. Each piece of luggage punctuated her steps with a loud bang. The suitcases were big enough to double as body bags. How long would we reside on the second floor?

"I can't believe you almost fell off the landing." I wasn't thrilled about moving down a story while the contractors replaced the floor in our apartment, but my mind was on my sister's near fall.

"Ezra needs to be more careful." Rachel made light of the incident of the crashing bannister, yet, judging by the quiver in her voice, I could tell she was still rattled.

"That's the thing. He's so thorough. He said the bannister was securely installed, and I believed him."

"He's a sweetie," Rachel conceded, "but everyone makes mistakes."

From the moment he'd laid eyes on my sister, Ezra was a goner. He followed her around the house like a little lost puppy dog and tried to engage her in conversation. Before today I'd wondered if she knew he existed.

"I hope we don't have any more mistakes that could end in someone losing their life." I hauled my belongings down the last few stairs.

Rachel claimed the regal red bedroom and wheeled in her luggage with a huff. The second-floor bedrooms had been the first ones renovated and were nearly ready for guests. I was grateful we had a place to stay since we were banned from our apartment.

"G'night, Mallory." Rachel collapsed on the bed and leaned over to shut the door.

I headed one door down with Whiskey, the calico, and Soda, the orange kitten, as they padded softly behind me. I selected the yellow bedroom, a small chamber located in the front tower. It was the smallest bedroom but the most charming, with an explosion of sunny fabrics and prints. Photographs of the yellow flowers that had bloomed over the summer on the grounds decorated the walls, from black-eyed Susans to daylilies to tiny buttercups. I settled into the poufy canopy bed, and the cats followed suit, curling into fluffy balls of fur. I reveled nestling into the downy mattress and breathed in the smell of fresh paint. I was out in minutes.

Snick. Snack.

I sat up in bed and glanced at the bedside alarm clock. Three in the morning.

Snick, snack. I heard a gentle but unmistakable sound emanating from somewhere in the room.

Whiskey opened one golden eye at the end of the bed and stretched. Soda remained sleeping, her paws twitching in kitty dreamland.

"Did you hear that?"

Whiskey stared at me and was about to lay her little black, white, and orange mottled head back down when the sound resumed.

Snick, snack. Snick, snack. The staccato rhythm paused.

The calico growled low in her throat and jumped to the floor, moving across it on her belly.

My stomach did a graceless flip-flop, and I tried to swallow the sour taste in my mouth.

Snick, snack, snick, snack.

Whiskey stopped her travel across the room and lifted her head.

Where is that sound coming from?

"Rachel?" I called out. It would be just like my sister to play a little prank, especially after Jesse's talk about ghosts. But no one answered.

I ignored the crushing weight on my chest and counted to three in my head. I threw back the heavy yellow comforter and swung my leaden legs off the side of the bed.

Snick, snack. My ears strained to figure out where the sound was coming from. I tiptoed over to the radiator, sure the sound was coming from that ancient apparatus. I pressed my ear to the lukewarm metal, but it was silent. The noise was coming from somewhere above. *Do mice make such precise movements?*

I roamed the room in the dark, trying to find the source of the sound.

"Okay, kitty, I'm as spooked as you." I made it to the light switch.

Snick, snack.

I flicked it on, and the room was bathed in safety, the chandelier illuminating every nook and cranny of the room.

The sound stopped.

"Well, time to go to bed!" I sang out cheerfully, begging whatever it was to stop the strange noise. I turned to go back to the bed when a waft of air hit my nose. I breathed in the heady, lush, unmistakable scent of lilacs.

Impossible. An enormous lilac bush threatened to take over the front porch, but the first frost had finished off the last few blooms weeks ago. Great, I was having olfactory hallucinations in addition to auditory ones.

Someone is gaslighting me.

I left the light on and crawled back into bed, and was almost asleep when the soft clicking sound returned, keeping its rhythm like a ghostly metronome. I flinched and drew the kitties near me on the comforter. I was exhausted and spooked by the mystery noises and smell, not to mention Jesse's little speech about rogue power tools and missing items, and the carved bannister that nearly took out my sister on its way to destroying the chandelier. I thought about what he'd said for another hour. The wind teased out odd rattles in my tower roost and didn't help to soothe my overactive imagination. When it abated, it was well past four. I fell into a fitful sleep, and I woke up whenever Whiskey and Soda stirred on the comforter.

I awoke the next day to the sun streaming through the sheer curtains, competing with the overhead light. The room was still and quiet.

"You want me to call Ghostbusters?"

I blinked back surprise and waited for Ezra to start laughing and clue me in on the joke. But he was as serious as a grave.

We were conversing in the octagonal breakfast room. The guests would eat in the dining room when the B and B was finished, and this room would remain private. Jesse and Ezra had cleverly disguised a commercial overhaul in the adjoining kitchen. We'd be able to cater large weddings, but the appliances were hidden behind wooden cabinet fronts so the room still seemed homey and fit with the old-fashioned grandeur of the house. I loved to retreat to the kitchen during the renovation because it was finished. It was the calm, Viking-outfitted eye of the money-pit storm.

"The contractors would feel better. We almost lost Rachel." Ezra's wide gray eyes filled with concern as he mentioned my sister. He had a crush on her wider than the Monongahela River. He was a sweetheart, and someone I'd be glad to see my sister with, so, of course, she didn't give him a single shred of reciprocal attention. He was quiet and boyish and serious, with a shock of thick copper hair and a wiry build. He graced my sister with lattes and compliments and shy smiles, and she barely knew he existed.

"I lost five years off my life watching Rachel on that landing. And I'm counting my lucky stars she's safe. But isn't there a logical explanation for the bannister detaching? It was just put in earlier that day. Why do you think it's ghosts?" It wasn't that I didn't think ghosts existed, I just didn't have any reason to believe they did. Just call me a ghost agnostic. Besides, the weekend had passed without incident, and I hadn't heard any more strange noises.

"I installed it myself." Ezra pressed his lips together, and his face tightened. "It was as sturdy as a slab of granite that morning. Whatever is going on in this house is ratcheting up, and it's time to call in professionals before it gets worse."

Professionals? Professional charlatans is more like it.

"Like who?" This wasn't the movies. I wasn't sure where we'd find Ghostbusters on an emergency basis.

"The Port Quincy Paranormal Society." I spun around to face my friend and historian, Tabitha Battles, who had dropped by to chat and try out my newest recipe. She closed the back door behind her and pulled up a chair. "Hi, Ezra."

Ezra nodded hello to Tabitha and took a seat. "My brother is the head of the Paranormal Society. Whether you believe in ghosts or not, they're the ones to call."

"And besides your current problems, this house is the perfect candidate for the ghost hunters to examine." Tabitha helped herself to a Chinese five-spice apple tart.

"But this place isn't haunted!" I thought back to all of the creaks and moans the house let out at night, the barely perceptible sighs one heard when it settled. In the cool light of day, it was easy to discount my feelings and observations from the yellow bedroom. "It's just old." But I sounded a little uncertain, even to myself.

"Believe it or not, it would be an honor if they want to examine Thistle Park. They're usually booked to the hilt in October, and they have a crazy busy schedule. Sylvia contacted them before she died. She was sure this house was haunted." Tabitha mentioned the woman who had left me the house as she swept her preternaturally red bangs off her forehead and took a delicate sip of tea.

"It isn't the best time to entertain ghost hunters, even to solve why strange things are happening. I moved up a wedding that was due to take place next summer, and it's going to be held the day after Halloween. If we finish this place on time." I took a viscous bite of my tart to assuage my worry. Its sweet, gooey, and spicy deliciousness helped, but not much.

Tabitha's gimlet eyes went wide. "You're going to hold the first wedding here in less than a *month?*"

"Yup. That's right."

"Well, of course you can pull it off," Tabitha sputtered, two dots of color on her cheeks turning as red as her hair.

"It's okay. I shouldn't have agreed to do it without consulting you," I turned to Ezra, "or Jesse. It turns out it'll be a miracle if this place is ready in time. I'm not sure if I can take on ghost hunters too. They might get in the way of renovations."

"My brother won't get in the way." Ezra's eyes pleaded with mine.

"Who's the bride? Anyone I know?" Tabitha deftly

changed the subject as she delicately cut into her
tart with a knife and popped another bite into
her mouth. "This is delicious." She closed her eyes
and sighed with contentedness.

"Thank you." I relaxed a bit, pleased with how
the tarts had turned out. "The bride is Whitney
Scanlon." My little beggar calico cat, Whiskey,
mewed softly at my feet, then pawed at my jeans
and sat with her two front paws in the air, doing her
Oliver Twist routine. I made sure Tabitha wasn't
looking down and fed her a tiny morsel of tart.
Soda shot Whiskey a disapproving look from her
bowl of food across the room. Soda had been an
inside cat since her early days of kittenhood and
eschewed begging for people food.

Tabitha opened her eyes wide for the second
time in five minutes, and she dropped her fork
onto her plate with a clatter. "Not the daughter of
Vanessa Scanlon? Port Quincy's most famous
missing person case?"

"The very one." I regretted spilling my woes.
Garrett was probably right. Whitney escaped Port
Quincy so she could have her own identity, and
not be known just as the infamous daughter of a
missing and murdered woman.

"What's this about ghost hunters?" My sister blew
into the cozy octagonal room like a hurricane. She
knocked into the back of my head with her giant
aqua canvas bag as she reached for a tart, and her
sweet perfume, redolent of jasmine and cupcakes,
tickled my nose. She wore her wavy caramel tresses
in a side ponytail, her long legs encased in tight
black leggings and purple leg warmers and her
gravity-defying chest bound by a lime-green sports

bra. A minuscule purple hoodie offered a bit of coverage. Soft feather earrings swished to her shoulders. Soda abandoned her kitty food and alighted on a chair, stretching to bat an earring. Rachel's eye makeup matched her outfit, and if time machines existed, she looked like she could sing backup for Pat Benatar. My sister always looked amazing, despite her outrageous style. She turned a lot of heads in Port Quincy. If I tried to pull off this look in October, people would assume I was wearing a Halloween costume. My sister narrowed her eyes at Tabitha, but she gently freed her earring from the orange kitten's paw and primly sat with her tart. She gave Ezra an easy smile. He couldn't even return it, he was so agog over her getup. He finally croaked out a throaty hello.

"After ninety minutes of hot yoga, I deserve at least two of these." Rachel licked a swath of cinnamon and sugar from her sparkly silver acrylics and sighed. I'd have to ask her how she managed to bake and do yoga and keep her hands looking nice, when mine looked like they'd been through a meat grinder.

"Is this the new tart recipe? It's a keeper."

"Thanks!" I lit up inside. Praise from my pastry-chef-in-training sister was always welcome, and it took my mind off my troubles for a split second.

"Ezra and I are trying to convince your sister to allow the Port Quincy Paranormal Society to examine the house." Tabitha shot my sister a cautious look, no doubt wondering if she would be amenable to any friendly overtures.

It was odd to see them even deigning to sit next to each other. Rachel was still tetchy that she and

Tabitha had once been interested in the same man. Whenever she and Tabitha met, they circled each other warily, like aloof cats sniffing each other out.

But today Rachel seemed willing to set aside her grudge momentarily. "Ooh, that sounds like so much fun! And it could help us drum up business!" She set down her treat and rubbed her hands together, dreaming up plans before I'd even formally agreed to let the ghost hunters examine the house.

"And you could make the B and B a stop on the official Port Quincy Haunted House Tour," Tabitha chimed in, giving my sister an appraising look. "Once this place gets a reputation as being haunted, you can schedule special ghost events, and it probably won't be too spooky to alienate regular guests. You could tie in the history of the town. There's an uptick of business throughout October to take advantage of the Port Quincy Fall Fest, hayrides, and corn mazes." Tabitha reveled in fall, and her appearance reflected it. She was dressed in a rust-colored corduroy jacket and a hunter-green wool skirt, with burgundy Mary Jane heels. Her vivid red hair was pinned with bobby pins in chunky waves.

Rachel nodded at her, still seeming a little cagey, but willing to make a rare alliance to get what she wanted.

Whatever that is. My sister antennae were alert and twitching.

Ezra frowned and bit into his pastry. "This is serious business, not just a ploy to book more guests." He blinked when Rachel shot him a disapproving look. "The other contractors are spooked, and the Paranormal Society can prove whether there are ghosts."

Rachel served herself another tart. "You'll barely notice they're here."

"Whoa! Hold the phone! Rach, I was just telling Tabitha there hasn't been any paranormal activity here." Not verified, anyway. I buried thoughts of the odd clicking noise in my room.

"C'mon, Mall, I almost bit it when the railing fell away! That wasn't a prank. And people did see lights on when no one was living here." Rachel started in on her second tart.

"But those were trespassers, not ghosts," I reminded her. Some lovers had used the third floor for clandestine dalliances before I inherited the house.

"Well, what about the night Shane Hartley was murdered?" Rachel's pretty green eyes gleamed as she presented her ace card. "You had that crazy dream about a woman screaming in a fire, and you didn't even know the history of this place."

Tabitha perked up and slid her chair closer to the scarred oak table. "You had a dream about someone who lived and died here eighty years ago?"

I shivered, remembering that dream and how I'd woken up to a dead man on the front lawn. A prickle of uncertainty danced up my spine. There were other odd things about this house, but I'd blocked them out. I'd misplaced a bunch of things and blamed them on my sister. When it came to my stuff, my sis was a kleptomaniac—whether it was perfume or a handbag or a shirt that was too small—the only possessions safe from her sticky fingers were shoes, since we wore different sizes.

"It was just a dream! Besides, I have more pressing

issues. The house isn't even rezoned to commercial yet, so it can't legally operate as a B and B or wedding venue, and I don't know what's holding up my application with the Planning Commission." There. I'd let my current commitments speak for me and get me out of these ghost-hunting shenanigans.

Tabitha let out a low whistle. "Good luck with that. They're notorious for holding things up, just because they can. They treat the Planning Commission as their own little fiefdom, and they jerk people around just for the fun of it. It's sadistic. Do you know anyone who could put in a good word for you? A little nepotism wouldn't hurt."

I shook my head slowly. "I don't know anyone. And I have a little too much on my plate. I'm sorry, but I'll have to pass." My voice was gentle yet firm, and I thought I'd put the matter to rest.

Ezra let out a gust of air and frowned at me.

Rachel blinked in disbelief, then carefully avoided my gaze. She fidgeted with the zipper on her hoody and finally stole a glance at me, looking up through her thick lashes.

"Spill it, Rach." I glowered at my little sister and collected our plates.

"Um. I spoke with the Paranormal Society today when they called the landline. I sort of promised they could examine the house during October."

I dropped the pretty blue and violet forget-me-knot platter on the way to the sink, and it smashed neatly into three pieces.

"Ezra and I thought you'd agree to it, so I saved you the trouble of discussing it with them. You're so busy!" Rachel bit one of her sparkly nails, then moved to pick up the pieces of the platter. "It was before I knew you'd moved up Whitney's wedding."

Rachel should have consulted with me before she promised the Paranormal Society access, but I should have consulted with Jesse and Rachel before I moved up Whitney's wedding. We'd have to make it work.

I accepted the broken platter from my sister and started to laugh at the preposterousness of this month. "What's done is done. We'll welcome the ghost hunters with open arms. At least I don't think anything else can go wrong."

Tabitha clapped her hands. "You won't regret it!"

"My brother will get to the bottom of this." Ezra instantly looked relieved, as if he were certain the Paranormal Society could solve the mystery of the odd happenings around Thistle Park.

I smiled at my friends and my sister and moved to wash dishes. The visage in the dark glass window startled me for a second before I realized it was just me. I took a deep breath.

"Tabitha, you know more about this house than anyone. What was the littlest bedroom on the second floor used for? The one in the middle, in the tower, that we painted yellow."

Tabitha cocked her head in thought. "I'm not sure. Why?"

I turned around and leaned on the sink.

"I heard some noises Friday night before I fell asleep."

Ezra's eyes went wide and he stopped staring at my sister. "What noises?"

"A kind of soft *snick, snack*." I shut my eyes and reimagined the persistent, regular rhythm that had stopped as soon as I tried to investigate. "I thought it was the radiator or a branch hitting the window, but I ruled those out. It seemed to be coming from everywhere and nowhere." Little hairs stood up on my arms as I described the phantom noise, and I tugged down my sweater sleeves. "It was almost like chopsticks."

Rachel had been listening with rapt attention, and she now sagged, her feather earrings falling to her shoulders. "We're okay, then. I doubt ghosts are noshing on Thai food from the great beyond."

Tabitha's pale skin turned an even lighter shade, and she gripped the table. "I remember what that room was used for. I think that was Mrs. McGavitt's sewing room. Yes, that's it. But she was known for being a knitter."

Snick, snack. Snick, snack. That was it. The sound I'd heard Friday night was the gentle cadence of knitting needles hitting each other. Mrs. McGavitt had been dead for more than eighty years. I shuddered and turned around to avoid everyone's stunned gazes and went back to the dishes.

The next day, I decided to tackle my problems from most to least pressing. That meant finding out what was going on with the rezoning of my property to include commercial use. The corners of my mouth curved in a smile as I drove my boat of a station wagon down the steep hill from Thistle Park into a valley flanked with houses, then crested another hill to reach downtown. Port Quincy had gone all out for the month of October, and the fall spirit was infectious. Pumpkins of all sizes leered with cheerful, gap-toothed smiles from front porches, and gangly scarecrows stood at attention next to mailboxes. Cotton-batting cobwebs stretched across windows, and fake bats with red eyes hung from eaves. Some yards sported headstones etched with silly names, and mums of every hue exploded along walkways in lush bunches.

The Planning Commission office was located in City Hall, across the street from the courthouse. If the courthouse was Cinderella at the ball, resplendent with pink marble and stained glass, City Hall was the ugly stepsister. The building was a squat, gray brutalist structure, with a kitschy, life-sized concrete statue of the town founder, Ebenezer Quincy, standing in front. Little brown sparrows perched on his tricorn hat, and he gave passersby a dopey smile with flat cement eyes. Some helpful citizen had drawn in irises with a purple ballpoint pen so it looked like he was crossing his eyes. His boots had been inked with permanent marker to resemble Converse All Stars, and little curlicues of chest hair drawn in red ink sprung from his concrete collar. I walked into the building with a spring in my step. I couldn't wait to straighten everything out and move on with my plans.

I found the Planning Commission office in the basement of the building and composed myself before entering. The sole person in the office had his back turned to me, facing his computer. The harsh fluorescent lights gleamed off the top of his head, and he ignored the little bell I rang at the counter.

I urged myself to keep an open mind and gently cleared my throat. "Sorry to interrupt you. I'm here to check on the status of my application to rezone my property from strictly residential to include a commercial business."

The man wheeled around and sat up straighter, making his round head seem to emerge from his green turtleneck sweater. He gave me a bored gaze, his eyes disproportionately large and impassive behind thick round frames. He said nothing but cocked his head to the left. Finally, Turtle Man sighed and wheeled back to face an ancient computer when his inertia didn't scare me away.

"Name and address?"

"Mallory Shepard, one twenty-seven Sycamore Street." I willed my leg to stop tapping and tried to appear serene and pleasant.

He stretched, and his neck moved out of the deep collar like an accordion. "I don't have any record of an application. You can start a new one. They're in that pile." He pointed to a stack of papers on the counter and lazily steered his chair back to his station, where a game of computer solitaire awaited.

I plastered on a smile. "I mailed the application over a month ago. I have the certified mail slip showing that it was signed for by a Mr. Troy Phelan. Is he around?" The name had been vaguely familiar to me, but I couldn't quite place it.

Turtle Man blushed and coughed. "I'm Troy." He abandoned his game and reluctantly returned to the counter, his mouth puckered as if he'd just eaten a Sour Patch Kid. "Let me see that."

I held the slip of paper high enough for him to see but wouldn't let him grab it, not that I stopped him from trying. He settled back into his chair with a thud. "Be that as it may, we still don't have your application. You'll have to reapply, *as I said,* and then you can get a hearing next month."

"Next month!" My voice was so loud a woman from the Fish and Game Commission across the hall poked her head out the door. "But your website said all applications were given a hearing that month if they were turned in by the first. I should have a hearing *this* month."

He shrugged and took a sip from a can of Tab.

Tab? Where did he get that? I felt like I'd stepped into a time warp in more ways than one.

"Are you new around here?" He straightened up and puffed out his chest. "Everyone knows you shoulda dropped it off. We're not responsible for lost mail."

His question about my status as a resident of Port Quincy hurt. I was new, but that didn't mean I should have divined that I needed to bring the application over in person.

"But it wasn't lost! You signed for it. And the website doesn't say to drop off the application in person. It says to send it via certified mail." Back in my days as an attorney, I'd followed procedural rules to a T. That didn't seem to be the way things were done in Port Quincy.

"Ma'am, if you don't calm down, I'm going to ask you to leave." He raised his eyebrow as if daring me to flip out.

"I have a wedding to put on in less than a month. This wouldn't be a problem if you'd managed to keep track of your mail! I'll just have to carry on without rezoning." I collected my bag.

"I wouldn't do that if I were you." Turtle Man

rolled back and smugly crossed his arms across his chest. "I'll flag your account, and we'll follow up. If the Planning Commission finds out you took money for a business venture and held it on your *residential* property, you'll never get your permit approved. Now, if you'll *excuse* me, it's time for lunch." He patted the counter next to him and frowned. "Where did I put my . . ."

"Troy, angel, you forgot your lunch!" A sprightly woman in a Halloween sweater vest, featuring a black cat with an arched back and a hand-stitched, leering Dracula, minced into the room on orange foam clogs, waving a brown paper bag. "Bologna sandwich, Twinkies, and pickles." She brushed past me and placed the bag into Troy's outstretched hand. "Honestly, how can I tend to my guests if you're always forgetting your lunch?" Her scolding was loving and warm, and she bustled around the counter.

"Thanks, dear. What would I do without you?" Troy leaned over, and his wife placed a prim peck on his cheek.

"Having trouble with your permits, Mallory?" The woman tossed her head, and her mousy brown hair swished over her shoulder.

I tried to place her. "As a matter of fact, I am having a bit of trouble." I flicked my eyes at the odious Troy and held up my chin. "A temporary bit of trouble."

The woman dug into the lunch bag and pulled out identical pink meat sandwiches, crustless and oozing with mayonnaise and mustard. "That's not what I hear. I don't think this town needs *two* bed-and-breakfasts, do you?"

My eyes nearly fell out of their sockets. *Was this a challenge?* "Who in the devil are you?"

"I'm Ingrid Phelan." She straightened up in her swivel chair and edged closer to her husband.

Turtle Man gave me a sly, smarmy smile and bit into his sandwich.

Aha. That was why I'd recognized the surname Phelan. Ingrid was the owner of the only other bed-and-breakfast in town. The Mountain Laurel Inn was housed in a small pastel Victorian overlooking the river, and it put the *shabby* in shabby chic, from the looks of the outdated photos on its website. It had once been a pretty, fusty, and florid bed-and-breakfast. But the reviews of the inn showed its service and décor had been slipping over the last decade. I hadn't worried too much about butting heads with the Mountain Laurel as we were soliciting different customers for different experiences and price points. Still, it gave me pause that the husband of the owner was delaying my rezoning.

"You're married to the owner of the Mountain Laurel Inn?"

Troy gave me a smug little nod, his neck retracting in his turtleneck.

"The *best* and *only* B and B in town," Ingrid reminded me, with a haughty jut of her chin. "If we have anything to do with it."

My eyes widened. "Your loss of my application is beginning to look like a dirty business tactic. It's unethical for you to stand in the way." My neck began to feel warm.

Troy placed his hand on his sweater in mock alarm. "You're not accusing me of bias, are you?"

Beside him, Ingrid's chest heaved, and she stood

like a tiny pugilist. "That's your interpretation, Ms. Shepard. My husband is an honorable man." She leaned over the counter, and I took a step back.

Troy whipped out a second bologna sandwich and flicked the glass partition closed in my surprised face, and he resumed his game of solitaire.

I arrived back at my car more determined than ever to find a way to finish the renovation on time and get the place rezoned, all while peacefully coexisting with ghost hunters underfoot. I wouldn't let the loathsome Ingrid and Troy Phelan and the dirty Planning Commission stand in my way. I headed to the east side of town and Pellegrino's restaurant to pick up Whitney. We were meeting to nail down specifics about her wedding. She hadn't been spooked enough by seeing Garrett to jettison her plans of getting married at Thistle Park.

Whitney's aunt Angela, Pellegrino's owner, met me at the maître d' stand. Rachel and I had taken a cooking class taught by Angela last month, and she had recommended the B and B to her niece for her wedding. Angela was a tall, big-boned woman, exquisitely dressed with finds from her various international travels. She always dressed beautifully, even when cooking. Today she wore a royal-blue silk shantung dress under a perfectly tailored inky-black velvet jacket. Her jet hair, with a smattering of silver strands, was scraped back in her usual severe bun. She was pleasant, but she missed nothing, and cooking in class had made me nervous. When she thought her students were underperforming, she could go from patient guide to Gordon Ramsey in a heartbeat. Angela had helped raise Whitney after her mother disappeared, and I felt a little bad since she'd had to grow up under her exacting standards. Still, Angela was an amazing teacher and had opened my eyes to new culinary vistas. Rachel and I had put her lessons to work and created our wedding menus based on her expert guidance. My sister considered Angela to be her mentor and wanted to impress her.

"Whitney will be just a few minutes. Let me get you a glass of wine."

We threaded our way through the dining room, back to the bar. Pellegrino's was the fanciest restaurant in Port Quincy, whose denizens liked prosaic but delicious standards like fettuccine alfredo and chicken scaloppine. The restaurant was hardly an epicenter of haute cuisine, and Angela catered to her customers. But she managed to slip in one daring dish each evening as the special. Tonight was no exception. The menu on the chalkboard featured steamed saffron and thyme mussels paired with pomegranate risotto. The dining room was subtly decorated for fall, with squat, square glass vases bursting with cranberries and tiny pumpkin-colored votives clustered on the tops of the intimate free-standing tables and within the deep wooden booths. The bar was similarly decorated, but with dimmer lighting and more hushed voices. I settled into a seat at the end of the row, which afforded a view of the dining room but partly concealed me behind a potted tree. It was the perfect place to people-watch the movers and shakers of Port Quincy settling down to their dinners and conversations.

"I'll let Whit know you're here." Angela gave me a rare smile and passed me a glass of Riesling. I took a sip of the sharp, sweet wine and sighed contentedly.

I'd sit in the quiet bar and pretend for a moment that everything was going swimmingly. I was doing just that when a voice from my nightmares carried over the dining room.

"I'll be just a moment, sweet pea."

Darnit. It was my ex-fiancé, Keith Pierce. I'd managed to avoid him for the past two months since he lived over an hour away in Pittsburgh and our paths had no reason to cross. A very blond woman with a stripe of dark hair at her center part gave him a sultry smile from the table then settled back to check out her appearance in a tiny handheld mirror. It was Becca Cunningham, the young associate I'd caught Keith cheating with a few weeks before our canceled wedding.

Keith headed my way, and in a moment of panic, I shimmied sideways behind a potted ficus.

"Arrgh!" My bar stool caught on the carpet, and I crashed to the floor, Riesling and all. The wineglass bounced and landed intact, but not before sloshing the sweet liquid over my jacket.

"I have that effect on the ladies." Keith smirked and stood over me.

The bar patrons who had jumped up to help me sat down now that my ex-fiancé had arrived. He'd grown back the beard Becca had made him shave off this summer.

"What brings you here, Mallory?"

"I'm meeting with a client," I smiled serenely from my spot on the floor.

"Yes, I heard you were starting a little wedding-planning business at Sylvia's home." He reminded me that the house had been his grandmother's once, before she'd disinherited him and left it to me.

"I've got to run. I have a very important question to ask a very important lady." He reached behind the bar, extracting a miniature pumpkin.

Oh no, oh no, oh no, this cannot be happening.

He stepped over me, strode purposefully through the dining room, and got down on one knee in front of Becca.

"Oh, *Keith!*" Her voice slid up the scale to a higher register, alerting all of the diners who hadn't yet taken in Keith's proposal stance. She tossed the tiny mirror on the table and flung her left hand atop her knee and waggled her fingers. Keith held up the tiny pumpkin and whipped off the stem with a flourish. A preposterously large diamond ring swung on a string like a pendulum from the top of the pumpkin.

"Will you make me the happiest man alive and be my wife?" Keith's voice boomed around the dining room as if he were on a megaphone.

My heart seized at the back of my throat. You never forget a proposal, and he'd said those exact words to me two years ago in the dining room of a little B and B in the Blue Ridge Mountains.

"Yes, yes, yes!" Becca leaped from her chair and embraced Keith, who swung her around in a bear hug. Keith seized Becca in a showman's kiss, complete with a dip, and the dining room erupted into applause. A few men catcalled and cheered.

Chapter Three

I consumed two swift shots of Jack Daniels while I waited for Whitney. I was on the clock but couldn't help myself. I chased them with Tic Tacs and hoped my breath didn't reek. Desperate times called for desperate measures.

Whitney sidled up ten minutes after Keith's performance. "Thanks for waiting! I'm sorry I flipped out the other day. I hadn't seen Garrett Davies since the day my mom's murderer was sentenced." She paused. "Quite frankly, I never thought I'd see him again. I'm sure you've heard all about it by now." She wrinkled her eyebrows in concern and peered into my face. "Shall we stay here or go somewhere else?"

"I'm great! Maybe we should meet somewhere else, where there's brighter light and we can talk more loudly." I stared at the exit sign, desperate to get out of Pellegrino's. From the corner of my eye, I could see men patting Keith on the back and women exclaiming over Becca's boulder of a ring, so big it could power a solar system.

"How about the Greasy Spoon? I haven't eaten there in years." We left her aunt's restaurant and crossed the street to Port Quincy's twenty-four-hour diner, its chrome and black-and-yellow vinyl interior outfitted with cheery plastic pumpkins and witches' hats and brooms suspended from the ceiling.

Whitney continued her ruminations about Garrett as we settled into a squeaky booth, the old springs twanging and sighing. "Then again, Port Quincy is such a small place, I'm not surprised I ran into him." Her gaze was far away.

"Tell me about it. I'm constantly running into friends and foes alike."

Whitney let out a surprisingly rich peal of laughter for her small size. "Oh, c'mon, you don't have any foes."

Between my ex, his tartlet, and the Phelans, I have more than I know what to do with at the moment.

I smiled and changed the subject to her wedding, opting to tackle the tough stuff first.

"The Port Quincy Paranormal Society would like to examine the B and B, and they have an opening in October." I neglected to say we desperately needed their services. "They've promised to be discreet, and they'll mainly be there at night, out of our hair. They should be finished with their . . . study of the house by the time of your rehearsal and wedding. Is that alright?"

Whitney's eyes lit up, and she leaned forward over the booth. "Ghost hunting?! It won't be a problem." Her face grew serious. "I've had my share of ghouls asking me questions about my mother. But this is the fun kind. October is my favorite

month. You get to pretend to be someone else."
She seemed wistful as she focused on something
out the window.

The waiter arrived with our food: an open-faced
turkey sandwich with cranberry sauce for me and
sweet-potato casserole for Whitney. No matter what
my troubles were, I could enjoy the tastes and
savory smells of fall.

I pressed on and bit my lip. "There's also a small
wrinkle with the zoning. The property hasn't been rezoned yet for commercial business. I have complete
faith it will be, but the Planning Commission is taking
their time." Okay, that was a small fib. "There's a
teeny-tiny possibility the house won't be rezoned by
the end of the month." Would the commission be
jerking me around if one of their members wasn't
married to my direct business competition?

Whitney laid her fork next to her plate, her meal
half gone. She could eat an impressive amount for
such a small person.

"The Planning Commission?" Her face relaxed.
"Don't worry about a thing! My aunt Lois is on the
board. I can't promise anything, but . . ." She
blushed, two bright spots of pink dressing up her
face. "I'll see what I can do. It's the least I can do in
exchange for you moving up my wedding on such
short notice." She shrugged as if to say, we'll see.

"Oh my God, really?" I abandoned all profession-
alism and nearly shouted, dropping my fork. This
was the best news I'd heard all month. "If you could
just put in a good word, I mean, I'm not asking for
special treatment, but I'm cutting it kind of close,
and they claim to have lost my application . . ." My
desperate prattle told Whit all she needed to know.

Despite the warm welcome I'd gotten in my new hometown, I sometimes felt like an outsider. I still wasn't sure how things worked around here, and it was a relief that Whitney would try to help me with the rezoning process.

"Don't worry about a thing, Mallory. I have a feeling your permit will be approved very soon." She winked conspiratorially, and a weight lifted from my shoulders.

With the two most pressing problems solved in a flash, the two of us got down to business planning her wedding. We'd covered a lot of ground when we met a month ago to discuss her nuptials next year, but I was sure much would change with the new wedding date.

"You'd envisioned getting married in the greenhouse, with a reception for a hundred people in the garden, and your color scheme was robin's-egg blue. We were going to serve picnic fare with a gourmet twist and cupcakes for dessert."

Whitney shook her head. "I don't think any of that fits with fall. I was actually thinking about my mom, and her favorite color—purple. Could we design the wedding around that, in honor of her?"

"That would be perfect for fall. Since time is of the essence, we need to let availability guide some of your choices. Like flowers, for instance. We can meet with the florist and choose flowers that are in season. I'm sure we can get something beautiful and purple."

We brainstormed and came up with a plan for a ceremony on the grand staircase, with Whitney and Ian marrying on the landing. Dinner and dancing would be in the front and back halls, and guests could mill about the house.

"Now, on to food. We could do fall comfort foods to echo the picnic theme from the summer. How do you feel about a chocolate hazelnut cake? And creamy lobster and squash bisque?" Rachel and I had come up with several preliminary menus last night to pitch to Whitney.

"Um, there's a problem with both of those dishes." Whitney looked nervous and extracted a bundle of papers from her purse. "There might be a problem with a *lot* of dishes. I'm a vegetarian. Dad is allergic to tree nuts and intolerant to gluten. My aunt Lois is allergic to shellfish. And my fiancé, Ian, is lactose intolerant. This is going to be hard."

My smile faltered, but I quickly composed myself.

"There are some issues with certain spices, too. Here, I made you a list." Whitney handed over a sheaf of papers stapled together. It was heavy and thick.

"Is there anything you guys *aren't* allergic to?" I blurted out, instantly regretting it.

A slow smile etched across Whitney's face. "Chocolate!"

"We could organize a theme around chocolate dishes!" Ideas exploded in my head of a fall, chocolate-themed reception.

Whitney clasped her hands together. "The first date Ian and I went on we had chocolate cake. I love it!"

We put our heads together for the next hour and decided to organize the wedding around a sweet, spicy, and savory chocolate theme as a nod to Ian and Whitney's first date, with a purple color scheme to honor Whitney's mother. I pictured rich plum decorations with chocolate accents, balanced with green, gold, and burgundy. The florist would be able to work with that on short notice, and we could have chocolate woven into the food courses.

Whitney scheduled a wedding tasting with her family in two days' time, and back home, armed with a list of prohibited foods, Rachel and I rolled up our sleeves and got to work.

"Have you seen my new wrap dress?" I shimmied into Spanx fortified enough to hold back the Hoover dam and tore through the wardrobe in my temporary second-floor bedroom. I could have sworn I'd hung the dress up right after I'd bought it a few days ago. But it was missing. Just like the contractors' tools. At least the sound of knitting needles hadn't returned in several days.

"Maybe the ghost took it?" I mused and pushed open the door to the bathroom shared with the adjoining red bedroom. *Or maybe my klepto sister took it.*

Rachel had the good sense to put down her mascara wand and freeze. She left one set of eyelashes rimmed in sable war paint, one set bare. But instead of taking off *my* new dress she crossed her arms protectively across her front. "It looks so good on me!"

I rolled my eyes and tried not to agree. The rose-colored dress draped to mid-calf on my frame, and I intended to wear a camisole underneath. On my sister it hit well above the knee, and her curvy figure stretched out the top to nearly bursting. A delicate carnelian bead necklace dipped down in the deep V-neck of the dress. She looked fantastic.

"That's my necklace, too!" This time I took a step toward my sister, who yelped and hurried around the claw-foot tub that took up the middle of the room.

"I know, I know! Tell you what, let's swap. I have the perfect dress for you." She maneuvered past me, barely evading my grasp. A minute later she returned with a gauzy, billowy, green-and-blue geometric print dress. "Put this on."

"I'd rather wear the dress I got for this wedding tasting, thank you very much." I was miffed at Rachel's sticky fingers and running out of time to get ready.

"C'mon. This will look better, I promise." Rachel tapped her foot with impatience and held out her dress.

"Fine." I pulled the airy fabric over my head. *This had better be good.*

Rachel studied me for a moment, then left the bathroom and quickly returned with a black patent-leather belt. She cinched the dress around the waist with the belt and handed me my knee-high black boots. "These will be perfect." She removed giant silver hoop earrings from her ears and shoved them in my hands. "Put these in." She undid my bun and fluffed out my curls.

I pulled on the boots and fastened the earrings.

Rachel spun me around to face the floor-length mirror on the back of the door. "Voilà!"

I tried to frown, then started laughing. I looked better than I would have in the wrap dress, and Rachel knew it. "Nice save, little sis."

"So I can keep the dress?" She picked up her

mascara wand and painted on another inky layer of lacquer.

"Just for today." I reached for a silver scarf hanging on the mirror and arranged it around my sister's neck, preventing anyone from staring down her chest. I undid the dramatic genie ponytail atop her head, tied half of her hair back with a black cloisonné clip, and handed her my dangly carnelian earrings. "There."

We smiled at each other in the giant mirror.

"What would I do without you?" she teased.

"Let's do this!"

We high-fived like we did when we were kids and descended the back stairs to the kitchen. It was going to be a busy day. First, we'd be giving the Paranormal Society a tour of the house, then we'd hold the wedding tasting. And our mom was due to arrive from Florida after the tasting. Rachel and I had labored until the wee hours of the morning crafting a menu for Whitney and her family, and I couldn't wait for them to try it. I knelt down and checked the oven, where the main dishes were warming. Rachel bustled over to the cakes on the counter and squinted at her handiwork.

The doorbell rang, and I glanced at my watch. "That'll be the Paranormal Society." We were headed for the front door when Delilah apprehended us, revving her scooter at top speed down the front hall. The contractors were holding off on renovations until after the wedding tasting was finished, but Jesse, Delilah, and Ezra had arrived at their usual time. The little black flag with a skull mounted on the back of Delilah's scooter waved in the motorized breeze.

"I read your cards today, girls, and I must warn you—"

"Save it, sister." Rachel wheeled around on her boots and held her hand up like a stop sign. "We don't want any of your heebie-jeebies predictions today, okay?"

Delilah sniffed and threw her bony shoulders back. "You'd do better to listen to me every once in a while, missy! Who warned you last week to be careful in your travels?"

Rachel dismissed Jesse's mother with a flick of her wrist. Her silver bangles chimed and jingled and seemed to mock the old woman. "Big deal. That was just a coincidence." But there was a harsh sliver of fear in Rachel's green eyes.

Eerie prickles danced up my vertebrae. I didn't believe in Delilah's pronouncements, but she had chased Rachel out the door, screeching about troubles with her short trip, and, sure enough, half an hour later Rachel was calling about the station wagon's flat tire.

"Fine," she spat and stared at my sister with scorn in her deeply lined eyes. "I won't bother with you."

Rachel gave her a mock curtsy and turned to go.

"But—you should know—beware the Aquarian!"

"We don't have an aquarium," I said gently. Was Delilah starting to lose it?

She tsked. "*Aquarian,* you silly girl! One born under the sign of the water bearer."

"Like astrology?" What the heck was she talking about?

"Come *on.*" Rachel pulled me to the front door,

and Delilah wheeled around to the library, where I
hoped she'd stay out of our hair.

I swung open the door to greet the ghost hunters,
two men and two women carrying bulky black nylon
cases of equipment.

"I'm Hunter. The ghost hunter," the man in
front said, in his best James Bond impression. He
held out his hand and enveloped mine in a pleasing, firm grip. He must be Ezra's brother. I smiled
at his goofy opening and turned to do a silent conference with my sister, but she was giggling like a
madwoman. *Oh no.* She was giving Hunter her
smitten look, and that was when I saw it. He had a
prominent cleft chin, a chin-dimple or chimple, as
Rachel called it, and chimples were like catnip for
my sister. He was also my sister's height, about five
foot nine, with thick, boyish chestnut hair that
flopped over his eyes in an endearing manner and
a toned, compact soccer player's build. His kind
gray eyes were the same as Ezra's, but other than
that, the brothers couldn't have been more different. He wore a white T-shirt with PQPS written on
the front. When he knelt down to place a heavy
canvas case on the floor, I saw the back emblazoned
with the words "Port Quincy Paranormal Society"
and a cartoon caricature of Ebenezer Quincy rising
over a profile of the town, dripping chartreuse ec-
toplasm. Hunter caught me looking at him and
flashed me a grin. His electric smile added two
more dimples. He was quite handsome, and he
seemed to know it.

"Come *in.*" Rachel placed her hand on his arm.
"Let me show you around." She delicately undid

the silver scarf and twirled it around her hand unconsciously, the better to lasso Hunter with.

Hunter smiled at my sister and hefted an expensive-looking video camera higher on his shoulder. My amusement faltered as I felt a mini wave of panic.

"Excuse me, will you be filming?" I blinked at the camera, not sure if I wanted the mess of renovations to be captured on film.

"Oh! I forgot. I have a release for you to sign. I just need your John Hancock right here." Hunter reached into his shoulder bag and pulled out a single sheet of paper, a release contract printed on one side in tiny letters. He'd highlighted the signature line in neon yellow and expectantly handed it and a pen over to me.

"I'd like to look at this first, before I sign it. Could you give me a day?"

Hunter frowned then shrugged. "That's reasonable. But no one ever really reads that thing. No filming until then, I guess." He dejectedly lowered the camera from his shoulder, and it hung limply at his side.

Rachel rolled her eyes at me behind his head.

"Is all of this equipment for filming?"

Hunter brightened and motioned his fellow ghost hunters forward. "This here is our EMF meter. It measures electromagnetic fields, which spike when there's a spectral presence. We'll take readings all over the house and the grounds."

I took the yellow instrument from him. It looked like an oversized remote control with a digital screen. I just managed to suppress a dubious eye roll.

"Won't this be set off by all the contractors'

equipment?" I turned the EMF over in my hands. Could it shed some light on the odd clicking in my bedroom?

"That's why we'll be here at night." Hunter replied to me, but his eyes never left Rachel.

"This is our EVP recorder." A slim, towheaded girl showed me a digital recorder that reminded me of the ones the older attorneys I once worked with used for dictation.

"What's an EVP?" I tried to keep the skeptical note out of my voice. I wanted the ghost hunters to feel welcome, even though I didn't really believe in their hobby.

"An electronic voice phenomenon. We'll be able to pick up any sounds made by ghosts."

The other ghost hunters showed us their infrared goggles and cameras, motion detectors, and complicated thermometers that looked like guns. I shivered as they described paranormal activity they'd picked up with their instruments at other sites. They seemed sincere about ghosts, and their enthusiasm was starting to rub off on me. I didn't want to accompany them on their nighttime wanderings of the house, but Rachel gladly volunteered to play host.

"Is that *the* Hunter Heyward?" Delilah's gravelly voice ricocheted down the hall and announced her presence before her scooter.

"Why is she meddling? Doesn't she have some tarot cards to read?" Rachel dropped Hunter's arm and whipped around.

Delilah motored over, stopping an inch from Hunter's knee.

"I can't believe my eyes!" Delilah fanned herself with her hand and blinked coquettishly.

Delilah was an incorrigible flirt, but she upped the ante for Hunter. The starstruck grin never left her face. She was more excited than my middle-school BFF Lindsay Watts, who peed her pants when we saw NSYNC in concert.

"I'm your biggest admirer." Delilah seemed surprisingly girly in her ardor, shedding several decades of age.

Was that a giggle?

"I'd love to be here when you hunt for spirits at night." She fluffed her gray curls and gave Hunter a toothy smile. "I'm sure Jesse can—"

"Thank you *so much*, Delilah." My sister gently removed Delilah's grasping hand from Hunter's arm and nudged him back a degree. "We really need to get going."

Delilah shot Rachel an acid glare, and Hunter seemed to stifle a chuckle with a well-timed sneeze.

"One more thing, Mallory." Hunter turned his infectious smile from my sister to me, and I relaxed. He was as friendly and assured as his brother, Ezra, just in a more gregarious way. I didn't quite believe in what he was doing, but if he and the other ghost hunters set the contractors' minds at ease, I was all for it.

"What can I do for you?"

"We'll need Wi-Fi access to upload our findings to the cloud."

"Sure thing. The network is the Thistle Park B and B and the password is 'Sylvia.'"

"We'll get out of your hair now," Hunter promised. He and the other ghost hunters moved toward the wide main stairs. I overheard Rachel explain about the falling bannister and shattered chandelier.

"My brother moves fast, doesn't he." Ezra materialized at my side and stared bleakly at his brother's arm, linked cozily and firmly with Rachel's.

"Not nearly as fast as Rachel," I mused and chucked him on the arm.

Ezra's head looked like it was about to explode. Somehow, I don't think he'd contemplated his brother whisking his crush away in five minutes flat. Ezra excused himself and stalked off, muttering about helping Jesse.

The other ghost hunters followed my sister with bemused expressions on their faces as she led them through the construction detritus. Rachel and I had agreed she would run interference with the ghost hunters, since she'd promised they could examine the B and B, and I would handle the bulk of Whitney's wedding tasting. Rachel disappeared up the main stairs with the ghost hunters in tow, not a moment too soon, as the doorbell rang.

It was Whitney and her entourage. They were a motley crew. Whitney introduced me to her father, Porter, a tall, thin, ailing man with a wan and gentle but strained smile. He had the same strawberry-blond hair as his daughter, but interwoven with strands of white. His skin hung on his frame, and you could tell he had been a beefy man when he was in good health. His fine gray suit was now several sizes too large. He shuffled in as if in pain, but seemed determined to put on a brave and joyful face. Angela, from Pellegrino's, gave me a nod in greeting and stepped aside, placing a steadying hand on her ill brother's arm.

"I can't thank you enough for moving my daughter's wedding up," Porter said in a near whisper. "It means a lot to me."

"It means a lot to me too, Mr. Scanlon." I quickly escorted him to the back porch, where we'd be having the tasting, so he could sit. It was a beautiful Indian summer day, warm and mild and pleasant. Porter's sister, Angela, helped him, and Whitney brought up the rear. Whitney and I circled back to the front porch to wait for our last guest.

"We're missing my aunt Lois. She said she'd be on time." She glanced at her delicate watch and let out a nervous gust of air.

"Hellooo! Hello, my darling!" Just then a tall woman swept onto the porch, her resemblance to her sister, Angela, clear, except for the extra fifty pounds clinging to her bones. Her black hair was woven around her head in a heavy braid. She wore a thick, marled-cream cowl-neck sweater, a brown and navy tweed skirt, and army-green wellies more suited to stalking pheasants in the Hebrides than taking part in a wedding tasting in Port Quincy. Three small dogs danced around her legs and anxiously barked.

"You must be Mallory. I'm charmed. I'm Whit's aunt Lois." She grabbed my shoulders and pulled me in. She applied two forceful air kisses to my cheeks, leaving me dumbfounded. She smelled of heather, lavender, and Earl Grey tea. Whitney was so petite in contrast to her father, Porter, and her aunts, Angela and Lois. *She must favor her mother's side of the family.* I followed Lois as she swept through the hallway to join her siblings on the back porch.

"And these are my loves." She pointed to the trio of lively, white West Highland terriers. "This is Miss Maisie." The small white dog yipped and seemed to grin when she heard her name. "And this is my Bruce." She patted a grumpy-looking Westie with impressive Wilford Brimley eyebrows and mustache. "And this is Fiona, their mother." The third white dog sat primly and sniffed the air with her little black nose. She seemed a bit more sedate than her two doggie progeny. Lois reached into her leather fanny pack and extracted three dog treats, which she threw in the air, causing a frenzy. The dogs leaped up in unison to catch the treats and promptly snarfed them down. Lois doted on her pups as if they were children. They were adorable, and I was amused that Lois had brought them to the tasting, until Bruce grabbed the tablecloth and began to pull.

"Bruce, stop that, you naughty fellow!" Whitney distracted the little dog, and he happily gave up the tablecloth to bound over to her. She knelt down in the grass in her khaki dress and scruffed him behind his tall, perky ears.

"Pleased to meet you, Lois," I mumbled, trying to walk without getting caught in the churning, zigzagging path of short doggie legs as Maisie bounded after her sibling to get some attention from Whitney too. Fiona maintained her perch on the porch and sent the other dogs what looked like a disapproving glance.

"Are those dogs wearing *Burberry?*" Rachel stuck

her head out of the back door with a whisper and craned her neck to see Lois's pups.

"It would appear to be so." I giggled, taking in the doggies' iconic plaid scarves tied just so around their necks. Bruce wore one in signature tan, and Maisie and Fiona were in pink and red, their scarves tied in jaunty bows.

"Those are three very spoiled dogs." Rachel's voice dripped with poorly concealed envy.

I sat Lois between her brother, Porter, and sister, Angela, and gave Whitney the seat of honor. The dogs continued to motor about, threatening to trip me as I served Whitney's family water and a deep claret wine.

Rachel rejoined me, and we served four courses: a spinach, beet, and cranberry salad with a shaving of dark chocolate in a curl on top; pumpkin soup with a heart-shaped dusting of cocoa; rosemary-crusted lamb and smoked salmon with capers and chervil accompanied by a side of root veggies; and portobello mushrooms and couscous with vegan soy cheese for vegetarian Whitney. I'd found a fussy, elaborate brown toile china set in the butler's pantry and mixed the antique plates with chocolate Fiestaware. It made for an intricate and modern tableau. I didn't interrupt the appreciative murmurs and cleared their plates in nervous and hopeful silence. Rachel wheeled out an impressive silver tea set with coffee and chocolate mint tea and three miniature cakes, each labeled with a discreet sign disclosing allergens: gluten-free, flourless red velvet torte; coconut spice cake with chocolate frosting; and key-lime white-chocolate pie.

Everyone tucked in, and I tried not to hover,

straining my ears between serving each dish. They cleaned their plates, all except Porter, who picked at his food with disinterest and smiled at his daughter. He was visibly ill, with ashen, papery skin, but when Whitney was enjoying herself, his face lit up.

The Westies yapped and barked at Lois's knees, and she fawned and doted on them like Queen Elizabeth with her corgis. I frowned when she tossed small pieces of lamb onto the lawn for the dogs to eat. The dogs deftly leaped into the air to claim their morsels, and I remembered how I liked to sneak Whiskey food from the table and relaxed.

Lois caught me watching her and crossed the porch when the meal was finished. "Bruce here is my troublemaker, but he's also a natural guard dog. Fiona is the matriarch. And Maisie is the princess." She spoke of her pups with pride and love.

"They're beautiful." I bent down to pet Maisie behind the ears.

Lois cleared her throat and leaned closer. "Whitney tells me you need Thistle Park rezoned from residential to mixed commercial by the day of the wedding."

I tensed and nodded, not wanting to push the issue. I gave Maisie a final pat and straightened up. I smoothed the gauzy print dress and dared to look Lois in the eye.

"I am the most senior member of the Planning Commission, and I could be of help with that." Lois opened her prodigious black-watch-plaid pocketbook and extracted an Altoids tin. She slipped a mint in her mouth, grimaced, and seemed to settle back to take in my reaction.

I blushed and nodded before I cautiously returned

her piercing gaze. "That would be fantastic. Anything you can do will be appreciated at this point. I turned in my application over a month ago and thought there would be a hearing by now. I hate to suspect anything, but the Phelans own the only other B and B in town, and they might—"

Lois held up her fleshy hand with a smile. "Say no more, Mallory. I *assume* this house can be re-zoned as a B and B. It can be . . . *arranged.*" She paused and leaned closer, her breath sharp and cool with icy mints. Her voice dropped to the soft-est of whispers. "Provided you make it worth my while." She raised her gray eyebrows expectantly, with a cunning smile, then whirled around, her wellies squeaking on the wood of the back porch. She returned to her chair and took a final sip of tea, her hand shaking almost imperceptibly. She set the fussy toile cup on the table, where it lolled to the side and spilled fragrant chocolate mint tea.

"Oh, dear." Lois's voice was raspy and wheezy and raw. She set the cup upright, and her hands fluttered to her face, then her throat. She let out a string of hoarse coughs and a trio of wheezes.

Whitney set down her cup and broke off conver-sation with her father. "Are you alright, Aunt Lois?" Concern deepened her delicate features, and she stood to help her aunt.

Lois rose unsteadily to her feet and made for the back door. She called over her shoulder as she entered the house, "I'm just going to go powder my nose." She seemed fine again and had stopped coughing. Whitney relaxed and sank into her seat.

I stood, stunned, at my post on the edge of the

porch, more alarmed by what she'd just said than her coughing and wheezing fit.

Did she just suggest a quid pro quo?

I couldn't pay Lois a bribe to get my permit approved. It would be entirely unethical, and even I wasn't that desperate.

That's what she just proposed, isn't it?

She was the picture of propriety, so maybe I'd just imagined it or misinterpreted what she said.

"Mallory!" Whitney's cry cut through my miserable thoughts, and she came bounding over to me. "Everything was absolutely delicious."

I glowed, Lois's shakedown momentarily forgotten.

"We'd like to go ahead with this exact menu. I can't believe you and Rachel put this together so quickly."

"We're glad you like it." My sister caught the tail end of Whitney's pronouncement as she walked around the side of the house. "The ghost hunters just left," she whispered.

I sighed with relief.

The dogs started to go nuts, keening and pawing at the door to the kitchen.

"What's wrong, little fella?" Whitney crouched down to calm Bruce.

I peered over her shoulder into the kitchen, where Lois's boots lay sideways on the ground, her panty-hose-clad legs sticking out at an odd angle.

"Oh my God." I pushed open the door, and Rachel followed.

"Oh, *no!*" Rachel hurried over to Lois, who was lying on the floor, her legs and arms askew. Her eyes were closed, and her chest rose and fell in time with raspy, labored breaths.

"Aunt Lois!" Whitney ran into the room, Angela on her heels, and Porter followed a few seconds behind, gasping and grabbing the chair railing.

Delilah scooted in and stopped just before she drove over Lois. "I knew it! I knew it! I drew the death card this morning." Her eyes roved wildly, and she stared in openmouthed shock at Bruce, who was barking and nudging his owner, his bushy doggy eyebrows dancing in alarm. "That creature! A white hound! He portends death!"

"Shut up! He's just a harmless little Westie!" Rachel gave Delilah's scooter a push while I started CPR on Lois.

As I felt for Lois's missing pulse, all I could think was, "Not again."

Chapter Four

"This house isn't haunted; it's cursed." It was hard for the chief of police to grill you when you were sort of dating his son and regularly met him over Friday pot roast dinner, but Truman Davies usually did his best. Except today, he seemed to be letting me off the hook.

"This wasn't your fault." Truman clapped his large hand on my back and shook his head somberly. "Accidents happen."

"It wasn't an accident. Healthy people don't just keel over." I handed Whitney a cold cup of chocolate mint tea.

She bawled into the purple tablecloth on the porch.

"The coroner just called me. We can't be sure just yet, but she thinks it was an anaphylactic reaction to an allergen." Truman patted Whitney's back with one hand and gave me a shrug with the other.

"It must have been shellfish of some kind! Why didn't she have her EpiPen?" Whitney dabbed at twin rivulets of mascara.

In the ensuing madness that had followed our discovery of Lois, Whitney had rushed in with her aunt's plaid purse and upended it on the kitchen floor, screaming about a missing EpiPen.

"She never, *ever* travels without it," Whitney insisted between jagged hiccups.

Angela joined Truman in patting her shoulder and murmured an ineffectual, "There, there." I'm sure she meant to be comforting, but she couldn't slip out of her cool, collected demeanor. But her hands shook, and her voice betrayed her discomfort.

Porter held his daughter's hand and slumped back in his chair, his eyes far away, stunned and glassy.

"It wouldn't take a lot," he muttered dejectedly. "Lois was highly allergic."

"Look, you're new at this. You probably didn't realize you had an allergen somewhere in the kitchen." Truman moved closer and delivered his opinion in a low voice.

"I was scrupulously clean! Fanatical, even! No *way* did any allergens touch her lips." I toned down my voice out of respect for Whitney's family.

"It's okay, Mallory. Don't beat yourself up about this. It could've happened to anyone."

"She said we didn't cook with Lois's allergen." Rachel glowered at Truman from her chair.

"We don't have a single bit of crab, lobster, or shrimp in this house," I insisted, trying to not seem like I was just deflecting. "No clams or mussels or anything."

Whitney shook her head. "It could have just been

a trace. This isn't your fault." Her eyes told a different story. "She should have had the EpiPen with her. I can't imagine why she didn't." She burst into a new gale of tears.

"We'd better go," Angela declared and ushered her niece and brother off the porch and to her car. Angela's car rolled down the drive, kicking up a small cloud of dust. They left Lois's Jaguar parked beneath a ginkgo tree, emblazoned with a "My terriers are smarter than your honor student" bumper sticker.

"They didn't take the dogs!" I could see the Westies through the kitchen window. They must have forgotten them in their shock and haste. Bruce sat in the corner, whimpering dolefully in the direction where Lois had lain, his voluminous eyebrows dancing up and down. Maisie milled about the kitchen, her little stumpy tail between her legs. She returned again and again to the spot where we'd found Lois's body. Fiona licked Maisie's face in what seemed like an attempt to calm her down.

Whiskey, my calico cat, marched into the kitchen, then screeched and alighted on the table when she saw the dogs. She arched her back and hissed in disdain at the canine interlopers. Soda was less perturbed, but she also hopped onto the table and swished her tail in annoyance. She gave the pups a quizzical look, then resumed washing herself in a patch of sunlight. The dogs barked in return and ran in frenzied circles around the oak table. Finally, Soda braved the dogs to get a bite of kibble. The little orange kitten wanted nothing to do with Bruce or Fiona, but she did a delicate, sniffing do-si-do with Maisie and swatted playfully at the Westie's nose. Maisie shied back as if Soda were a Doberman instead of a five-pound miniature ball of orange fluff.

I opened the door and whistled, and the three little dogs ran out onto the porch. Little Maisie placed her snowy paws on my calves, and I reflexively bent down to pick her up.

"There goes *that* wedding." Rachel frowned.

"*Rachel!* A woman has died!" I was outwardly aghast at her comment, but inside I was thinking the same thing. I stroked the small white dog and buried my nose in her fur. She missed her human mommy and shook like a leaf.

"I know, and it's awful, but you can't tell me you weren't thinking the same thing."

Garrett relieved me from responding with his arrival. He crossed the last few feet of the backyard that connected our houses and enveloped me in a bear hug, stopping at the last minute to avoid crushing Maisie.

"Dad told me what happened," he whispered into my hair. He patted Maisie, and the Westie licked his hand. "I came as soon as I could." Garrett and his daughter, Summer, lived with his mother and his father, Chief Truman.

"Can it get any worse?" I pulled back and gestured around me. "This renovation has been plagued with accidents, there's no time to pull off Whitney's wedding, and now Lois is dead. Not to mention," I snuck a glance at my sister, "the wedding is probably off now."

"I was just telling Mallory she's not to blame."

Truman sidled up next to his son and shot me a pleading look. "There was probably a trace of allergen in the food, but that couldn't be helped."

I stepped away from father and son and held my chin high. I placed Maisie on the ground, and she snuggled next to my feet. "That kitchen was spotless. Whitney gave me a list of every allergen for her family, and I made sure none of them were near the wedding tasting."

"It was most likely some kind of shellfish, but we won't know the official cause for a few days," a cheerful voice said behind me. I whirled around to face a small, buoyant, pretty young woman with nutmeg-colored hair and eyes and freckles dancing across her ski-jump nose. Her whole demeanor was bouncy. She had bouncy hair, a bouncy step, and a girlishly enthusiastic voice. She must have been a cheerleader in a former life.

"Mallory, this is Natalie Nelson, the coroner." Truman smiled at the peppy woman, who held out her hand.

I shook it in a daze. *This woman is the coroner?*

"Don't feel bad, Mallory. It could have been a minute bit of shellfish from anywhere."

Thank you, voice of reason.

"Although," she cocked her pert head, "it was likely in the food you just served." I dropped her hand like a hot coal and bristled as I picked up Maisie.

"Garrett!" Natalie stood on tiptoe and enveloped my sort-of-boyfriend in an embrace just long and familiar enough to make me uncomfortable. "It's *so* nice to see you!"

Garrett looked appropriately sheepish and broke off the hug before Natalie did.

"How's it going, Nat?" He took a step back and rewarded her with a slow but flustered smile.

She returned it with a billion-kilowatt grin and kept her eyes locked on his.

Nat? What the heck is going on?

"I haven't seen you in a while." She continued mugging, like an adorable, pint-sized jack-o'-lantern, and I could stand it no longer.

"Would anyone like a piece of cake? We have a lot left over." I stuttered and wondered if it was bad form to serve something that might have killed Lois.

"I'd love some!" Natalie chirped. "But I bet Truman will need it for evidence. I could go for a cup of coffee, though." She smiled at me expectantly, and I had no choice but to leave her on the back porch gazing at Garrett and retreat to the kitchen. I set Maisie on the floor, and Bruce and Fiona raced in behind me, to the chagrin of my cats, who retreated to the breakfast room and their perch on the table again.

"Alert, alert," Rachel whispered as she followed close behind. "That chick has designs on your man."

"He's not my man," I retorted with a touch of irritation in my voice. I banged the percolator around the counter. "We haven't even been on a single real date!" I shook coffee beans into the grinder with an unsteady hand, and several spilled over the counter and onto the floor, where they pinged around like marbles. I hated to admit the woman flirting with Garrett had unnerved me more than Lois's untimely death.

"He is so," Rachel soothed and emerged from the closet with a broom to sweep up the beans. "You guys have just been too busy to go out on a proper date. But I know men, and this one is absolutely crazy about you. Now go out there and get 'im." She shooed me out of the kitchen and took over the coffee-making duties.

I must have been imagining things, because when I returned to the back porch, Natalie, the cute-as-a-button coroner, was gone. She hadn't stayed for a cup of coffee, and she didn't have designs on Garrett. She was just dropping in to inform her colleague Truman about Lois's cause of death. From the corner of the porch, I could see a lemon-yellow VW Bug exiting the drive, a pink flower attached to the antenna.

She even has an adorable car.

Garrett and Truman were deep in conversation.

"This family doesn't need any more tragedy." Truman stroked his chin. "This year will be the twentieth anniversary of Vanessa Scanlon's disappearance."

"And the tenth since an innocent man was wrongly convicted." Garrett squinted his hazel eyes, an exact replica of his father's.

"Don't start with that again." Truman snorted and waved his hand, making light of Garrett's comment.

"Your department's investigation was sloppy at best." Garrett's voice was clipped and strained, and his hands were fisted at his sides.

I frowned and took a step closer. I'd never seen him this worked up.

"It wasn't *my* department. I wasn't chief yet. Rusty Dalton was still in charge. And, son, it was your very first homicide case." A warning note pierced his dismissal. "I know you'd like to do things differently, but you can't turn back time."

"Eugene Newton is innocent." Garrett's nostrils flared, and he turned to me. His eyes softened, and he dropped a kiss on top of my head. "I'm sorry. I need some air. I'll call later." The right side of his mouth crooked up, and he turned to leave, threading his way through the newly manicured gardens and fields of purple thistle and goldenrod back to his house.

Truman shook his head. "I apologize for my son's behavior." He stated this as if Garrett were a two-year-old who'd just pitched a tantrum. "But someday he'll admit that his client murdered Vanessa Scanlon in cold blood."

I trembled and went back to the kitchen to settle my nerves with a cup of coffee.

Truman strode away with leftovers from the wedding tasting in evidence bags. Before he left, he reiterated that Lois's death wasn't a homicide, just a horrific accident. Rachel and I cleared the tasting table.

We only had a few minutes to spare before my mother arrived, and she always showed up a tad early, the better to catch us straightening up.

"My daughters!" She surprised us in the kitchen. "This house is a *disaster*," she said cheerfully as she advanced for a hug.

"We must've left the front door open," I whispered to Rachel.

Mom held us both back at arm's length for a

quick inspection, while Bruce, Maisie, and Fiona sniffed Mom's pants, probably picking up the scent of her pug back in Florida.

A pack of Skittles had nothing on my mom's wardrobe. For as long as I could remember, she always dressed in a sweater set in a bold hue, with matching accessories. She even worked this look down in the heat and humidity of Pensacola, where she and my stepfather, Doug, had retired and never managed to sweat a drop. Today was kelly green. She wore a wool sweater set in the vivid color, with matching suede loafers and a jade elephant nestled just below her throat. Had her monochromaticism inspired confidence from her decorating and staging clients? Ever since she'd retired five years ago, she'd commandeered Doug's wardrobe. He'd stayed in Florida for Mom's short trip, but I bet he was sporting a matching green polo shirt today, with his usual defiantly white socks. He had to draw the line somewhere.

Mom tucked a piece of hair behind Rachel's ear and scanned her outfit. "This dress is just stunning on you, dear." She gave us each a kiss.

Rachel sent me a victorious smile.

Mom took in all of the food in the kitchen. "I see you girls have been working hard on the wedding-planning business. This all looks absolutely divine!" She switched to one of her favorite topics, my love life.

"How is Garrett and that darling daughter of his? You'd make a wonderful stepmother someday."

Rachel looked torn between laughing, with amusement dancing in her pretty green eyes, and helping me distract Mom.

"Garrett and I haven't even been on a proper date yet, unless you count the family dinners I've had over at his and Truman's house." I needed to set the record straight.

My mother made a tsk-tsk noise and opened her mouth to say more.

"Check out our newest guests at the B and B." Rachel knelt down to pat Lois's dogs, and I sent my sister a grateful look.

Rachel and I caught Mom up on the happenings from the morning, just as the rest of the contractors arrived. We had to raise our voices to be heard over the cacophony of drills and hammering. They'd graciously postponed their workday until the afternoon after the wedding tasting.

"That's dreadful!" My mother dropped the cookie she'd been noshing on as if it contained poison and clasped the jade elephant at her throat.

Bruce motored over and deftly gobbled the cookie.

My mom moved her pendant up and down on the chain around her neck with nervous, jerky movements. "You girls ought to have been more careful!"

"I fully expect the police will find no shellfish in any of our cooking. I could use your expertise with decorating the place," I offered, trying to kill my mom with kindness.

Her green eyes lit up, and she clapped her hands together.

"That would be wonderful! I can just see it now." She dramatically shut her eyes, then flicked them open, shining with ideas. "We'll do a tropical vacation theme. It'll be just the thing for guests looking for a getaway when it's cold and gray here in Pennsylvania. We can reupholster everything and brighten up this heavy, dark wood. I'll mix sumptuous fabrics with playful ones. It'll be magnificent!"

"Whoa, who said anything about a vacation theme?" I stepped back in alarm.

Maisie picked up on my dismay and began to whine.

"Besides, that sounds expensive. I've got a strict budget, Mom, and I'm applying for this house to earn historical status. Maybe you'd like to consult with the local historian before you jump in. I plan on using existing pieces of furniture."

"Don't worry your little head about those pesky details, Mallory. Leave it all to me. I'll get right on it." Mom spun on the heel of her green loafer and began to take stock of the house, with Fiona the Westie trotting to keep up with her.

"Whew! You got her out of our hair, and I didn't even have to say a word." Rachel slumped in a chair and undid her cloisonné clip. "I'm exhausted, and she's been here for what, five minutes?"

"She'll be back in a second with some sweet comment," I mused. "Do you really think she'll try to decorate with a Florida theme?" I regretted asking my mother for decorating help, even though she was the expert.

"It's not like we can stop her if she does."

A bloodcurdling shriek pierced the air. Maisie went wild, yapping and turning around in nervous circles. Whiskey hissed and streaked up the back stairs to a calmer area of the house, a blur of black, white, and orange.

"What now?" Rachel and I hightailed it to the hallway, expecting the worst.

Delilah had scooted within ten feet of my mother. She pointed her knobby index finger at her and stabbed at the air. She looked like a pirate, marauding around with big gold earrings, a red bandana restraining her gray curls, and a flag attached to the pole on her scooter with a Dia de los Muertos skull. "You! You came back!" Delilah stared at my mom as if she were a damp gym sock left in the bottom of a bag.

Mom had a similar reaction to Delilah, her lips pursed and screwed in a scowl.

Rachel positioned herself between Mom and Delilah. "Don't talk to my mom like that! Who do you think you are?"

"How in the heck does Delilah know you?" I gasped.

Jesse stepped out of the shadows and stared at my mom. He glanced at Rachel and me and seemed to consider what he was going to say. Finally, he addressed my mother instead of us. "She's the one that got away."

"*That* is the hussy who broke my son's heart!" Delilah screeched, peering around Rachel at my now ashen mother.

Chapter Five

Jesse took a step toward Mom, as if he wanted to gather her up in his giant arms. But he faltered at the last second and took a hesitant step back. Mom stared back and forth between the triangle of her daughters and Jesse and Delilah, then burst into tears and tore up the bannisterless stairs. She called over her shoulder, "I need to touch up my makeup!"

"Whoa! You and Mom used to date?" I stared at Jesse. I couldn't picture it.

Delilah must be going crazy.

"I offered to marry her."

"Say *what?*" Rachel reached out for the bannister that wasn't there and almost fell over. She grabbed my shoulder and steadied herself.

"Quit joking around, Jesse." I playfully punched his colossal arm, and he barely moved, a pillar of stone.

"It's no joke. She didn't accept." Jesse stared off into the middle distance, right where my mother had last been on the stair landing.

Delilah snapped her gnarled fingers and awakened him from his trance.

"It's a good thing she didn't! I foretold awful things about your union, as you recall. And it appears she's married to someone else, so you can stop looking so hangdog."

Jesse whirled around and glowered at Delilah. "This is all your fault, Mother." He stomped off to the second floor like a six-foot-eight toddler.

"C'mon. We have to get to the bottom of this." Rachel grabbed my elbow and hauled me up the stairs in search of our mother.

She didn't have to twist my arm. I was as curious as she was about my mother's former relationship with my contractor.

We found my mother calmly seated at an antique dressing table in the green bedroom. She carefully patted on a new layer of foundation and expertly covered the red blotchy patches her crying had raised.

"Mom, you have some splainin' to do." Rachel pulled up a frilly chair and sat next to our mother.

"When did you date Jesse? Did he really propose?" I tried to not sound gossipy and eager.

My mother slid down farther, and her ears betrayed her, turning red, since she hadn't slathered them with foundation.

"It was a long time ago. I was just shocked to see him again. I don't want to talk about it." She buried her face in her hands and waited for us to leave.

"Not so fast, Mom. We know it was a long time ago. You and Doug have been married for ages."

"It was right after your father left us." Mom let her hands fall to her lap and nervously twisted her elephant pendant. "He was renovating a house in Coal Valley, and I was decorating it." She named a town halfway between Port Quincy and Pittsburgh. "I never had you girls meet anyone I was"—she paused and blushed—"dating, unless it was serious."

She'd only introduced us to Doug very carefully, very slowly. By the time they were engaged and got married, it felt like a natural progression, and we were happy to be adopted by Doug and take his last name. I'd never caught a whiff of a relationship with Jesse Flowers.

"I was lonely . . . ," Mom began tentatively, picking a minuscule dot of lint from her sweater sleeve. "And Jesse was so handsome, and . . ." A slow flush of pink began at her neckline and crept upward, stopping where she'd applied the foundation.

"It's okay, Mom." I placed a hand on her shoulder. But I really wanted to scream *Stop the story!* Picturing my mom together with Jesse in a romantic rendezvous made me wish they made Magic Erasers for upsetting thoughts.

"Ooh, Jesse was your rebound!" Rachel leaned in as if hearing an especially juicy bit of gossip. She raised her brows and went in for the kill. "Was this before or after Doug?"

"That's it! Forget I said anything." Mom stood and minced out the door. "I'm going to bring in the rest of my luggage," she called over her shoulder in a huffy tone.

"You ruined it!" I threw up my hands in exasperation. "I wanted to hear about Jesse's proposal and why Mom didn't marry him. But the other stuff I could do without. Yuck."

"C'mon, we know why she didn't marry him.

He's tied to his mama's purse strings, and Mom probably couldn't stand to live with Delilah. Thank God." Rachel cringed. "I'd hate to have her as a stepgrandma."

I had to agree. And I wished more than anything that Doug was here. Rachel must've read my mind.

"Should we call Doug and let him know Mom's former . . . ," she faltered for the word.

Flame? Almost-fiancé? Great love of her life?

"Former boyfriend is here?" I filled in.

Rachel nodded.

I thought for a moment. "No, that's Mom's business. We'll just keep an eye on them."

Rachel gave me a reluctant nod, and we uneasily went back to planning Whit's wedding, just in case she didn't cancel.

My mother moped around for the rest of the week, while Jesse gave her a wide berth. I gathered all of the documentation I needed for the Planning Commission and put it in a file to take to City Hall next week.

It was Friday night dinner at the Davies household, or date night, as I liked to think of it. Garrett and I had yet to go on a formal date, but I'd been joining his family for their end of the work week meal for the last couple months. I got to chat with his lovely thirteen-year-old daughter, Summer, and his charming mother, Lorraine, and hear the latest police goings on from Truman. Not to mention seeing Garrett.

I knocked on the door of the Davies' tidy brick ranch. An autumn-leaf wreath was mounted on the front door, its sparkly orange bow set at a jaunty angle. Carved pumpkins with gap-toothed smiles huddled squat on either side of the entrance, and twinkling lights lined the picture window. Summer must have convinced her grandma to decorate for Halloween. Lorraine Davies opened the door, and I presented her with a pumpkin-rum cake.

"Sweetie, you shouldn't have." She always said the same thing, then offered a shy smile and accepted the dessert. Garrett's family were my guinea pigs as I tried out recipes for the B and B. Lorraine was decked out for fall in a brown turtleneck sweater with a scattering of yellow and red leaves knitted along the bottom hem.

"No trouble at all. I love the decorations."

"Summer did them. Isn't she sweet?" Lorraine bustled into the kitchen and assembled a pot roast on a platter already laden with potatoes and carrots. It smelled heavenly.

"Can I help with anything?"

"Why don't you help Summer set the table?"

"Mallory!" Summer bounded into the kitchen with her black kitten, Jeeves, in her arms. She set him down, and the little guy sniffed carefully at my jeans, no doubt searching out the smell of his mother, Whiskey, and sister, Soda. He jumped back in alarm, then renewed his sniffing with vigor. He probably picked up canine smells in addition to the usual cats.

"You need to help me change Grandma's mind," Summer whispered as we set the table for five. "All of my friends are going as zombies for Halloween, and she won't let me be one too."

"What does she want you to be?" I didn't want to get in the middle of it, but maybe I could help Summer think up a compromise costume that would be acceptable to her grandma.

She wrinkled her cute elfin nose. "A Disney princess." Summer was thirteen going on twenty, and I agreed that she was probably too old to be a princess.

"Can you think of anything that isn't a princess or a zombie that you'd like to be? Something your grandma would be okay with?"

Summer ran a hand through her short blond hair and sighed dramatically. "That's not the point. Phoebe and Jocelyn are going to be zombies. I won't match!" She shuddered at the thought of a Halloween where she couldn't coordinate with her best friends' theme.

"What does your dad say?" I thought I'd deflect and defer to Garrett.

"He thinks a zombie is okay, just tacky."

I stifled a smile.

"But Grandpa told me to listen to my grand-mother, and he's doing it just to get back at Dad. Dad and Grandpa aren't talking."

"What?" I said it a little too sharply because Lorraine leaned her head into the dining room.

"Do you need something, Mallory?"

"No, thank you, Lorraine."

Summer dropped her voice after her grand-mother left. "It's because of that case a million years ago. Daddy says his client is innocent, and Grandpa called him a fool. Grandpa also said he was just doing his job back then, upholding justice, not defending losers who are guilty like Dad did."

I grimaced, but Summer seemed to relish her report.

"That was two days ago, and they haven't spoken since."

I was sure Garrett and Truman would think differently about volleying insults at each other if they knew Summer was parroting them back.

Just then Truman ambled into the room in his off-duty outfit of light washed jeans and a West Virginia University sweatshirt. Garrett entered from the kitchen. He carried the pot roast and blatantly ignored his father.

"Good to see you." He squeezed my arm and sat across from his daughter. "The pumpkin cake looks delicious."

"Summer, will you tell your father he forgot to bring in the peas?" Truman stared at a spot above Garrett's head.

Summer giggled and ignored her grandfather.

"Summer, tell him to get the darn peas himself if he noticed they're missing."

Summer tossed me an "I told you so" look.

Just then the doorbell rang.

"Oh, dear, I wasn't expecting anyone else." Lorraine looked flustered. She was a tidy, precise woman, from her tight gray curls to her trim leaf apron that matched her sweater. She didn't like surprises.

"I'll get it!" Summer leaped to her feet and ran to the front door, Jeeves bounding after her like a furry black pinball.

"Look who's here." Her voice was flat as she returned with a perky, grinning Natalie Nelson.

"Natalie! My word!" Lorraine shoved the mandarin Jell-O salad she'd been carrying onto the table and crossed the room in three quick strides to embrace the pert coroner.

"Great to see you, Mrs. Davies." Natalie presented Lorraine with a cheery fall arrangement of tiger lilies and black-eyed Susans erupting out of a ceramic cornucopia. It was as cute, bright, and adorable as its giver.

"These are just lovely." Lorraine beamed as if she'd been handed a bouquet as the winner of the Miss America pageant and shoved my pumpkin cake out of the way to make room for Natalie's flowers.

What is she *doing here?*

"Care to stay for dinner, Natty?" Truman asked, although I was sure that was her intention all along. He called her *Natty?*

"Don't mind if I do." Natalie flashed a triumphant grin and slyly cut a glance in my direction, as if to observe me. She plopped down on the chair next to Garrett, the one I always sat in.

I tried to not glower and surreptitiously gauged his reaction. He looked impassive and took his seat next to the coroner and across from his daughter. Summer looked furious and stroked Jeeves until he yelped and twisted out of her arms. I lamely took the chair next to Summer, catty-corner to Garrett and across from Natalie. She turned her sunny smile to me, and I swear I saw a challenge in her sweet nutmeg eyes.

"I love what you've done with the dining room," she simpered, showing me she'd spent time here before. "When did you put in this wallpaper?" She turned around to further admire the new accent wall of cream and mint stripes.

"Just a month ago, dear." Lorraine served a helping of potatoes onto Natalie's plate. I grimaced at the *dear* part, but that was what Lorraine called everyone.

"I see you still have the place mats I crocheted!" Every other sentence from Natalie ended in an exclamation point. I stared at the cheerful red place mats, and Summer appeared to do the same.

"And how are you, kiddo?" Natalie turned her megawatt smile on Summer and waited expectantly. I saw Summer wince at being called a kid.

"I'm doing just fine, Natalie," Summer responded politely, if not a bit coolly.

"Summer and I were talking about Halloween costumes." I offered up a change of subject.

"With her delicate good looks, I think she should be something pretty, like a princess." Lorraine smiled. "What about Elsa, from *Frozen?*"

Summer shook her head, her short blond hair fluffing out. Just this July, Rachel and I had convinced her to cut off all of the inky Goth black hair she'd dyed. I didn't think she'd ever go for Elsa.

"I think I'm a little too old to be anything princessy, Grandma. I'm sorry," she added to soften the blow. She took a deep breath and braced her hands on the dining room table. "I'd like to be a zombie."

Natalie drew in a sharp breath. "The deceased I work with deserve dignity and respect. Not the mockery I see in all of these zombie movies and shows. I don't think a zombie is an appropriate costume."

Summer appeared mortified. She chewed on her lower lip and pulled her cloth napkin into a taut line. Her eyes filled with embarrassment. Garrett looked furious. He opened his mouth to speak when Natalie beat him to the punch.

"Tell you what," Natalie continued. "I was Glinda the Good Witch last Halloween for the police department party, and we're about the same height. It's an impressive costume, and I'd be happy to lend it to you!" How was this perky, adorable woman a death examiner? *Does. Not. Compute.*

"Natalie, how wonderful!" Lorraine actually clapped her hands together, and I tried to not stare. I'd thought I had a good relationship with Garrett's mother, but Natalie made her practically manic with happiness. "Say thank you, Summer." Lorraine cast a look at her granddaughter that brooked no wiggle room.

"Thank you for the offer, Natalie." Summer set down her fork. "But Grandma," Summer continued with real fear in her eyes, "I'll be the laughing stock of the whole eighth grade if I show up in a princess costume." She abandoned her dinner. "Did you come over tonight just to offer me a Halloween costume?" she asked Natalie, her big hazel eyes wide and questioning.

Bingo. Leave it to Summer to get to the heart of the matter. I'd been wondering the same thing myself.

"Actually, I'm here to give Mallory some good news! The lab informed me there was no shellfish in the food you cooked for the wedding tasting."

That was *fantastic* news.

"So that means—," I began.

"Oh no, don't start." Truman held up his large hand in a halt. "I can see where you're going with this. Lois wasn't murdered, Mallory. Just because there was no shellfish in the dishes you cooked doesn't mean she didn't ingest them elsewhere, by accident."

"That's right!" Natalie chimed in, as buoyant as a cruise ship director. "The anaphylaxis didn't have to be immediate. And the contents of her stomach showed she ate a big breakfast and probably several snacks, any of which could have contained—"

"Thank you, Natalie," Garrett said with a tight smile. He placed his hand gently over hers to stop her dissertation on the digested contents of Lois's stomach, which had turned Lorraine an interesting shade of green.

I was glad to see Garrett quickly remove his hand.

The rest of the meal passed in a blur. Garrett and I waited until dessert was over and Summer was excused. We slipped out of the house while Summer and Lorraine did dishes and Truman and Natalie talked shop, and we went for a short walk back to my car. I was pleased that not a crumb of my pumpkin cake remained and glad Rachel and I had been cleared of making allergenic goods in our kitchen.

"So how long did you and Natalie date?" I breathed in the damp, early-evening air and held it in my lungs. It had turned hot and stuffy in the dining room, and I was glad to be out of there. A light rain began to fall, and we didn't have umbrellas.

Garrett put his arm around my shoulders and drew me closer. The drizzle drenched my curls, probably turning them to frizz, and little beads of moisture adorned Garrett's dark hair.

"It doesn't matter, Mallory. What matters is I'm dating you right now."

So they had dated.

I stepped out of his embrace and turned to face him. Rivulets of rain ran down his face and under his jacket collar. "We've yet to go out on a real date."

Garrett took my hand and looked carefully into my eyes. "Let's go out on a real date. Just you and me."

I shook my head. "I love eating with your family. I don't want to take you away from your Friday dinners. I just wish we had more time." *And I can't help but wonder why Natalie keeps showing up, and why now.*

"We have all the time in the world." He leaned over and planted a slow kiss on my lips that quickly crescendoed to firework proportions. I no longer felt cold, but warm to the bone.

BEEP! BEEEEEEEEP! BEEEEP!

I yelped and jumped back, expecting to see an oncoming car. We broke apart and peered down the street to his driveway, where a frenziedly grinning Natalie peered sheepishly at us from behind the wheel of her yellow Bug. She rolled down her window and raised her eyes to meet mine.

"Sorry! I hit the horn by accident!" She reversed down the drive, nearly taking out a jack-o'-lantern in the process, and peeled down the street.

"You're over her?"

Garrett cast a frustrated look at Natalie and pivoted back to me. "Completely." There was a steely edge to his voice.

"It seems like she didn't get the memo."

Garrett flushed red and opened his mouth to explain, but there was no time for a response.

"Mallory! I need to talk to you." Truman burst out of the house and placed his hands on his hips, a sour look on his face. His jaw worked back and forth, making his jowls dance.

I dropped my hands to my side. "Looks like we're in trouble."

The two of us shuffled back to the stoop like chastened teenagers.

"You were right." Truman said the words softly, with great regret. "It was no accident. Lois Scanlon was murdered."

I hurried home to tell Rachel the bad-yet-good news. Lois had been murdered, which was inconceivable and devastating. But that definitely got Rachel and me off the hook for accidentally killing her with allergens.

"Bloody Mary mix in her mints?" Rachel frowned and returned to chopping cranberries for a new biscotti recipe we were trying out. Bruce sat at her feet and stared dolefully at her with his white mustache quivering.

"Doggies can't eat cranberries," I counseled and scruffed him behind his ears. I got him a biscuit, and he gratefully gulped it down. Fiona sat contentedly nearby, and Maisie was stretched out on her back with her little white paws windmilling in the air, dreaming doggy dreams.

"Truman explained Lois's mints were coated with Bloody Mary mix containing clam juice." I gasped as

I recalled her popping an Altoid into her mouth right after she solicited me for a bribe. "I saw her eat that mint! Who would have laced her mints with shellfish, and better yet, when and why?"

Before we could ponder the motive for killing Lois, my phone trilled out to announce a new text. "It's from Whitney." I bit my lip as I opened it, and Rachel crowded in to read the screen.

The wedding is still on. Can you meet to discuss?

I let out a breath I didn't know I'd been holding and sat back with relief.

"That's great news!" Rachel resumed chopping while I texted Whitney back to affirm a meeting with her on Monday.

"She wants me to meet her at her maid of honor's house. She was staying with Lois and doesn't feel she can go back there."

"Who is her maid of honor?"

I dropped the phone with a clatter on the table and stared at the address on the screen in shock. It couldn't be. I clicked on the address, and it opened up a map website on my phone. I was astonished when a grid of streets materialized on the screen.

"You've *got* to be kidding me."

"What is it?"

"Do you recognize this address?" I spun the phone around and showed it to Rachel. She shrugged. "Should I?"

"It's the place Helene bought for Keith and me." Before I called off my wedding to Keith Pierce, his mother had bought us a barren plot of land in a development of mega McMansions.

"But there couldn't be a house there already, could there? It was just a foundation this summer. We know from renovations here that it's impossible to throw up a structure that fast."

Rachel reached for my phone. She clicked off my screen with a decisive tap of her long, strawberry-colored nail. "Don't go into that den of vipers. I smell a trap."

"I have to go." I took a cleansing breath and tried to whoosh the panicked tone out of my voice. "Whit is my client, and we're lucky she still wants to have the wedding here."

On Monday afternoon, I took a fortifying slug of coffee and climbed into my vintage, rattling Volvo station wagon, a hulking tan vehicle I'd christened the Butterscotch Monster. Bruce, Fiona, and Maisie sat in the backseat, sliding down the long bank of tan leather each time I made a turn. I didn't relish meeting Whitney at my ex's address.

I pulled into the circular driveway and stared at the four-car garage, trying to discern whether Keith's navy BMW was already parked inside. When I last saw this plot of land in the summer, there had been a skeleton of a foundation rising out of the mud. The contractors had worked at a dizzyingly fast speed, because a monstrous, eclectic edifice stood complete and imposing on a new sod lawn, where seams of grass met together like green jigsaw puzzle pieces. The house was a maroon brick study in modernism, with cubes and angles jutting out in alarming, unpredictable patterns. Floor-to-ceiling windows of glass block graced each level, and a garish copper roof crowned the hulking colossus, reflecting the autumn sun in long, blinding slices. The landscaping echoed the abstract architecture, with Lilliputian topiary trees cut in geometric shapes, clustered together like nervous passersby on a crowded sidewalk. Red-leafed Japanese maples stood at attention, flanking the wide, double front door. The house would have been at home perched on a canyon in Los Angeles but looked out of place in Port Quincy. How had it been built so quickly? I shook my head. *Silly me.* Keith's mother, Helene, practically ran Port Quincy, and she'd no doubt commandeered the best and swiftest contractors to throw the house up in record time. When the doyenne of Port Quincy cracked the whip, things happened fast.

It was utterly arresting, but not my style. All of this could have been mine, if I'd gone through with my marriage to Keith. I breathed a sigh of relief and was glad this wasn't my alternate reality.

"Arf!" Bruce let out a gruff bark, and I nodded at him. "I'm alarmed too, buddy."

I must have stalled too long, my mouth agape, because someone tapped at my window.

"Eeek!" I whipped my head left and scared Whitney. She laughed weakly when she saw that I was okay and motioned for me to roll down my window. Since my car was from the 1970s, I actually did roll it down.

"I'm sorry! You were sitting here so long, I wondered if you were okay."

"I was just taking in the house. It's very . . . eye-catching."

Whitney motioned for me to follow her, and I

reluctantly left the cocoon of the station wagon, the little dogs churning their legs to keep up.

"I'm so glad you brought the dogs. I can't believe we left them at Thistle Park. We were in shock." Whitney stopped at the front door and bent to pet the pups.

They stood on their hind legs and tried to give her doggie kisses.

"I'm sorry about your aunt Lois." I gave Whitney a swift hug, which she returned with surprising force.

"It wasn't your fault," she assured me. "It could have been anything, and it wasn't like her to not have her EpiPen. She was the best aunt a girl could have." Whitney dabbed at her swollen eyes with a worn tissue. "My fiancé, Ian, my dad, and I talked about whether we should go on with the wedding. We decided life is so short. My dad's health is getting worse"—her voice caught in her throat—"so we'll carry on and get married while he's still here. Lois and my dad were so close; she would've wanted that."

Not to mention the fact it wasn't the meal Rachel and I cooked that killed her. I handed Whit a packet of tissues from my purse.

"Thanks. I'm all out." She sheepishly accepted the tissues and opened the red lacquered front door for me. She smiled at the dogs and shooed them inside. They dutifully trailed in behind her and followed her around like a small school of furry white minnows.

I carried a sample board of fabrics and flowers for Whitney to approve. I stepped over the threshold and would have been less surprised to find myself in

Oz with the munchkins. A massive open floor plan revealed peach tile, peach pillars, poufy peach window treatments, and a peach ceiling. Bridesmaid-sea-foam green and gold accents were woven throughout the room, from the rugs in the living room area to the wallpaper border that hugged the walls. Impractical cream furniture was scattered through the house. Everything was frothy and shiny and stiff with yards and yards of chintz and silk and brocade. If the outside looked like it had been designed by Pablo Picasso, the inside was mid-1980s bridal boutique chic. It was like being teleported into Helene Pierce's living room. The outside juxtaposed with the inside showed this house was suffering from a serious case of multiple personality disorder. The dogs loped around the pastel room and sniffed each piece of furniture with glee. Whitney got them a dish of water and some kibble, and they happily settled in the kitchen.

Whitney wrinkled her nose. "My cousin Becca designed the outside of the house. Isn't it daring?" She sat on a shiny, vanilla-colored couch embroidered with seashells and starfish and poured me a cup of coffee with shaking hands.

"It's something!" I said with an even tone.

"Becca's my only cousin on my mom's side. She's a little outrageous but a lot of fun. And her future mother-in-law, Helene, decorated the inside. She's so pushy."

Better Becca than me. I settled into a peach damask wing-backed chair.

"They just got engaged this week. Isn't it exciting?" Whitney picked up a picture from the coffee table of Keith and Becca together in the snow holding skis.

"That's why I was late the other day. I had to help her fiancé plant the ring in a miniature pumpkin."

Keith and I had broken off our engagement in July, and he'd obviously been skiing with Becca all winter. I thought back to the many weekends during ski season when he'd claimed to be out of town.

Whitney dropped her voice conspiratorially. "Becca's fiancé was involved with someone else, so she kept her relationship hush-hush. She wouldn't let any of us meet Keith."

"How scandalous," I said dryly.

"I'm so glad they're out in the open now and getting married!"

"You don't say. I made a mockup of your color scheme and some fabric and floral choices." I changed the subject before I got mired irrevocably in the past. Plus, I wanted to wrap up our meeting and skedaddle before Keith and Becca arrived. "The linens vendor can do deep plum tablecloths with chocolate overlays, and I'm sure the florist can handle an explosion of mums, since it's October." I unfolded the triptych poster board with swatches of fabric for the tables and a photograph of a representative table I'd set up with mums flowing down the center in a lush, curving river. Chunky pillar candles in cranberry, evergreen, and plum rested on brass candlesticks of various heights.

"Mums are probably the only flowers the florist can pull off this late in the game. But we can make a wide swath of flowers marching down each banquet table, and it'll look full and lovely."

Whitney ran her fingers over the luxe fabrics and squealed with delight. "This will honor my mom and look perfect for fall. I think this will turn out better than the wedding planned for June. I just wish Lois could be there too. And my mom. But Dad being there makes it all worth it."

"It's beautiful that you're including your mom in other ways," I said gently.

Whitney's electric smile faltered, and I swear she shivered as she stood and crossed the long room to the giant glass doors facing a red deck and rock garden. "I'm not the only one who still thinks about my mom. I've been getting letters about her." She wheeled around and wrung her small hands together.

"From whom? About what?"

"I don't know who's sending them. I got two in Baltimore before I came here. They upset me so much Ian wrote 'Return to sender' and dumped them back in the mail. But whoever's sending them knows I'm in Port Quincy now."

I abandoned the fabric samples and crossed the room to where she stood, clutching a slim white envelope. "Did they send that here?"

"No, this one was addressed to me care of my aunt's restaurant." She placed the envelope in my hand. I opened it and read the letter.

Eugene Newton is innocent. Your mother's killer is still free.

The note looked like it had been composed on a typewriter, as the letters were lightly embossed on the page. The paper was generic white notepaper, college-ruled and with three holes for a binder. A frisson of dread ran through me. I'd probably already marred it with my fingerprints.

"You have to give this to the police. We shouldn't even be handling it." I tentatively held the paper by the edges.

Whitney snatched the paper as if I were going to abscond with it and tucked it under a pile of junk mail on a white wicker table. "No police!" Her voice was high and reedy and frantic. "I don't trust them." She slowed her breathing. "I just want to get married. I don't want any more problems." Her face was white. "And I don't want to upset my dad when he has so little time left. Our time together is one of the most important things in the world to me. I took a leave of absence at my job to spend this month with Dad, and I don't want it to be stressful."

I frowned but grudgingly agreed. "Okay. But let me know if you get any more letters."

A flood of relief rushed over Whitney's pale face, and she sat in a chair and stared at her engagement ring.

"The timing is so odd," she mused, daring to look up. "First the letters arrived, and now Lois is dead."

"You think they're connected?" I picked my head up sharply.

"My mother was murdered twenty years ago, and her killer was put away a decade ago. Why did these letters show up now, postmarked Port Quincy, right before Aunt Lois was killed with clam juice in a Bloody Mary mix? It can't be a coincidence."

I opened my mouth to agree.

A key rustled in the door, and we both swiveled our heads.

I didn't leave soon enough.

Becca and Keith scampered into the house,

holding hands like two coeds. They didn't see me at first, since I was seated behind a giant peach pillar, but I could see them.

"How're you holding up, Whit?" Becca paused at the doorway to slip off her shoes. I did a double take. When she was a new associate and Keith mentored her, she wore sky-high heels with her dresses and suits. Today she wore flats. She was about one inch taller than Keith, and she probably didn't wear heels anymore to avoid upstaging him.

"Mallory, what a pleasant surprise." A reptilian smile crept over Keith's face, and he wrapped his arm around Becca, pulling her in close.

"So nice to see you," Becca simpered, looking like a cat that had caught a coveted mouse. A paunchy, balding, jerky mouse, whom I used to be in love with. She looked fantastic in a slim black skirt suit and vivid pink silk shirt. Her boulder of a ring winked merrily from her left hand as she ran her fingers through her blond hair. The stripe of her dark part stood out against her gleaming blond tresses like a skunk in reverse. I wondered for a moment what had happened to the engagement ring I'd tossed down the street in July.

"It is wonderful." I beamed and moved to fold up my table sample board.

"You know each other?" Whitney blinked in surprise and took the board from me, unfolding it to show to Keith and Becca. "Isn't this amazing? Mallory is pulling this all together in record time."

Becca's eyes flicked toward the samples and then back to Keith.

"It's very nice." Becca didn't look at the board

and dismissed my hard work. She turned to Keith. "Honey, we need to convince your mother that a winter wedding in Barbados will be just the thing." She held her hand out and gazed at the sparkling diamond.

"We'll have a lot to celebrate." Keith stared adoringly at his fiancée. "Our marriage and your successful passing of the bar. You should get the results any day now."

"I've had a wonderful teacher," she cooed.

"I think I'll be going now." I sidestepped the lovebirds and mustered up a tight smile for Whitney. "I'll call you to set up a time to see the florist. I'm sorry about Lois."

"Wait." Keith doled out a smug smile. His new fiancée and Whitney were exclaiming over the fabric swatches and out of earshot. "I heard you were having some trouble with the Planning Commission and rezoning my grandmother's house to commercial."

I stiffened and cursed the gossip mill in this small town.

"It'll be approved in time," I replied, though I was anything but sure.

"It's a shame Lois isn't here to help you with that." His smile spread from ear to ear.

Just then Maisie streaked down the stairs, a very expensive Italian leather shoe dangling from her quivering white jaws. Bruce scampered after her, nipping at her heels, in doggie chase heaven. Fiona woke up from her nap in the kitchen and decided to join in the fun, frolicking and barking around the living room.

"What the . . . ," Keith's face darkened, and he made a move to lunge for the Westie. "She has my shoe! That's a Salvatore Ferragamo, not a chew toy!"

Becca squeaked as if the dogs were rats instead of cute little terriers. Maisie skidded to a stop and dropped the shoe at my feet, the front end of the buttery mahogany leather torn to shreds and dripping with saliva.

I chuckled and picked up the Westie. "Is that a present for me, sweetheart?"

Keith nearly collided with me, quaking with rage. "Get these mutts out of my house!"

"They aren't mutts!" Whitney sidled up next to me and picked up Fiona.

"It's okay, Whitney. Why don't I just take them back to Thistle Park with me? Keith isn't a fan of pets."

A flash of recognition swept across Whitney's face, and she toggled her surprised look between me and my ex-fiancé.

"Th-that would be an excellent idea," she stammered.

"Yes, I want them out *now*." Keith delivered this pronouncement through clenched teeth, his words dripping with acid.

Bruce glared up at Keith and lifted his hind leg.

"Oh *no!*" Whitney divined what was going to happen before I did and reached down for Bruce, but it was too late. The Westie peed all over Keith's trouser leg, then executed a neat little hop over to my feet.

"You little—" Keith was rendered speechless for once and stared at his sodden, dripping cuff. His face contorted with disgust, and he started to strip off his pants right then and there. I took that as my cue to leave.

"Talk to you soon, Whit!" I cried out gaily.

Whitney was shaking with suppressed laughter at Keith. I retrieved the dogs' leashes from my purse and stalked out of Keith's house with Fiona, Bruce, and Maisie leading the way.

Chapter Six

The dogs settled into the back bench seat, and I drove out of Keith's development in a daze. All of the fall decorations blurred together in a haze of orange and black, and the station wagon seemed to steer itself. I turned out of Windsor Meadows and right toward town, and before I knew it, I was back at Thistle Park, a cacophony of hammering cascading out the open window of the front room that was to be my and Rachel's office. I felt the stress of seeing Becca and Keith roll off my shoulders and mustered up a smile for the Westies. "Looks like we'll be seeing a lot more of each other, pups."

A green Prius pulled in behind me with a raven-haired woman at the wheel and my sister in the passenger seat. They both got out of the car in yoga gear, and I realized the driver was the most fit woman I'd ever seen. She was built like a gymnast, short and sinewy, yet she walked with a gazelle-like grace, each step toward the front porch languid and precise.

"Mallory, this is Charity Jones. She teaches my yoga class." Rachel took the dogs' leashes, and I shook hands with the young woman. She had pretty black Irish looks, her blue forget-me-not eyes contrasting with her blue-black hair. Tiny smile lines crinkled at the corners of her eyes, which danced with mirth. She gripped my hand with some force and cracked a dazzling smile. She was a stunner.

"I'm also your neighbor, as it happens." She tilted her head to the right, where I could barely see the peaked roof of the old stone cottage through the copse of deciduous and evergreen trees. "I moved in at the end of the summer."

"Welcome to the neighborhood. What brought you to Port Quincy?"

"I grew up here but left for college. I was with Cirque du Soleil in Las Vegas, and then an injury ended my career. I took up yoga as therapy and fell in love, and I decided to open a new studio back home." So that explained her chiseled yet graceful physique. "You should stop by some time."

Rachel nodded, her feather earrings beating against her shoulders like little wrens. "It's amazing, Mallory! All of the stress of this house just melts away after one of Charity's classes."

Charity gave my sister a grateful look and glanced at her green wristwatch.

"It was nice to meet you, Mallory. I've got to get going." She shook my hand vigorously again and nodded at my sister. "I'll see you in class, Rachel."

A loud bang emanated from the office, and Jesse swore. Charity cringed as if she were in the room.

"I'm sorry this renovation is so loud." I cocked

my head toward the window. "Thankfully it will be over soon, within a fortnight." *At least I pray it will.*

"About that . . ." Charity's luminescent countenance dimmed a degree. "It's been awfully loud. I'm not home much during the day, since I have the studio to run, but when I've been back, it has been hard to relax." Her pretty face was burdened with regret, and I guessed it was hard for her to bring it up.

"I'll ask the contractors to close the windows so the noise is contained."

"You must be planning something big with all of these upgrades."

"As a matter of fact, the house will open as a bed-and-breakfast starting next month!" Rachel gushed.

"And we'll be holding weddings here as well." I smiled and gestured to the wide green lawn and acres behind the house.

Charity's brows furrowed and a deep line formed between her eyes. "*Outdoor* weddings?"

Uh-oh.

"Some," I admitted. "But others will be completely indoors."

"How many people will be descending on Sycamore Street?" Her eyes swept to the quiet end of our road, which dead-ended in front of Thistle Park.

"Er, we can accommodate weddings with two hundred guests," Rachel mumbled, studying the dogs as they sniffed a rake leaning up against the front porch.

"What about traffic?" Charity was positively alarmed. She plucked at the sleeves of her pink warm-up jacket, her movements erratic and agitated, like a bird captured under a bell jar.

"I had a traffic study done as part of the process to rezone the property." I didn't bother to tell Charity it was still in limbo. "The street can handle it, and parking will be located right on the side yard."

"The yard adjoining my property?" Charity's voice wavered, and she actually flinched when I gave her a weak nod.

"We can plant more trees between our yards." My promise was laced with desperation. "And set up the tents for summer weddings on the southern side of the house, away from you."

"*Tents?!* This is worse than I expected." She rubbed the back of her neck as if it pained her.

"Arf!" Bruce strained at his leash as a squirrel bounded up a tree, and Charity nearly jumped out of her black leggings.

"I knew something fishy was going on, but I never dreamed it was of this magnitude. I'm sorry, I have to go meditate." She marched back to her Prius.

"Uh-oh." I watched her reverse down the drive, her face pale and drawn.

"Uh-oh is right." Rachel sighed heavily, and her arms dropped to her sides. "She's been letting me take her classes for free. What if she reneges?"

I started to laugh. "I think that's the least of our troubles with Charity. What if she finds out there's still a chance for us to be denied a rezone? I need to talk to the landscapers about adding more trees to

soundproof." I pinched my temples and wondered
how to address this new wrinkle.

Does anyone want my new business venture to succeed?

"She's just mad we're harshing her Zen." Rachel
blinked after Charity. "She's super into concentration
and quiet. She's the calmest person I've ever met,
until she catches you chitchatting during yoga."
Rachel flinched as if she'd been on the receiving
end of one of Charity's tongue-lashings.

"Good fences make good neighbors. I'll see what
I can do for Charity."

The weather the next day mirrored my mood as
I drove to the Port Quincy Historical Society. What
had been clear warm weather was now increasingly
gray and murky. After a short trip through town, I
parked outside the Historical Society. I needed to
vent, and Rachel was busy catching Hunter up on
the history of the house and giving him yet another
personal tour. And I didn't want to discuss my
troubles with Mom, who seemed to be in her own
mental hot water over her reunion with Jesse.

As I stepped out of the station wagon, a fat, cold
drop of rain hit my nose. The sky opened as I
rushed up the stairs of the old home that housed
the Historical Society.

"I'll be . . . ," I muttered.

This morning Delilah had revved her scooter up
behind me and waved an umbrella beneath my
nose. "It's going to rain, Mallory. Take this."

"But the forecast online predicts a clear day." I'd

swung the front door open and motioned to the flinty but dry sky.

Delilah shook the umbrella a little more forcefully. "Mark my words!" Her silver bracelets jingled and pinged with her rattling movements.

"It's just your arthritis acting up," Rachel called over her shoulder as she shimmied past us with Hunter to check out the carriage house with the EMF meter. "We're not afraid of getting wet!"

I'd thought Delilah's shtick was a load of hooey, but now that it was coursing rain, I was a little more open to the idea. But my personal jury was still out on whether ghosts existed or not.

I hoped Tabitha could give me some information on Vanessa Scanlon's murder.

"Come in!" Tabitha ushered me into her office and offered me a plate of shortbread cookies. With her flame-red hair and magenta tweed jacket over a tawny yellow dress, she looked like an exotic bird of paradise.

"Tell me about Vanessa Scanlon," I pleaded before I nibbled on a cookie.

Tabitha leaned back in her chair and rested her hands in her lap. "Well, it's the most famous murder here in Port Quincy. I was about thirteen when Mrs. Scanlon disappeared. She was a pretty woman, so it made the national news." She whirled her swivel chair around to her computer and brought up the website for the Port Quincy *Eagle Herald* newspaper. "They've archived their old issues online, so we can read the stories from when Vanessa disappeared." Her manicured fingers flew over the keys, and she turned the monitor around so I'd have a better look.

I gasped. MISSING read the jarring headline in three-inch print. "She looks just like Whitney." There in black and white was a giant picture of a beautiful woman with delicate facial features and a poufy, feathery nineties perm. "Well, except for the hair."

Tabitha skimmed the article. "It was a crummy time. Port Quincy was kind of innocent before that. Bad things happened, but no one expected to have a family member snatched off the street. My parents stopped letting me walk unaccompanied to my friends' houses."

"Why didn't people just think she left Porter?"

"Some people did." Tabitha cocked her head in thought. "But what kind of woman would run away and leave her child behind?" I thought of Summer's mother and how she left her daughter with Garrett but didn't remind Tabitha. "And some people thought Porter murdered his wife and hid the body."

"So where does the man who was convicted fit into all this?" Garrett's client Eugene Newton had been convicted of Vanessa's murder, but it didn't sound like he was a suspect at first.

Tabitha skimmed the article for a moment. "The prosecution relied a lot on Whitney's memory of the event. The day her mother disappeared, Whitney heard Vanessa arguing with a man in the living room. She hid in the closet while the voices were loud, then crept out when they stopped. She saw a man in white leading her mother down the driveway."

I shuddered.

"And appearances aren't everything, because it turns out Vanessa and Porter did have a rocky marriage. Vanessa was having an affair with Eugene." She stopped to skim another article. "He painted their house that summer. Eugene wore a white painter's uniform while working on the Scanlons' house. Vanessa's body was found in the woods behind his property ten years after she disappeared, and that's when he admitted the affair." Tabitha typed in a new search and brought up an article from the mid two thousands. VANESSA SCANLON'S BODY FOUND, this headline screamed, with a picture of woods behind a tidy cabin.

"Why are you interested? Because of Whitney?" Tabitha gave me a level gaze and turned her computer monitor back around.

"I guess . . ." I didn't want to seem morbid. I wanted to tell Tabitha about the letters Whit had received, but I'd promised not to. "And because Garrett is still so remorseful about how his case defending Eugene ended up."

I decided to switch the subject. "Not to speak ill of the dead, but I think Lois tried to get me to entertain a bribe in exchange for rezoning the B and B, right before she was murdered."

Tabitha dropped her cookie, and it broke on top of her keyboard. "Ugh, crumbs!" She picked it up and shook cookie dust out of the keys. "No way. You must have imagined it."

"Maybe." Doubt crept into my voice, and I tentatively glanced up through the curls forming on my forehead from being out in the rain. "But I don't think so. Maybe that's why she was murdered. Do you think her death could be connected to Vanessa's somehow, even though twenty years have passed?"

Tabitha guffawed and reached for another cookie. "Lois wasn't murdered; it was a horrible accident." She took in my frown and softened her tone. "Lots of people couldn't stand Lois Scanlon. She worked in human resources at the Senator Hotel in town. She had a reputation for being pretty hard on the employees, just like her sister, Angela, is at Pellegrino's. But she wasn't murdered," she reiterated gently.

"It hasn't made the papers yet, but it turns out she was murdered." I filled Tabitha in on the mints laced with Bloody Mary mix, and she gasped.

"At least you're off the hook now. But who would want to murder Lois?"

"Now that she's dead, I'm even more sure she offered me a bribe." And some denizen of Port Quincy hadn't taken her propositions lightly.

Tabitha's eyes widened. "I'll keep my ear to the ground." She blew out a breath that raised the bright red hair off her brow. "And I hate to say it, but now that's the least of your problems. Your mother stopped by to see me today."

"My mother?" I squeaked.

"Yup. You asked her to consult with me about redecorating the B and B. Well, her ideas of historically accurate are a bit different from yours and mine."

I hid my face in my hands and shook my head.

"She wants to go with a more . . . modern theme."

"Spill it." Keith and Becca's cubist monstrosity flashed before my eyes.

"Picture *Miami Vice* meets Lilly Pulitzer. Lots of tropical colors and whimsical fabrics. Flamingoes and mangoes and that kind of thing."

I started to laugh. "This is a joke, right?" *So my mother was serious.* I thought back to Whitney's plum and harvest theme. Not many weddings would fit with my mother's proposed redecoration.

"We'll just have to convince her otherwise." Tabitha offered me a weak smile that let me know she thought my mother was a formidable character and it would be nearly impossible to convince her of anything.

I closed my eyes with trepidation and tried to picture my mom's vision for the B and B. I didn't relish telling her a tropical vacation theme wouldn't work for a late-nineteenth-century Italianate mansion in western Pennsylvania. Ever since her retirement, her heart had been with the Emerald Coast, and it seemed like her creative inspiration was there too.

I switched subjects to something else that had been bothering me. "You told me Evelyn McGavitt used to knit in the tower bedroom." I suppressed a shiver even though Tabitha's office was cozy and warm.

Tabitha arched an eyebrow.

I reminded her about the strange noises I'd heard, and her eyes lit up. "The ghost of Mrs. McGavitt is in your bedroom!" she said, wide-eyed and suppressing a smile.

"Let's not be hasty. It could have been the house settling, or an animal in the walls or something." I didn't sound convincing even to myself. "There was

one other odd thing, too. I smelled lilacs, but the
bush outside has been dead for weeks."

Tabitha's mouth dropped open, and her hand flew
to her chest. "She was known for her lilac perfume!"
She stood, and her chair knocked into the bookcase
behind her desk. She bit her lip and ran her hands
over the books. "Check this out."

It was a catalog of antique glass, and Tabitha's
finger flew down an index and flipped to a specific
page.

"An 'Evelyn' model glass lilac perfume decanter,
McGavitt Glass Company, 1927," I read the entry
aloud. "What does this mean?"

"Lilacs were her favorite scent. The McGavitt
Glass Company had these purple lilac perfume decanters made in her honor, and they were some of
their best sellers. There are thousands of these
decanters scattered in antique stores all over the
country. You know what this means."

"Don't say it."

"You have a real, bona fide ghost!" Tabitha
paced in front of her window, a slow smile softening her sharp features. "Mrs. McGavitt returning
to haunt you now would make sense. She suppos-
edly liked her house just so. Sylvia kept it like a
museum in homage to her mother. The ghost of
Evelyn McGavitt must be mad you're renovating
and changing her beloved Thistle Park."

"Ghosts can't get mad because they don't exist,"
I said with a firm shake of my head. "And possible
hauntings aren't the only thing on my mind." I fiddled with the small citrine pendant at my neck.

"Let's see." Tabitha ticked items off on her

slender fingers. "House trouble, permit trouble, ghost trouble. That leaves . . . man trouble?"

I nodded and polished off the last piece of short-bread. "How long did Garrett and Natalie date?"

Tabitha scowled at the mention of Natalie's name. "For about a year." She cocked her head and seemed to consider going on. "She pressured him for a ring."

I mulled this information over carefully. "A ring?" I hadn't been able to discern this history between Garrett and Natalie, just that she was still way into him.

Tabitha shook her head. "That's just it, though. There was no ring. You can't pressure Garrett, especially when it comes to dating. He's not Port Quincy's most eligible bachelor for nothing. He hasn't been truly serious for a long time." She smiled. "Until you."

"We haven't even been on a single proper date!" I wailed. I stood and peered out the side window, where the rain danced down in buckets, soaking the fallen leaves and leaving passersby with sodden jackets and shoes.

"I wouldn't worry about it, Mallory," Tabitha soothed. "I know Garrett, and things between you two are progressing just fine." She sent me off with a giant smile, and I gratefully huddled under Delilah's umbrella.

"I quit! I never want to set foot in this creepy castle again." The master tiler who'd restored all

eleven decorative fireplaces knocked into me on
the way out the door and didn't stop to apologize.

Jesse bounded after him, muttering about con-
tracts and ghosts. He chased him halfway down the
driveway, sputtering and begging and pleading.
His size-sixteen shoes connected with each puddle
and stream of water and sent up splashing geysers.
Finally he gave up and bent over, heaving for air.

I turned around to the hallway. "What's going on?"

Rachel and Hunter sprang down the stairs, holding fast to the newly replaced bannister. My sister
looked wild, exhilarated, and beautiful.

Uh oh.

It was her falling-in-love face. Hunter mirrored
her syrupy gaze.

"That was freaking *awesome!*" Rachel bounced on
the balls of her feet and clasped Hunter's arm.

Hunter rubbed his hands together and nodded
at his video camera. "I caught it all, too." He sheepishly looked at me and tried to push the camera
behind his back a second too late.

Why does he want to film so badly?

"I haven't decided whether to sign the film release
or not." I paused for a moment. "What happened?"

"We were in the rose bedroom—," Rachel began
breathlessly.

"And we heard a genuine spirit!" Hunter grinned
and patted his camera. "All on tape." He waggled
his eyebrows. "That is, if you'll let me keep it."

"I'll sign the release."

If he was going to film anyway.

Hunter whooped and put his dimples on full display. Rachel batted her eyelashes at him and placed
her hand possessively on his arm.

"Let me guess: the tiler was in the room." The ghost hunters' mission was already proving more trouble than it was worth if it lost us the best decorative tiler this side of the Alleghenies.

"Mallory, you're not listening!" Rachel squawked. "I heard it! A real, live ghost! It whispered, 'Help!'"

"Well, not a live one, Rach, because, you know—"

"Stop being so analytical! There are ghosts in the house!" She turned in the thrill of the moment and planted a giant pucker on Hunter's lips.

He got over his initial shock and returned my sister's kiss.

A horrible buzzing noise grated through the stillness and forced the lovebirds apart.

"What the . . ." Hunter stared at the ceiling and cocked his head.

I cupped my ear. "It's coming from the library."

Hunter, Rachel, and I rushed into the room. The noise got louder and louder. A soft dusting of plaster shook itself off the wreaths and vines carved into the ceiling and coated our heads like the finest snow. Above our heads, the blade of a circular saw suddenly broke through, the sound now deafening. It churned and whirred through the decorative plaster ceiling like a hot knife through buttercream frosting.

"Get out of the way!" I heaved my sister to the left and landed on top of her with a clatter. The saw finished slicing through the layers of floor and ceiling above us. A whole patch of plaster surrounding the cut gave way, and the saw crashed through to the carpet, still plugged in to a bright orange extension cord and spinning its large silver teeth.

"Turn it off, turn it off!" Rachel jumped back and screamed.

Hunter gallantly approached the saw as if it were a grizzly bear and switched it off in one deft movement. A delicate dusting of plaster coated his thick chestnut hair, and he solemnly peered up through the ceiling at his brother, Ezra. Hunter was shaking and breathing in sharp, wheezy gusts of air.

"It was turned off when I left the room! I swear! This place . . ." He peered down through the hole in the ceiling at Rachel, who was now nestled in Hunter's arms.

Hunter stroked my sister's hair and planted a kiss on top of her head.

"I'm going to be sick." Ezra stepped away from the hole in the ceiling.

I couldn't tell what had rattled him more—that a buzz saw turned itself on and sawed through a perfectly good ceiling or that his crush was canoodling with his brother. His footsteps retreated.

My mother entered the library and looked stricken.

But she wasn't looking at the mysterious hole in the ceiling. She gazed in lovesick agony at Jesse, who'd just come in the library door. Rain poured off his hat and squished from his shoes with each step he took. He stopped when he saw my mother and mutely stared at her, the misery meter on his face falling another few notches. He was equally stricken. My mother turned and fled from the room and up the stairs.

* * *

The rain continued, and the next day dawned cold and gray. Fall had truly arrived, with a chilly mist that seemed to permeate the house with clammy moisture. The red leaves from the maples stood against the sky like flames, and the leaves from the sycamore trees popped like golden coins against the leaden clouds. The driveway was slick with matted fallen leaves. I minced down the path and dodged puddles to return with the sodden mail. At the bottom of the pile was a slim envelope from the Planning Commission.

"What's that?" Rachel peered over my shoulder.

A wave of optimism crested, despite the gloomy day. "Maybe they mysteriously found my first application." I unfurled the sheet of paper within and scrunched up my nose.

"Good news or bad?"

I read the letter as I walked through the hall to the breakfast room. "A little good, a lot bad. They acknowledge they received my original application to make this a B and B. But now they want more documentation above and beyond my business plan, financials, and building permits."

"Let me see that." Rachel squinted at the tiny print enumerating the bajillion other documents I would have to scrounge up for the Planning Commission, some rather personal.

"What does your tax return have to do with re-zoning this place?"

"Absolutely nothing. I can't believe they need to dig further into my financials. I already gave them a stack of paper half a foot high—everything they asked for, and more. This has to be the work of

Troy Phelan, acting on behalf of his wife. She wants to make sure hers is the only B and B in Port Quincy. This smells so fishy." I reached for my laptop. "They're trying to change the requirements. It isn't fair. The ones in place when I originally applied should govern, not some fake, made-up ones. Troy probably cooked up some special new requirements just for me."

But the website told a different story.

"Well, this is interesting," I smirked and turned the screen around for my sister.

"Keith is a member of the Planning Commission?" she squeaked.

"Newly appointed as of Friday, by the mayor."

So that's why he hinted my permit won't be approved.

The application section of the website enumerated the new ridiculous documentation requirements.

"What's the big deal?" My mother shuffled into the room, looking slightly less spiffy than usual. I squinted at her, trying to decide what was off. "Keith is a reasonable human being. Just talk to him, and you'll get your permits approved."

I raised my eyebrows at my mother.

"It's too bad Lois had to kick the bucket before you could bribe her," Rachel mused, picking at a cuticle.

"Rachel Marie Shepard! I raised you better than that! Do not speak ill of the dead!" My mother regained some vigor to chastise my sister, but then sunk into a chair and rested her chin on her hand.

I shook my head. "No, it's true, Mom. Lois made

it sound like I could get this place rezoned if I sweetened the deal for her."

"You don't know how messed up the local government is," Rachel chimed in.

My mother wasn't listening. She moved wordlessly to the kitchen. Rachel and I exchanged a glance and followed her, in time to see her pour a healthy slug of orange juice into her coffee.

"Um, did you just wake up, Mom?" I asked tentatively.

Her usually smooth hair, dyed to match Rachel's, was crunched next to her ear on one side of her head, and the other side lay flat against her scalp. Her eyes were red, and she was wearing a quilted bathrobe. Something was definitely up. My mom was always made up and ready to go before the sun rose, and she wouldn't even get the mail if she happened to not look her best.

"I'm fine, just a little under the weather," she snapped and ran a hand through her hair. "This place is so dusty. You really need to do something about it. It's exacerbating my allergies."

"It's Jesse," Rachel mouthed beside her.

"I heard that!" My mother flounced up the back stairs to her room and barricaded herself inside for the rest of the morning.

I retired to the yellow bedroom early that evening after compiling all of the documents the Planning Commission claimed they needed. I had my first real date with Garrett scheduled for that night, a late dinner and a movie, and I wanted to decompress

first. I tried to think of the finished product that
would now have to happen in less than two weeks.
I thought of the cracked ceiling in the parlor and
the peeling and fading mural there. I hadn't been
able to find a muralist to work on it and doubted I
would on such short notice. I'd probably just paint
it light blue with some clouds and call it a day. Not
to mention the gaping hole in the library ceiling,
compliments of a poltergeist or, more likely, a flustered worker. Though Ezra claimed the saw had
been off, I couldn't really chalk it up to a ghost.

Though I was knee-deep in renovations, I knew
this was what I was supposed to do. I loved the history in this big hulking mansion and couldn't wait
to show my guests hospitality like the people here had
shown me. I had inherited the place this summer
from my ex's grandmother, Sylvia, and I vowed to
make her proud. I closed my eyes and pictured the
B and B perfectly renovated. It was going to work.
It was going to be awesome.

And though Natalie obviously had designs on
Garrett, he'd made his preference known.

The wind howled, and the rain pelted down
faster, and I realized, with a start, that my kitties
were nowhere to be seen. They had the run of the
house on the weekends, but they always made their
way up to me by early evening. By the time I went
to bed, they nestled around me as I slept. Bruce
and Fiona had taken a liking to Rachel and could
be found curled up at the bottom of her bed most
evenings, and Maisie liked to sleep beside me on
the opposite side of the bed from the cats. I left
the room and padded around the second floor,

listening for any signs of them. Maisie trotted next to me and stopped to sniff the carpet every few feet.

"What're you doing, sneaking around in the dark?" Rachel popped her head around the back staircase, a cup of cocoa in hand.

"Ugh, don't scare me like that!" I explained the missing cats, and Rachel, Maisie, and I set off to find them.

We paused at the back stairs, and I craned my head back to take in the entrance to the third floor.

"It's off limits now," Rachel reminded me, since the contractors were working like mad to replace the water-damaged floor.

"It's the last place to look."

My sister shrugged, and we climbed the stairs anyway and pushed open the door. Maisie scampered in. I padded around the plywood subfloor and reached for a light switch. None of the lights worked.

"That's odd," Rachel let out a gust of nervous breath.

"They must be working on the electrical, too." The hair on the back of my neck stood up.

We felt our way around the third floor. A bead of sweat trickled down my back, despite the frigid air. My mind was hyper alert. Maisie trotted ahead, her little nails clicking on the new subfloor. Finally I reached the end of the hallway. No kitties.

I was about to retreat downstairs when Maisie stopped and cocked her head, her pointy white ears quivering in the near darkness. Like a switch had flipped, she let out a piercing series of barks and jogged to the last door on the third floor. She looked up. I heard a soft mewling above me and gasped. The cries were coming from the small flight of stairs leading to the widow's walk. I took them two at a time and flung open the door to find my two kitties, soaking wet, huddled and scrabbling against the door to get back in. I scooped up the matted balls of fur.

"You poor dears!"

A soft, sibilant whisper slipped between the raindrops and barely reached my ears. "Beware . . ."

A low guttural growl started in Maisie's throat.

"Arrgh!" I grabbed Whiskey and pivoted down the slick short staircase.

"Ohmigodohmigodohmigod." Rachel grabbed Soda and banged the door shut behind us.

Chapter Seven

"Just try to blame *that* on my overactive imagination." Rachel grabbed a kitchen towel and briskly rubbed Soda until she returned to her normal fluffy orange self. My sister was spooked and excited and triumphant all at the same time. The battling emotions made her pretty features appear even more animated than usual.

"I heard it too," I admitted, with a guarded note in my voice. I clutched Whiskey close to me and enveloped her in my fleece robe. We'd retreated to the kitchen to tend to the frightened and damp cats. Rachel and I nuzzled and doted on the two kitties until they were purring and warm, then set them on the ground before dishes of albacore tuna, a special treat after their ordeal in the rain. Maisie hadn't left our side, and now she nosed in to sniff the fish. She backed off when Whiskey stood her ground and hissed. The pint-sized calico guarded her dish of food with jealous, narrowed ochre eyes.

She stared dolefully at the dog, not impressed with the canine.

"Maisie saved one of your nine lives," I admonished the calico as I scratched under her chin. "You should share your food." I put the electric kettle on to make us some tea. I was chilled to the bone from my brief dash onto the roof to get the cats and hoped some honey tea would warm us up.

Soda was more grateful. Maisie tentatively licked the orange fluff ball on the nose, and the little cat let the Westie tend to her before she returned to her bowl of tuna, her tail jaunty and held high, no worse for wear.

"Let's go back up and see if we can find any evidence on the widow's walk. Someone must have been up there to lock out the cats and to whisper that warning." I stood and grabbed my raincoat from the hook near the fridge.

"I'm not going back up there. Are you crazy? The sun's set already. And we know the source of the noise—Evelyn McGavitt's ghost!" Rachel's teeth began to chatter, from the cold seeping through her damp sweater or from fear, I wasn't sure which.

"Who would put two cats out in the driving rain?" I was baffled and wanted to throttle whoever had played this heartless and cruel joke.

"Thank goodness Maisie let us know." Rachel knelt down to scratch the little white dog behind the ears.

I frowned and did a double take. The pretty tartan fabric tying back my sister's hair looked vaguely familiar. *Why haven't I noticed it before?*

"Are you wearing Maisie's scarf?"

Rachel blushed and adjusted the petal-colored

plaid fabric. It hung jauntily down her back, tied around her ponytail. The soft pastel perfectly matched her angora sweater, which was shrunken enough to moonlight as a child's mitten.

"She let me borrow it," Rachel began ruefully.

The Westie gazed adoringly at my sister and blinked her large sable eyes rimmed with white. "Ruff!" She barked and sat closer to Rachel and nuzzled her outstretched hand with her black button nose.

"See?" Rach cocked her head approvingly in Maisie's direction and tied the scarf more firmly around her ponytail.

"She's a dog! She can't give you permission to borrow her stuff."

"Oh, c'mon. Dogs shouldn't have *stuff*. And I had it dry cleaned and everything!" But Rachel gave an exaggerated sigh and undid the scarf. She carefully tied it back around the little dog's neck, and Maisie batted her eyes at my sister, placing a paw on her knee.

"Maybe one of the contractors let them out." Rachel neatly deflected my attention from the subject of her pilfering designer textiles from a dog and focused blame on someone else.

"Maybe it was the ghost hunters who let our cats out on the roof." I tried to gauge my sister's reaction since she was so smitten with Hunter. "We're lucky they didn't try to climb down!"

Rachel scoffed. "Impossible! The ghost hunters weren't here today, and they don't have access to the third floor. Whenever they're here, I personally accompany them."

"You mean you flirt with Hunter," I amended, a slow smile twitching up the corners of my mouth.

"Why can't you just believe in the supernatural?"

I shrugged. "I'm a ghost agnostic. I don't believe in them, but I *could* believe. I guess it's a matter of unproven possibility." I hadn't heard the knitting needles or smelled lilacs since the ghost hunters had arrived, and with each passing day, I was more willing to chalk the incident up to my vivid imagination.

"Stop being so practical," Rachel grumped as she flicked through an upholstery sample book. "When we were kids, you reasoned Santa out of existence."

"Maybe so. But when you found your presents in Mom's trunk, necessitating an explanation, I tried to tell you Mom was helping Santa out because he was so busy."

"You two girls always were very curious," our mother startled us by speaking from the other room.

"How long have you been listening in?" Rachel poked her head out the kitchen doorway to converse with our mother.

"I just got back a few minutes ago from the hairdresser. They squeezed me in as their last appointment. Why are you all wet, Rachel?"

My sister ignored my mom's question and dashed back into the kitchen.

Rachel leaned close to my ear and hissed out a whisper, "Mom got her hair done." Rachel looked stricken. "She did this for Jesse. She's out of control, like a lovesick teenager. I'm scared. What does it mean?" Her green eyes were wide with panic, and she gripped my damp sleeve with her sharp acrylics.

I laughed and dropped my voice so Mom wouldn't hear. "She's never out of control, Rach. Mom *invented* control. And what do you mean, 'What does it mean?' Like she's trying to win Jesse back?" I poured hot water into three mugs and inhaled the sweet, mellow fragrance of Lady Grey tea and honey.

"You don't get it!" Rachel wheeled me around, and I sloshed hot tea over my foot with a yelp.

I resettled the mugs on a tray and took a step back.

She gently pushed me into the breakfast room, where our mother sat at the table, tentatively touching her hair.

I was mesmerized by her, and Rachel plucked the tray out of my arms as I stopped and stared.

"See what I mean?" she hissed. Rachel did have a point.

Mom's hair had been the same for decades—a layered bob that brushed her shoulders and gently curled under, dyed to match Rachel's natural shade, with subtle golden highlights woven in. Today her pretty face was framed by edgy layers up to her chin in the front that reached a dramatically short shelf of feathered fringe at the nape of her neck. Wide highlights were painted through her locks, in shades of burnt sienna and wheat, and the look was great, but startling.

"Spill it, Mom." I thrust a mug of tea into her hands and sat on one side of her.

"Yeah, is this makeover for Jesse?" Rachel sandwiched herself on the other side of our mom.

"Of course not! I just decided to freshen up my look." Mom ran a hand uncertainly through her short, razor-cut hair and burst into tears.

"It's alright, Mom." I patted her back and glanced over her at Rachel. "Your hair looks great, by the way."

"Thank you, dear. It's just a shock seeing him, that's all. Things ended rather badly, and I didn't think I'd ever see him again." She sniffed and accepted the box of tissues I handed her. "And it was time for a new look. I didn't cut my hair because of Jesse."

Yeah, right.

"Did you cheat on Doug with Jesse?" Rachel clapped a hand over her mouth as soon as the words were out, but it was too late.

Our mother jumped up, spilling tea down her front and whirled around to place her hands on her hips.

"I've never cheated on your stepfather! How could you make that assumption! Seeing Jesse just dredged up memories of a very vulnerable and chaotic time in my life. One I worked very hard to shield you girls from experiencing." She drew in a shaky breath and sat down again, opting for a rocking chair facing the breakfast table rather than resume her seat between her daughters, the inquisitors.

"I dated Jesse for a brief period after your father left, and before I met Doug." Our mother smoothed down the front of her sweater set, a dull gray merino wool, uncharacteristically bland for her. It was jarring with her new haircut. She must have been dressing to mirror her mood.

"It's just . . . Jesse mentioned that he proposed, Mom. I wonder why we never heard about him? And why you turned him down?" I didn't want to pry, but things were getting uncomfortable around here. And Mom's new haircut was downright bizarre.

"Isn't it obvious?" My mother's voice was nearly hysterical, pitched high enough I was surprised a dog didn't come running. She cleared her throat and took a delicate swig of tea. "That woman! Delilah is the reason I broke things off with Jesse, and he countered with a proposal I couldn't accept. I wasn't going to bring a man like that into our family, regardless of how I felt about him. He let her run his life then, and I see he hasn't changed in a quarter of a century."

"We won't bother you again about it, Mom," Rachel said, contrition softening her tone.

"I'm fine. It's all in the past." But her rheumy red eyes told a different story. "Just don't be rude again, dears. I raised you better than that. Now," she brightened a degree, "tell me about your new beau, Rachel. That ghost hunter is awfully cute, and he has one of those chin dimples I know you adore."

Rachel picked at a thread on her cuff, and two spots of color appeared on her cheeks. "I'm not interested in Hunter because of his chimple. He's an amazing guy."

"Nonsense," my mother smiled. "In high school there was Jason Sparks. He was a lovely boy, and he had a chin dimple, and then there was Derek Lampher, who had a butt chin and wasn't nice."

Rachel's eyebrows shot skyward at my mom's use of the term "butt chin."

"That young man has been spending a lot of time around here in the evenings, taking his measurements." Our mother paused and fluffed her new hairdo. "I wanted to remind you not to move so fast."

"Mom!" Rachel's embarrassment curdled to annoyance, and I decided to switch gears to rescue my sister.

"Tabitha told me you had some ideas about decorating the first floor. I can't wait to see them."

My mother brightened and excused herself to get her presentation board.

"Whew! That was intense." Rachel let out a sigh. "She just brought up Hunter to get us to stop talking about Jesse."

"She's not over him," I whispered. "And Doug doesn't know what's going on."

Rachel smirked. "I wanted to tell him from the get-go."

I glanced out the window at the lashing raindrops and sodden night. I wondered about my mother and Doug, but now wasn't the time. Mom had returned with a spring in her step, even though her eyes were still puffy and red. Maybe this trip back to Pennsylvania would be good for her. She carried a large presentation board and set it up on a small collapsible easel she'd brought. The board was covered in white cloth.

I put on my best poker face. Mom was retired, but she was a professional, and her clients always loved the rooms she'd staged and redecorated. The house had good old bones, and it had come a long way since the day Rachel and I first moved in. The first floor was an empty canvas right now, with most of the furniture removed and stored in the carriage house and shed. It was bare and cavernous except for the workers' tools and equipment, when before it used to suffer from the opposite problem, being stuffed with dusty knickknacks and glass from long ago. I wasn't sure what pieces to bring back, or what effect I was going for. Elegant or cozy? Slavishly following the time period when it was built or a focus on modern comfort? I felt my eyes widen in confusion, and my mother picked up on it.

"Leave it all to me, Mallory. You're going to love this."

The task before us at Thistle Park would require an especially deft hand and needed to be completed in record time, no less. There were 1950s chrome appliances, late 1800s photographs, and modern amenities like the large flat screen in the library. My mother needed to meld it all together. It would take a special touch to make it not look like an eclectic estate sale.

"I'm so excited to show you girls." She took a deep breath, shifting into pitch mode. "Picture this—a study in contrasts. Heavy and light, mahogany and sherbet, historical and whimsical." She whipped the white sheet off and unveiled the design board.

My eyes swept over the display. It was early *Golden Girls* with a touch of Versailles. My vision swam as I took in wicker, rattan, and cane furniture reupholstered with lime-green stripes. Silk melon plaids mixed with heavy Louis Quatorze–style furniture. I squinted at particular elements. There were turquoise chevron ottomans and a fainting couch redone in fist-sized canary polka dots. Live, twenty-foot-high palm trees would grace the entrance hall. Holy tamale! Maybe this was where Rachel got her sense of style. It was perfect for an opulent B and B located on the Emerald Coast, but rural western Pennsylvania?

"What do you think?" My mother flashed a smile and waited for me to understand how awesome it would be.

"It's stunning," I began. Then, at a loss for words, I added, "Simply stunning."

My mom nodded, her new hairdo sending strands flying into her eyes, which she impatiently brushed out of the way.

"And I'd love to live in a house designed like this," I continued cautiously. "But see," I rushed on, "I was thinking of something more neutral. Something that would go with any kind of wedding." I tried to imagine Whitney's plum, gold, and chocolate theme nestled next to this tropical paradise.

"That's so worn and dated, Mallory dear. This is fresh and breezy, like a vacation down in the Caribbean." Mom touched a fabric swatch with a loving hand. "This is cozy and sophisticated and delightful, just like you wanted, and it incorporates each existing piece of furniture, bringing in the historical elements you mentioned."

"Um, how is it historical?" I offered my question with a small smile.

"Like if Malibu Barbie redesigned Buckingham Palace?" Rachel arched her eyebrows, staring at the design with frank confusion.

"You don't understand the genius of it. It will be simply *marvelous*." My mom snatched up her presentation board, snapped it shut, and huffed up the back stairs.

Rachel and I were charitable and counted ten seconds before we grabbed our bellies and howled into the cushions on the breakfast room chairs.

"Great. I think she's more upset with our reaction to her decorating scheme than she was about us probing her former romantic tryst with Jesse."

"It would be funny if we had a few more months," I moaned. "But we really do need to decorate within two weeks." My phone vibrated in my pocket, and I answered with relief when I saw who was calling.

"Thank God." It was Tabitha.

"How did your mom's presentation go? She told me she was showing you tonight." Tabitha's voice was both hesitant and sprinkled with mirth.

"Did you see the presentation board?"

"Um . . . yes. Yes, I did."

"So then you know."

Tabitha sighed. "It would be a great idea for a B and B a thousand miles south of here, perhaps on the water. But, yeah. It's a no-go."

"You have to help me figure out a way to convince her to design something more historically accurate. If we had more time . . ." I felt awful. Mom had put her everything into the design, and it was gorgeous, but it just didn't fit with the house and the region.

We were silent for a moment.

"What if we sweetened the deal?" Tabitha's voice was pensive.

"There is no deal. Mom is doing this out of the goodness of her heart." I felt a stab of pain and vowed to chase after Mom and apologize. It was a stunning design, and she had put a lot of hard work into it.

"No, I mean like an extra incentive? A contest!"

"Hmm." I paced around the breakfast room and knitted my eyebrows together. "A contest for the most accurate renovation?"

"You don't want it to be completely accurate," Tabitha reminded me. "That would lead to anti-macassars on horsehair couches. You want it warm and inviting, not fusty and frumpy. What about a contest for the most successful combination of historically accurate and cozy amenities?" I could hear her smile over the phone. "An unofficial contest, that is."

"Tabitha, I think you just saved the day."

"I'll whip up some contest rules. It's worth a shot."

"I owe you big-time." A beep cut through our conversation. "I have to go. I have another call."

Tabitha and I bade each other good-bye, and I answered the other call with a grin. It was Garrett, and we had our first real, official, out-to-a-restaurant date scheduled for tonight.

"I can't make it." His voice was tight and clipped and funny-sounding. "Something has happened."

I took the steps two at a time when I reached Garrett's office building. The rain had picked up and slanted nearly sideways against the crumbling art deco building. The days had grown shorter, and it was completely dark. It might as well have been midnight.

"You can't come in here, ma'am." I nearly collided with the young cop standing in the doorway to the waiting room. He puffed out his chest and took a step toward me to block the entrance. "This is a crime scene."

"It's okay." Truman motioned me in, to the surprise of the young man, and gestured toward the corner. "Just don't touch anything, Mallory."

I nodded and craned my head down the hall for any sign of Garrett. He emerged a second later and hurried over to give me a quick hug.

"Sorry about our date." His shoulders were hunched up, and his eyes held no small amount of shock.

"You had a good reason for calling it off. What happened?" I looked around the small waiting room, which appeared untouched. There were piles of popular magazines and a chair and small couch for clients. Everything appeared in superficial order.

"This way." He gently steered me down the hall to his office. It was an utter disaster. Papers and files littered the floor like oversized pieces of confetti. A filing cabinet was upended, belching accordion files and manila folders over the carpet. His computer lay on its side on the floor, and someone had tried to break in the side of his desk with a hammer or other heavy object—there were golf-ball-sized indentations all along the metal frame, but the assailant hadn't been successful.

"What did they want?"

"All of my files on Eugene Newton's case." Garrett motioned to the tipped-over filing cabinet with the scattered contents. "Three drawers worth, every scrap of information. I have most of it scanned electronically, thank goodness, but someone wanted the information badly. The funny thing," Garrett rubbed the back of his neck, "is the odd timing. Yesterday I received an anonymous letter stating that Eugene is innocent and that I should revive the case to prove it."

A shallow wave of dread doused my nerves. I would have to tell him about Whitney's identical letters, even though I'd promised to stay mum.

"I still believe he's innocent, but I exhausted his appeals years ago. Who would want to revisit his case? Why now, when Whitney's in town? And how does it relate to someone trashing my office and stealing the files?"

"Or Lois's death?" I was about to continue when I was interrupted.

"Someone should have locked all of their file cabinets." Truman appeared in the doorway and jutted his chin out defiantly in the direction of his son.

Garrett crossed his arms over his chest. I couldn't believe they still weren't talking, what with Garrett's office being tossed.

"Tell my father the front door to the building was locked, as was the door to the ante-office and my inner office. If someone wanted the information badly enough, a small filing-cabinet lock wouldn't have stopped them. The locks to the office doors were picked, and probably not by an amateur."

Garrett's eyes flashed, and he threw a glare at his father, even though he technically hadn't been addressing him.

"Humph." Truman spun on his heel and stalked out.

I let out a sigh and hoped he would pursue this crime as vigilantly as he would if he weren't sparring with his only son.

Garrett's face was weary and pale from the ordeal and arguing with his father. "The cops said it would take a while to check for fingerprints. I'd ask my dad if they could speed up the process, but under the circumstances, forget it." His handsome face was suddenly lined and exhausted. He ran a hand from the top of his forehead to the bottom of his chin.

"You need to end your feud. It's ridiculous to argue over a case from a decade ago."

"If I hadn't gotten the call from Whitney, I wouldn't have come back to the office to even discover this mess until tomorrow."

"Whitney?" I frowned and rubbed my arms. It was warm in the office, but the crime gave me the chills. Garrett's office had been worked over, and not delicately. If the person who stole the files about Vanessa's convicted murderer had picked the locks to get into the office, they didn't need to break everything in sight. They had sent a message.

"I'm the executor for Lois's will, and Whitney wanted to meet first thing tomorrow to discuss it. I wanted to look it over tonight."

"Did she pull a Leona Helmsley?" I pictured the Westies outfitted in more than just designer scarves. Perhaps they'd have the run of Lois's house or spend the rest of their doggy days traveling in the lap of luxury.

A small smile ticked up the corners of Garrett's mouth. "She left the bulk of her estate to Whitney, including the dogs, except for a small donation to Westie Rescue USA. Her estate was quite a bit larger than expected." He frowned. "Lois was thrifty, except for the dogs and her annual trip to Scotland. She was an inveterate penny-pincher. And even though she spoiled the dogs like children, I never would have guessed at the fortune she amassed."

"Is that a problem?" A chill skipped down my spine as I remembered Lois's hint about greasing the wheels of the Planning Commission if only I'd grease her palm in return.

"I don't know where she got the money. It worries me." Garrett's gaze was intense.

I blushed and turned to tell Garrett about Lois's offer, but I was cut off before I could confess.

Truman burst into the room, his jaw tight and his eyes fuming. "I have another crime to investigate," he announced with frigid importance, just as my phone rang. It was Whitney, and she was so hysterical I couldn't understand her.

Chapter Eight

"It'll be alright, sweetie." I patted Whitney on the back and blinked in disbelief. It would not be alright, but I couldn't tell her that. She'd just gotten off the phone with her fiancé, Ian, describing for him the scene I now took in.

Her room in Keith and Becca's house resembled Garrett's office, but the perpetrator for this crime had used a knife instead of a blunt object. Everything was slashed. Whitney's black luggage, the pillows, and the curtains had jagged rips running down their lengths. It had been decorated like a shiny peach bordello turned into a set for a slasher film. The downy apricot bedspread spewed feathers from a wide gash in the middle, as if a flock of geese had duked it out in this room.

But the worst of it was reserved for her wedding dress. The garment bag that had carefully preserved the gown she was to be married in was ripped diagonally from one shoulder to the ground, leaving the bag and the gown within it in tatters. I couldn't touch the gown, but I could see it hanging open in front, a strip torn through the middle, right where Whitney's stomach would have been had she been wearing it. The delicate stark white sheath, covered in silver beads and seed pearls, was beyond repair. And sticking out above the dress, where the wearer's head would be, was a note cleaved to the door by a butcher's knife. It was printed with the message:

GO BACK TO BALTIMORE

An icy trickle ran down my back, and I turned from the sight. "Thank goodness the dogs are back at the B and B. And that you weren't here, either."

"I was visiting my dad." Whitney trembled. "I headed back to look over paperwork for a meeting with Garrett tomorrow to talk about Aunt Lois's will. If I'd gotten here earlier . . ." She took in the scene again.

Did she know she was now the heiress of a considerable fortune?

Whitney burst into fresh sobs and backed away from the room. "I want to go home. I thought Port Quincy was my home, but I made a mistake. I'd be safer in Baltimore."

"Safer? Why not completely safe?" Truman's ears perked up, and he strode over to Whitney.

Faith Hendricks, his young police partner, stopped taking pictures of the slashed items and put down her camera. Her dark blond ponytail bounced off her shoulders as she looked back and forth between Whitney and Truman with interest.

"Tell him about the letters," I urged, giving Whitney's shoulder a soft squeeze, effectively announcing their existence.

"What letters?" Truman turned to me with a laser-beam focus, and I felt my features melting under his strict gaze. "Has someone been threatening you, Whitney?" His tone softened considerably, and the jowls on his face relaxed. He gave me an "I'll deal with you later" look.

"They started to arrive six months ago. They were sent to the hotel where I work in Baltimore. You can figure out my place of employment online. I guess they didn't know my home address."

"Can I see them?" Truman was the picture of patience, as he probably didn't want to disturb Whitney any more than necessary in her agitated state.

"May I touch that?" She gingerly pointed to a small tan valise on a dresser, and Faith handed it to her. It appeared intact and untouched by the slashing knife. Whitney riffled through the contents once, twice, and a third time, her features growing more agitated with each search.

"Th-they're gone!" Whitney dropped the small bag. She walked away from the room, and Truman and I quickly followed her down the cutaway exposed staircase to the peach great room below.

Truman picked up the pace to keep up as she told him what she'd told me: the letters were anonymous, appeared to have been typed on a typewriter, and claimed Eugene Newton hadn't murdered her mother twenty years ago.

"Garrett also received letters about Eugene," I offered to Truman as I jogged to keep up.

"*What?*" He paused on the stairs, and I ran into him with a thunk. "He didn't tell me that. He's purposely concealing information from my investigation." Dark thunderclouds gathered in his eyes to mirror the weather outside.

"Give me a break! If you'd deign to talk to him, maybe he'd tell you."

Truman deftly ignored me and continued down the stairs to talk to Whitney.

"Our wedding rings were stolen too." Whitney rubbed her bleary eyes. "Ian wants me to leave Port Quincy immediately. He's coming here tomorrow, and we'll leave for Baltimore later in the day."

I squeezed Whitney's hand and nodded. I didn't blame her for calling off the wedding this time.

"Then we'll be back to get married."

My mouth dropped open for a moment.

Whitney sniffed and turned to me. "I'm not canceling the wedding. If anything, this drives home how delicate everything is. I'm getting married, and my dad will see it, and we are full steam ahead."

I tried to hide my shock. Keith and Becca ran into the room, clad in their work clothes. The red and blue lights from Truman's police car streamed in the door behind them. Becca swept Whitney up in a hug, and Keith paced the room, talking animatedly on his phone.

"May I have a word, Mallory?" Truman motioned me over to the sliding glass doors.

The sun was long gone, and the wet black sky met the solid dark wall of the tree line beyond the modernist rock garden. I braced myself for a mini lecture and thought that if things had gone as planned, I'd be on my first official date with

Truman's son, rather than discussing secret letters with him in my ex-fiancé's living room.

"Why didn't you tell me Whitney has been receiving letters about her mother's murder?"

I stood my ground and turned from the view. I went with the most simple explanation. "It wasn't my information to tell."

Truman sighed and ran a tired hand through his salt-and-pepper hair. He didn't ream me out. "I'm worried." His face fell, and he dropped his voice so only the two of us could hear. "The Vanessa Scanlon case was bad business. We didn't get a lot of murders in Port Quincy back then. That is, until you came to town." He smirked. "We weren't equipped to handle a kidnapping turned missing person and eventually a murder case. Garrett is right."

He stopped and cringed, as if it hurt him to admit it and drop the façade of his tiff with his son. Seeing his office ransacked tonight must have shaken him. Truman shook his head and went on. "From the way it was investigated, to the amount of time between Vanessa Scanlon's disappearance and the discovery of her body, all of it was a bit of a mess. And now it's resurfacing."

I stood in shock.

Truman hated to admit he was wrong. It must be worse than I thought.

"Sweetie beans, we can't stay here." Becca's shrill voice cut through Truman's musings. She stood with one hand on Whitney's shoulder, the other on her cocked hip. "Keith, be a doll and find us a hotel. Preferably one with an in-house dry cleaner, room service, and a gym."

Keith slapped his cell phone down on the kitchen island and shook his head. "There's some kind of Marcellus Shale drilling convention in town, and every hotel, motel, and inn is full. We can drive back to Pittsburgh, but it's getting dark."

Becca thrust her plump, rose-colored bottom lip out in a maudlin pout. "But I don't feel safe here! There must be somewhere we can stay." She batted her tarantula-like lashes, and a sly smile played on her lips.

"Let's stay with my mother. I'm sure she won't mind." Keith picked up his cell to make the call.

"No!" Becca's smile faltered, and her voice ricocheted around the room. "I mean, I don't think that's a good idea. Your mother goes to bed so early, I wouldn't want to disturb her."

I suppressed a smirk. I wouldn't want to stay with Helene either.

"Mallory can certainly accommodate us at her little B and B, right?" Becca's smile returned and broke freely across her face, revealing even, blinding teeth, enhanced by some kind of whitening solution.

"The house is still being renovated, and the contractors will start work tomorrow at six AM." I wouldn't mind taking in Whitney, but I wasn't so sure about Keith and Becca. Keith had been absolutely inhospitable to Lois's dogs, and he'd be reunited with them. But then I pictured the guest room upstairs, its hideous peach and sea-foam equanimity slashed to ribbons and bits. Even I couldn't be so callous as to lie about there being no room at the proverbial inn.

Keith and Becca weren't my first choice for guests, but it was undeniable that Becca would be a calming influence on a now hysterical Whitney. "But there are three bedrooms ready enough to accommodate you."

The last time Keith had been in my home, he was skulking about trying to find some valuable paintings. Tonight he strode around grandly as if he owned the place.

"I love what you've done with the house." Keith smirked as he guided Becca around a pyramid of paint cans lined up in the middle of the back hall. "Are you sure it'll be done in time for Whitney and Ian's wedding?"

Whitney gave a firm nod. "I'm getting married here, and it will be done by the day after Halloween. Right, Mallory?"

"That's right," I affirmed and led everyone up the grand staircase with a new balustrade and bannister firmly in place. I knew because I gave the gleaming dark wood a subtle practice shove before we advanced up the stairs.

Rachel peeked her head out of the last bedroom I'd assigned to my first guests and gave me a thumbs-up. I'd called her on the way over, and she'd made up all of the beds and placed toiletries in the bathrooms. The bedrooms were finished enough for guests, with fresh paint, buffed wood floors, beautiful modern bathrooms carved out of what were once large closets, and the original, massive beds appointed with new pillow-top mattresses. The decorations were a little spare, since most of them were still stored in the carriage house, but the rooms were cozy, clean, and, more importantly, nearly finished.

"Ahem." Keith and Becca peeked into each room as I led them to the one I'd picked for them.

"This is the room I always played hide-and-seek in," Keith mused, gesturing toward the green bedroom, where my mom was staying. "Grandma Sylvia had a huge wardrobe in here with a trick hollow back. When I was six or seven, I could just squeeze into it."

Becca stared with naked envy at the house. It was still a showstopper, despite the renovations not being finished.

I opened the door to the blue bedroom and gestured them in.

"Ooh, this is lovely." Becca spun around in the room, outfitted in alternating pale and deep blue stripes, irises, cornflowers, and lots of frothy eyelet lace. It was the most complete bedroom, and I was giving it to them free of charge.

Becca dropped her bag on the floor and slipped off her shoes. "What will you serve for breakfast?" She cocked a dark eyebrow and waited expectantly for the answer.

"Excuse me?"

Becca flicked her eyes dismissively around the room. "This *is* a bed-and-breakfast, right?"

I bristled. "Of course it is! It's just that we're not officially open . . ."

Becca exchanged a simpering glance with Keith. As of now, my unexpected guests could dine on Rice Krispies, yogurt, and oatmeal, but I wasn't going to serve them that.

"We're having avocado eggs benedict, bananas Foster French toast, fruit compote, and south-western omelets."

"That sounds wonderful, Mallory." Whitney looked exhausted.

I left Keith and Becca and led Whit down the hall to the most elegant bedroom of all, the purple room.

"This is what will be billed as the honeymoon suite," I told her, flicking on the light. Bruce, Fiona, and Maisie had been following Whitney and happily jumped on her bed.

"It's gorgeous," she breathed, turning around in the room, painted a heavy French cream with a deep orchid accent wall. She knelt down, and the doggies leaped from the bed, yipping and jumping up to give her kisses. It was a sweet reunion, and the pups looked ecstatic to see her.

"I'm just going to head out to get some things for breakfast. Call me if you need anything. I'll leave you with a key to the front door so you can step out with the dogs if you need to."

"Thanks again." Whitney gave me a big hug, and I headed out for provisions.

Shopping at three in the morning was a fantastic experience. I had the grocery store to myself and quickly filled my cart to the brim with delectable ingredients for several days' worth of breakfasts. I didn't know how long it would take the crime team to process Keith and Becca's guest bedroom and when my unexpected guests would feel safe enough to go back.

I carefully steered the Butterscotch Monster through the near-empty streets and kept close watch for deer and other critters roaming in the cool fall night. The clouds and rain had cleared off, and I stepped out under inky black skies with a latticework of twinkling stars. I smiled as I headed back to my boat of a station wagon for my third and final trip. A feeling of serenity washed over me as I contemplated the house. It felt wonderful that nearly all the rooms were occupied, even if not by paying guests. I was energized as I hefted the heaviest bags onto my wrists and set off to prep a delicious breakfast.

I gazed at Thistle Park, hulking and solid in the moonlight, and swallowed a scream that came out as a strangled gurgle. Up on the widow's walk stood a figure in a heavy bell skirt, her hair in a tidy bun. I dropped my bags and backed up to take in the woman from a better angle, but she was gone.

"There's no such thing as ghosts. There's no such thingasghosts. There's nosuchthingasghosts," I chanted to myself in hyperventilation speed. The front door creaked open, and this time I did scream, before Rachel clapped her hand over my mouth.

"Shh! We actually have guests, in case you forgot! You're really spooked." She cracked a big bubble of gum, and the scent of spearmint permeated the air.

"The widow's walk . . . I saw her . . . the ghost!" I gasped this out between short puffs of cold air.

Rachel rolled her eyes so hard the whites shone by the light of the moon.

"Stop making fun of me! I know you don't believe

in them, but that's no reason to tease me, especially today, when so much has happened."

"I'm not kidding." Breathlessly I told Rachel about the apparition on the roof as I heaved the last of the heavy bags into the front hall.

"Well, let's go see!" Rachel rubbed her hands together as goose bumps stood out on her arms.

"The food will go bad." My voice wavered. "How about you put it away? I'll run upstairs and poke my head outside to catch the ghost."

"Are you sure?" Rachel's eyes went wide.

"I'm sure. You need to stay inside. You must be freezing."

Rach was dressed for bedtime in a short satin robe that barely covered the silk shorts she wore. I'd be freezing in a getup like that. I couldn't wait to don my cozy but threadbare flannel PJs with the black cat and pumpkin pattern. *Maybe that's why I have yet to go on a real date with the man I'm seeing.* I slowly headed for the widow's walk.

I climbed the steep back staircase to the third floor, then advanced with tiny steps. Each footfall groaned with my weight, and I wished, not for the first time, that Jesse's renovations had de-creaked the noisy stairs. Finally I reached the third floor. It appeared to be empty and still. I made my way to the back of the apartment for the second time in less than twenty-four hours and to the door to the widow's walk.

I placed my hand on the doorknob, which was ice-cold, as if the door had been left open. I hoped my kitties were still inside this time. I flung open the door, and I peered up the short flight of stairs to the roof and saw nothing. I let out a shaky breath and climbed to the top, where it was eerily calm. No ghost occupied the widow's walk. The moon seemed even larger up on the roof, a wide, silver-white wafer in the sky. I stood on my tiptoes and could just see the outline of a barge traversing its way slowly down the Monongahela, low and flat to the water like a submerged hippopotamus. I looked up at the stars winking merrily at me. It was a beautiful, cold, velvety night, and the world seemed peaceful after the day's tumultuous events.

"Phew." My heart rate began to decelerate to normal. "I must have imagined it," I whispered to myself.

But what is that smell? The delicate, old-fashioned aroma of lilacs wafted to my nose. I spun around in a circle, expecting to come face-to-face with Evelyn McGavitt's ghost. I was still alone. My eyes swept the landing again and alighted on something gleaming on the ground. It was a small scrap of cloth, a dainty lace handkerchief. It was stained, aged, and fragile.

My heart accelerated again, and I wheeled around. I carefully placed my foot on the top stair of the widow's walk. With a shaking hand, I pushed the scrap of cloth into my pocket. "There's no such thing as ghosts." I shut the door firmly behind me and made my way to the top of the back stairs on my way to the second floor.

The lights went out, and an earsplitting scream echoed from below me.

I stumbled down the last few stairs to the second floor, falling on the last step. I swore and rubbed my twisted ankle and felt the walls with trepidation.

"Mallory?" Mom reached out in the dark and grabbed my hand. "Oh, this is just awful!"

I held her hand, and the two of us did an awkward crab walk in the dark down the last flight of stairs, following the sounds of the bedlam below, ending in the kitchen. Rachel turned on a flashlight, and I could see her, Keith, Becca, Whitney, and my mother in the weak glow. And Hunter. *Hunter?*

"What are you doing here?" I blurted out. My face heated.

Rachel's silky robe suddenly made sense.

"I wanted to observe the house at night, and Rachel graciously invited me," Hunter said gallantly, without a shred of embarrassment. "The EMF went nuts right before the spectral event."

"It's true, dear," my mother said with a worried frown. "I set my alarm to wake up and join in the fun, and that little instrument went haywire right before all the commotion."

My mother, the moonlighting ghost hunter? All of the consternation about her rejected design plans had evaporated in her excitement.

"The spectral event?" Keith's mouth turned down in a forceful sneer. "What's the meaning of this?" He crossed his arms and blustered over to Hunter. He was decked out in a navy robe and a grade A-scowl. His browbeating of Hunter was put to a merciful end by the scrabbling sound of the dogs and cats. They were meowing and barking one flight up.

"Why aren't they coming downstairs?" I grabbed a flashlight from the small stash in the kitchen drawer. *Mental note, get more flashlights, one for each guest room.* I had a lot of things to tweak before our official grand opening. I raced up the stairs, the flashlight bobbing with each step. I stopped in front of the white bedroom, where no one was staying.

"They're locked inside," I whispered. I used the key ring I'd snatched from what would be the check-in area in the front hall and unlocked the door. Whiskey and Soda came tumbling out, followed by Fiona, Bruce, and Maisie. I heard a crash and swung my flashlight into the hall. The McGavitt family's factory was famous for their miniature decorative menageries of whimsical crystal animals. Our real menagerie of animals caromed around the corner in the hallway and collided in a mass of churning legs, fur, barks, hisses, and meows, straight into a built-in wall curio display. The delicate glass menagerie shook and rattled. A spotted giraffe and a striped tiger teetered off the edge and met their shattered and splintered demise. The rest of the animals slid off the shelf, and the little crystal critters were dashed to pieces.

"Kitties! Doggies! Stop it!"

I broke up the dog and cat kerfuffle, and the cats ran for the third floor, while the dogs trotted down the stairs to the first floor. I tried each door on the second floor, but they were all locked.

Rachel and Hunter joined me, growing more and more excited.

"Whitney, Keith, and Becca heard their doors lock, and Becca screamed when she couldn't get out at first," Hunter explained. "This is the strongest, most clear manifestation I've ever witnessed." His gray eyes sparkled.

Clearly, everyone about me had lost their wits. "This is hooey. Someone locked those doors, and they weren't of the supernatural persuasion. I'm calling the police."

Chapter Nine

"No crime has been committed." Truman glanced at his watch and yawned. "This was a harmless prank gone wrong." He stopped to address my mother, who started to speak up in annoyance. "Although, I can see why you're so spooked. You shouldn't use real keys."

The lights were on again. Faith had discovered that every fuse had blown in the basement.

"You should upgrade the electrical around here," she tsked, and my face went red.

"Jesse did do electrical upgrades!"

Disdain was etched on Truman's tired face.

"Ghosts have very strong electrical fields." Hunter's face was flushed with excitement, and he nearly bounced on the balls of his feet. "The fuses were blown by their presence!"

"Or someone sent us a message," I muttered. "Why wasn't the security system tripped?"

"Um." Rachel's voice was very small, and she studied her mule bedroom slippers. "I took the security system offline for ghost hunting tonight.

We were roaming around outside and didn't want to trip it."

Truman groaned.

"I should sue you!" Keith clenched his hands.

"Most B and Bs use real keys." I turned to address Truman and ignored Keith. I wanted to keep the quaint skeleton keys, but not if they were a security risk for my guests.

"I work hotel security at the Senator," Hunter broke in. "I can help you set up a key card system. Your guests will be much more secure."

"But someone must have broken in to do it," I protested. "I'll change the locks, but right now I'm more concerned that someone was able to get into the house."

"There are a lot of people here." Truman's tired eyes swept the room to take in all of us assembled around the breakfast table, clutching cups of strong coffee. "Any one of you could have orchestrated these shenanigans. It wasn't someone from outside."

"Are you accusing us of staging this fiasco?" Keith puffed his chest out. His navy robe rose and fell with each blustery breath, but it didn't work.

"Keith," Truman began, drawing himself up to his full height, "I've spent the night processing your house after a genuine crime and my son's office after another break-in. I don't mind making sure the premises are secure here, but I won't be told how to do my job." Truman looked imposing, though exhausted, still in his full uniform. "I'll check the grounds, as a courtesy, but don't expect me to find anything. You need to take a close look at each other and figure out who would want to do this." Truman looked us each in the eyes briefly in turn and stalked out the back door, flooding the grounds with a flick of the spotlights out back.

"It was a ghost," Hunter affirmed calmly, his clear and pleasant voice filling the dead air.

Keith threw up his hands and scowled at Hunter. "There are no such things as ghosts." He turned his searing gaze on me. "If this is how you run your B and B, you'll be out of business in less than a year. Ingrid Phelan is right." He turned and left the kitchen, Becca following him, mincing off on low-heeled satin bedroom slippers.

"I'm not quite sure what you ever saw in him," sniffed my mother. She'd apparently forgotten counseling me to go through with the wedding to Keith.

Whitney looked sleepy and appalled, and she hugged Bruce to her and sipped her coffee. Maisie and Fiona sat at her feet.

I nonchalantly tried to make everyone feel at home, despite the recent events. It was now five in the morning, and the contractors would be arriving in an hour.

"I may as well make breakfast. Are you guys hungry?"

I was met with enthusiastic nods and cheers for food, and it was too late for everyone to go back to bed. So I began to make the inaugural breakfast for the B and B under the strangest circumstances I could imagine.

"Need any help?" Hunter appeared at my elbow as I chopped peppers, onions, and mushrooms for southwestern omelets.

"Thanks for offering." I gave him a smile. "You

could set the table for me. You worked with Lois at the Senator Hotel. What was she like?"

He blushed and stacked plates for the guests. "Honestly? We called her the Stasi."

I stopped chopping in surprise right before I almost hacked off my left thumb. "She seemed so nice." A little pushy, but pleasant.

"She was a pretty cheerful lady. An institution at the Senator. She cheerfully stuck her nose into people's professional *and* personal lives. She was the head of HR, and I work in security, so our paths crossed a lot. The ghost hunting is just a hobby, one I hope will pan out into a reality TV show."

Had he told Rachel that? It was one of her dearest ambitions to be on TV.

I steered our conversation back to Lois. "So she busted people's balls, huh?"

"Yeah. It sounds awful, but I'm not surprised she was murdered. She cracked down on people for legit things, like when she caught them moonlighting on company time. But she was also plain old nosy. She made it her business to be in everyone's personal business, things that had nothing to do with work. It was a little unethical." He stroked his cleft chin for a moment.

Unethical, just like her shaking me down for a bribe in return for my permits getting approved.

"Her snooping must not have endeared her to the other employees." I added a tidy mountain of mushrooms to the skillet, and they sizzled and popped.

"She had a lot of enemies." Hunter blinked, his large gray eyes filled with sadness. "But that doesn't mean she deserved to be murdered."

Truman opened the back door and gave my jangly nerves a start.

"I don't like to be proven wrong," he muttered and wiped his feet on the mat. "There are footsteps in the mud under the tree closest to the fire escape. They lead around the house to the front and the driveway, where the puddles washed away any trace of them. Someone shimmied down the ladder and hightailed it out of here."

Hunter looked more shocked than I did. "Then why did my EMF go off?" The deep furrow of disappointment between his brows matched his cleft chin. "And Mallory saw a ghost. Mrs. McGavitt's ghost."

All eyes lasered on me.

I recalled the woman on the widow's walk. After Garrett's office break-in and Whitney's guest room being ransacked, I would have happily welcomed a prank of the supernatural variety.

"I thought I saw *something*," I admitted.

Someone rapped on the back door.

Truman opened it, and Charity Jones stalked in, bleary-eyed and furious in a fluffy bamboo robe.

"And you are?" Truman inquired with a sardonic smile.

"Charity Jones." She sniffed and looked around the room until she spotted me and my sister. "Their neighbor." She drew her robe around her like a cocoon and wrinkled her nose. "I don't know how to put this."

Truman interrupted. "We're plenty busy here, Ms. Jones. If you could return home, it would be

helpful. There's a crime scene out back, and I don't
want you—"

"Do you have any idea what time it is? What's
with the flashing strobe lights and all of this
racket?" Charity addressed Truman, her nose an
inch from his.

"Those 'strobe lights' are from my police vehicle,
ma'am. And I suggest you take a step back."

Charity's eyes glinted, and she stood her ground.
"Believe it or not, some of us are trying to sleep!"

She whipped around and faced Rachel and me.
"I thought this was a quiet neighborhood. I left
Vegas for some much-needed peace and quiet.
What a mistake I made." She wheeled around on
her heel and stalked back across our yards.

"What got her panties in a twist?" Truman shook
his head and tried to suppress the rueful smirk
spreading across his face.

"There go my free yoga classes," Rachel moaned.

The contractors arrived as we tucked into breakfast. I'd made triple the amount we needed, and
they helped themselves, chatting with Whitney,
Rachel, Hunter, and my mom. The bananas Foster
French toast was a big hit, and every bite was de-
voured. I was grateful they were willing to start
working so early in the morning in a bid to finish
the B and B on time. They were happy for the over-
time.

Ezra fixed himself a plate and gave his brother,
Hunter, and Rachel a frosty hello before retreating to the third floor. It seemed like it would take
him a while to get over my sister hooking up with

his brother. It had to be hard to compete with Hunter, and it bothered him to see his older brother sweep Rachel off her feet.

Delilah rolled into the kitchen and looked my sister up and down. Rachel had the good sense to blush. She still hadn't changed out of her silk robe and shorts getup. She tied the sash around her waist a bit tighter and held her head high.

"I see the apple doesn't fall far from the tree," Delilah muttered under her breath in a loud whisper.

"Excuse me?" Rachel bounded forth like a pugilist, and Hunter neatly stepped between her and Delilah.

He gathered Rachel's hand in his and gave it a squeeze.

"Now, Delilah, that's no way to talk about a lady." His smile didn't reach his eyes. It was a good thing my mother had left the room to let the Westies out or there would have been hell to pay.

Rachel sighed as if he'd sung her a troubadour's song, and Delilah immediately hung her head. She grumpily picked at her omelet.

Jesse wasn't quite as soothed by Hunter's performance. "And just what were you insinuating, Mother?" He glowered over Delilah.

"I'm sorry, son. I just don't want you to forget how Carole broke your heart." She glanced up to make sure my mother was still out of the room.

"Losing Carole was the biggest mistake of my life. Loving and losing really is worse than winning it all." Jesse carried his dish to the sink and stalked out of the room. I stifled a chuckle at his malaprop.

After Jesse left, everyone calmed down, and

breakfast continued with pin-drop silence and scratching silverware on plates. I wanted to take a nap, but I had three guests to take care of. Keith and Becca left for work, and Whitney was visiting her father. Rachel and I stood outside of Keith and Becca's room.

"You don't have to do this," Rachel carefully wiped down the door handle, blackened from the police's attempts to take prints. After Truman's admission that someone had entered and exited the house via the fire escape, they had gone into high gear, dusting for prints on the bedroom doors and around the circuit breakers. They hadn't found any.

"It's okay. I can handle it. I'm sure we'll have other guests someday that give me the creeps. I may as well get used to it."

Rachel unlocked the door with our master key. I breathed a sigh of relief. It looked like a normal hotel room. The bed was turned down, there was luggage scattered about, and the curtains were drawn. We got to work freshening up the room.

Until I saw the panties.

"Ack!" I jumped back as if the offending scrap of lace were a hissing copperhead.

"What is it? Oh." Rachel stared at a pair of red crotchless panties marring the smooth fawn carpet. "I bet she put them there to get a rise out of you."

Well, it worked. I stared at the undies as if they were nuclear refuse and made no moves.

Rachel picked up the offending scraps of cloth with a pen from the desk and tossed them on top of Becca's suitcase. We hurried through the rest of our task, prettying up the room and wiping down the bathroom.

We took our time in Whitney's room.

"Hunter still thinks it was a ghost." Rachel fluffed Whit's pillows.

"But Truman found actual footprints, Rach. The ghosts are just a front."

Rachel put down the pillow and placed her hand on her hip. "Are you insinuating the ghost hunters were behind that stunt, locking everyone in their rooms? Why don't you just come out and accuse them? Besides, it's impossible. Hunter was with Mom when everyone was locked in. And you saw the ghost!"

"I saw something, or someone. It didn't have to be a ghost." I told Rachel about the old lace handkerchief I'd found and hidden from Hunter on the widow's walk.

We finished the room and padded downstairs.

"Mom, tell Mallory where Hunter was last night."

"Well, we were all looking at that ghost-o-meter thing around three-thirty in the morning when the mêlée began," my mom offered.

"Ghost-o-meter?"

"Yes. The needle was dancing all over the place. It was so fun. We were drinking coffee and making a night of it. We were about to walk through the rest of the house when the lights went off."

I frowned. My mom's corroboration let Hunter off the hook. But that didn't mean other ghost hunters weren't afoot in the house.

"Maybe it was the contractors," Rachel mused.

This time my mother got upset. "Jesse would never do something like that! He's an honorable man." She stopped and blushed. "And it wouldn't be in his interest to sabotage this project."

"Then who did it?" I asked. "And the same evening Garrett's office was ransacked and Whitney's room was tossed at Keith and Becca's house. Who knew we'd all be here?"

The three of us racked our brains but couldn't come up with a suitable answer. We went about the rest of our day.

"I'm sure it was an intruder, not a ghost."

It was after six, and Becca and Keith had returned from work in Pittsburgh. I silently agreed with him. Ghosts didn't shimmy down ladders and leave footprints in the mud.

"If this is the way you run this establishment, you can kiss a rezoning to commercial business goodbye." Keith was still dressed in his work suit, and he pulled his and Becca's matched luggage behind him. Becca brought up the rear, peering down her nose at me.

"Don't threaten me."

"That's what he does best," said a dry voice behind me. Garrett entered the kitchen.

Keith startled. "Davies. What are you doing here?"

"They finally finished processing my office. My dad told me what happened here."

I gave him a grateful smile and moved closer to him. I was ecstatic to see him, although it could have been under better circumstances, like our canceled date. "I'm happy you're here. Are we on for another time?"

Keith jerked his head to stare first at me and then Garrett and redoubled his efforts to rattle me.

"What I said about the rezoning is true. This isn't

a professional establishment. You can barely keep this circus under control. It's a mockery of my Grandma Sylvia's house. She never would have wanted her home to be a place of business. And the Planning Commission will agree."

"Cool your jets. She loved people and excitement and fellowship and celebrations and, most of all, talking about and showing off the history of this house. Of course she'd want it to be a B and B!"

Keith shook his head. "I will strongly recommend to the other members of the committee that they deny your application to turn this into a place of business."

"Don't try to intimidate her." Garrett's voice was deceptively soft, and menace clouded his hazel eyes.

"Stay out of things that don't concern you." Keith gestured to his luggage. "We're leaving. I like our chances back at my house better than here." He strode out of the room.

"That was intense."

Garrett shook his head. "It's not unexpected. I've been thinking, though. Is it really wise for Whitney to go through with the wedding?"

"What do you mean?" I didn't like the sound of this.

"My office was ransacked, the locks picked by a professional, from the looks of it. My entire case file on Eugene Newton's defense for the murder of Vanessa Scanlon was stolen. Then Whitney's room was destroyed, and she was warned to go back to Baltimore. And your bed-and-breakfast was broken into and everyone scared to pieces. I don't like it." Garrett echoed his father, and an icy shiver ran through me. I'd never seen both Truman and

Garrett so unsettled. But a kernel of annoyance bubbled up too.

"Whitney wants to get married. It's still two weeks away. She's going to get married, and I'm going to throw her the wedding, and everything will be alright." I hoped I could deliver on that promise.

"I just want you to be safe."

"I will be. Don't worry."

His concern was sweet and annoying all at the same time. I appreciated his chivalrous worry, but there was no way I was canceling the wedding.

Whitney emerged from the back stairs, a borrowed backpack of belongings slung over her shoulder, since all of her luggage had been torn to smithereens. Bruce in a black sweater, and Maisie and Fiona in matching white sweaters sat obediently at her feet, like doggie salt and pepper shakers.

"I heard Keith going on at you from the second floor. I can't believe Becca is marrying him." Her face twisted in a frown, equal parts sadness and disbelief. "But I'm going back with them. The police are done with the room I was staying in, and Becca assured me I can stay in another guest room." Her mouth ticked up in a wistful smile. "Maybe I can convince my cousin to not marry that horrible man. And besides," she smiled and knelt to pat the pups, "these guys can act as guard dogs." Bruce barked once in assent, and with that, Whitney left Thistle Park with Keith and Becca.

"I can't say I'll miss the dogs." Rachel held up one acid-green snakeskin Jimmy Choo, the heel chewed down to the nub.

Chapter Ten

The next day I woke up and fumbled for my alarm clock.

Something was missing.

I'd placed the delicate, aged lace handkerchief I'd found on the widow's walk under my alarm clock, and it was gone.

"You must've put it somewhere else and forgotten it," Rachel said airily, but I detected a thin current of fear threading its way through her dismissal.

I shook off my doubts and drove to my friend Bev Mitchell's new bridal shop to meet Whitney and find her a dress. She had called the store in Baltimore where she'd bought the gown destroyed at Keith and Becca's, but the owner sadly informed her they couldn't get another one in time for her wedding. I hoped Bev would have something in stock that would please Whitney and that we could get it delivered in time and alter it, or better yet, that she'd fall in love with a dress right off the rack.

I parked and hurried over to the store. I was ten minutes early, and if Bev could spare me a minute,

I wanted to pick her brain about Lois. Bev was the biggest gossip in town. Although her mouth sometimes got her into trouble, I couldn't resist. If anyone knew about Lois's bribe attempts, it would be Bev.

Bev's store, Silver Bells, was nestled at the corner of Poplar and Main Streets, and she'd gone all out in her decorations for fall. A dress form stood in the window clad in a dazzling ball gown. Tiny crystals scattered over a full tulle skirt sparkled like a mini galaxy of gold stars. A chocolate sash circling the waist and a vibrant paprika-colored scarf around the shoulders completed the look. Bev had suspended hundreds of leaves from the display ceiling in rich shades of yellow, sienna, and orange, so it looked like they were blowing in a gentle wind around the bride. I stood spellbound in front of the display and heard the tinkling of bells as Bev bustled into the street.

"Come in!" Her excitement was infectious, and I found myself grinning as I stepped over the threshold. Bells chimed again as the door closed behind me. Her store was cozy and sophisticated all at once, with plush gray velour couches lining the walls, three-way mirrors, and discreet dressing rooms tucked into nooks along the sides. Dress forms were placed at different depths throughout the store displaying showstopper gowns. Shorter dress forms with bridesmaids' dresses surrounded the bridal gowns.

Bev enveloped me in a crushing hug, and I breathed in her familiar Snickerdoodle smell of cinnamon and sugar.

"Two new business owners! Can you believe it?"

She gestured around her store, pride lighting up her pretty plump face.

"I hear things are going well. This space is lovely."

Bev nodded, her acorn earrings jingling. "Sales are booming. I can hardly keep up with my regular seamstress work. How's the wedding planning going?"

I filled her in on Whitney's drastically moved-up wedding and gave her the truncated version of the demise of her dress.

"That's awful!" Bev clucked her tongue. "Things like that don't happen around here. What a dreadful welcome back to her hometown. We'll have to find her something she loves and feels comfortable in. I'll start looking."

I described Whit's ruined dress to Bev, and she pulled samples off her racks, clearly knowledgeable about her inventory. She amassed ten gowns similar to Whitney's original dress, all sheaths with elaborate beadwork.

How should I broach the subject of Lois? Bev's curiosity opened the door for me.

"I can't believe what happened to Lois Scanlon." She moved to select veils to accompany the dresses and flipped through frothy confections of netting and rhinestones. "I hear she left Whitney quite the bequest. She was already wealthy, due to inheriting from her mother, Vanessa, once it was proven she was murdered, although I'm sure she'd rather have her mother than the money."

I checked myself from gasping, but said, "How do you know Lois left Whitney a lot of money?" Garrett hadn't said not to tell anyone, but surely it wasn't common knowledge.

Bev dropped her eyes, suddenly sheepish, and murmured, "I have my sources. And I'm sure Whitney Scanlon would rather have her aunt, too, than her money."

Now that Bev had cracked the door, I could plunge in. "Lois seemed like a jolly sort of woman. Who would want to kill her?" I didn't add I knew from Hunter that she spied on her fellow employees at the Senator Hotel.

Bev fingered a pretty veil laced with luminescent seed pearls and dropped her voice, though we were the only ones in the shop. "This space used to be a soda fountain. I had to make some structural changes, but luckily I know someone who did it quickly for me." Her eyes twinkled. "But I did have to apply for a construction code permit." Her dancing eyes clouded over. "When I applied for the permit, Lois tried to get me to pay her a bribe."

Bingo.

"I think she did the same to me, about thirty seconds before she died."

Bev's eyes opened wide, and she nodded. "We're not the only ones. I asked around a bit after it happened—"

Of course she did.

"—and no one would confirm it, but I saw the fear in their eyes. I think several people ended up paying Lois."

"You didn't, though."

"Of course not!"

Relief flooded over me in a small wave.

Bev drew herself up to her full height, which wasn't very tall, and her heavy chest heaved. "I do things on the straight and narrow. I don't need

nepotism or secret handshakes, just this right here."
She stopped and tapped the side of her beehive. "I
told that silly old coot she must be joking, to give
her an out. And she took it, grumbling about a misunderstanding. I would have a little chat with the
new florist and chocolatier, if I were you." Bev raised
her blond eyebrows.

"Maybe that's where Lois got all of her money.
And blackmailing all of the new business owners
would create some pretty powerful enemies." I
liked running my theories past Bev.

She opened her mouth, but the silver bells on
the door rang in a merry peal, announcing some
shoppers. It was Whitney, on the arm of her father,
Porter, who grimaced with each step, leaning heavily on a new cane.

"Welcome, sweetheart." Bev rushed over to settle
the bride and her father on a love seat and get them
champagne. Porter declined, but Whitney nervously
took a sip of the clear, bubbly, gold liquid.

"I hope I can find a dress. I'm running out of
time." She looked near tears, not excited like a
bride should be.

Her father squeezed her hand. "You'll look radiant in anything, Whit."

Whitney gave Bev a dubious look. Bev's style was
eclectic, and today tiny sparkly pumpkins nestled in
her voluminous blond beehive.

"These are gorgeous." Whitney fingered the
elaborate beading on each dress and held a few up
against her petite frame, promptly bursting into tears.

"It's okay, honey," Bev put her arm around
Whitney.

"It's just—I'm not sure if I want to wear this style

anymore. All I can see is that dress slashed down the middle. I'm sorry. I'm so confused!"

Bev raised her eyes over Whitney's head, and we silently pondered.

"Ahem." The three of us wheeled around, and Porter sheepishly spoke from the love seat. "I have a surprise for you, Whitney, in the trunk of my car. If you ladies could help me . . ." He seemed embarrassed that he couldn't get the item himself, so I quickly hurried out to his car and emerged with a heavy box from the trunk. It was covered in aging pink satin fabric and closed with a bow. I placed it on the floor in front of the love seat, where Whitney now sat, dabbing her eyes and looking puzzled.

"Open it," Porter gently urged. "I'm not sure if you'll like it, and you don't have to wear it, but I thought . . ."

Whitney peeled back brittle tissue paper and emerged with an old but pristine wedding gown. It was heavy satin, probably once a cream color that had deepened over time to a rich champagne. It featured a foam of frothy lace cascading down a high collar, a stiff, full skirt, and round puff sleeves that would make Princess Diana proud.

"Mom's wedding dress," Whitney gasped. She held the dress up to her in front of the three-way mirror and promptly burst into tears again.

"Oh, Whit. Did I do the wrong thing?" Porter turned his sad eyes anxiously to his daughter, and they went wide.

"No! It's lovely, Dad." Whitney bawled into a clump of tissues offered by Bev, and I took the dress from her. It was beautiful, but it screamed 1980s haute couture.

"It's gorgeous," Bev offered diplomatically. "And with some subtle updates, it will be just stunning." Her seamstress eyes flicked over the gown, cutting here, streamlining there.

Whitney's eyes lit up. "You can do that?" A wave of relief seemed to wash over her.

"Sure thing, honey. Come right over here."

Whitney stood on a short raised platform in front of a mirror, where Bev discussed removing the puff sleeves, lace collar, and insert and making a new dramatic V neckline.

"It would go perfectly with your chocolate theme with a sash like the one in the window," I suggested.

Whitney nodded, a light going back on in her dark eyes. "It's the perfect color for fall." She held the dress close to her and spun around. The heavy silk satin rustled and fell in pretty pleats. "Let's do it!"

Bev ushered her into a fitting room, and Whitney emerged, wearing the heavy gown.

"It fits perfectly." She stood in front of the mirror, and a small smile played on her lips. "It'll be stunning with some updates."

"There's more in the box, honey." Porter shuffled over and held a small lacquered jewelry box. "These were your mother's as well."

We all crowded in as Whitney lifted the lid and displayed a striking amethyst and diamond pendant necklace, fashioned as an iris touched by snow, and an ornate diamond and emerald band on a bed of black velvet. Whitney gasped. "These are gorgeous, Dad."

"I've been waiting for years for the right moment to give these to you."

Whitney slipped the pendant over her head and placed the ring on her finger. "They're beautiful." Tears came anew, but this time they were joyful ones. Whitney hugged her father, and Bev turned away, wiping at her eyes behind her purple cat's-eye glasses.

"Are these family pieces?" I peered at the distinctive jewelry and wondered if they were Whitney's style.

Porter shook his head slowly. "I'm not sure. Vanessa loved jewelry. She collected it and sometimes brought in old pieces to exchange for new."

A gasp tore through the store. We turned to see Angela in the doorway, transfixed by Whitney in her mother's dress and jewelry.

"Sweetheart, you're so beautiful." Angela slowly walked over and joined Whitney, clearly choked up. After embracing her niece, she leaned back and took her in again. "You look so much like your mother. You nearly startled me. Amethysts were her favorite." Angela's voice was hollow with emotion. She gently picked the necklace up from Whitney's throat and studied the large stone in the light.

"Isn't it gorgeous? Dad's been saving it all these years." Whitney stepped from the platform and turned to Bev. "Are you sure you have enough time for the alterations?"

Bev grinned at the bride. "For you, we'll get it done. Now, slip out of that dress and I'll get started today."

"Eeek!" Whitney hid behind a dress display and peeked her head out. "Ian's here. He can't see me in my dress!" She shimmied into a dressing room.

"Where's my girl?" The tinkling of bells announced Ian's arrival.

"You can't see her in her dress," Angela sniffed as she echoed her niece. Her warmth evaporated, and her ramrod posture returned, transforming her into a schoolmarm.

Ian gave her a wide smile. "That's why I walked in with my eyes closed. Right, guys?" Ian had brought the Westies with him, and they strained their tartan leashes, sniffing around the store.

I finally got to introduce myself to Whit's fiancé. He was a foot taller than her, with a shock of blond hair that neatly framed his wide face and deep-set blue eyes. His smile was kind, and he gave me a warm, charming, chipped-tooth smile.

"Hi there, little guy." Bev leaned over to pet Bruce. "Why, hello there, sweet peas." Maisie stood on her hind legs, showing off for Bev, and Fiona yapped with glee.

Whitney emerged from the dressing room and ran to her fiancé. "Here's my favorite ring bearer!" She leaned down to accept a doggy kiss from Bruce. I smiled. The dogs would make adorable ring bearers.

"Wow, what's this?" Ian gently picked up the heavy amethyst pendant from Whitney's grasp and swung it back and forth. It glistened like a sparkly plum on a pendulum in the light, ripe and heavy and full. It was too enticing for Bruce. He leaped up in a surprisingly graceful doggie arc and nimbly plucked it out of the air with his mouth.

"Bruce!" Whitney lunged for the dog, but he evaded her and shook his head back and forth. I joined Whitney in chasing the dog around the room, and we cornered him under a gilt chair near the entrance to the fitting rooms. The chain slithered to the floor, but he still held the jewel in his jowls.

"Drop the amethyst, sweetie," Whitney cooed. She petted Bruce on the head and made to grab him when he chewed the purple stone, with a yelp, and swallowed it whole, his Fu Manchu mustache quivering.

He broke out into a doggie smile. "Arf!"

"Oh no," I moaned. "Bruce, that couldn't have felt good."

But the Westie settled back on his haunches and looked quite pleased with himself. His pink tongue darted out, and he licked his lips, then sat back and dangled his front paws, seemingly delighted with his trick.

"Let's take him to the vet." Whitney's elation at wearing her mother's dress evaporated over concern for her dog. "It looks like we'll be staying in Port Quincy after all." She and Ian scooped up their charges and hurried off.

Whitney called me on Monday with the verdict. The vet's advice was to become intimately familiar with Bruce's bathroom habits over the next week.

Ian offered to be the one to follow Bruce around and hunt through the doggy doo-doo. His bride was more concerned about Bruce's discomfort, but the vet assured Whitney that Bruce would be fine.

My mother was measuring furniture in the

parlor when I walked by, and she quickly hid a large upholstery sample book behind her back. She was in official decorator mode. A pencil was nestled behind her ear, holding back a lock of her new haircut. She held a clipboard and was all business.

"Hi, Mom." I tried to hide the trepidation in my voice.

"Just getting some dimensions for the furniture." The upholstery book landed on the floor behind her with a dull thud, and she whipped around to close it before I could see the fabric.

"I know you're nervous." She set the book on a table.

"Nervous?" I squeaked like a mouse. "No, Mom, I'm not nervous. I trust you." I had no choice but to hope my mom had gotten the memo. I needed her decorating expertise, even if it meant palm trees and coconut rattan, because Whitney's wedding was due to take place in less than two weeks.

My mother's face relaxed, and she clasped my hand. "Sweetie, it'll be beautiful. Tabitha told me about the contest the Historical Society's sponsoring, and this redecoration is going to win. I'm sure of it."

This time I actually did relax a bit as my mother told me the parameters of the contest I'd secretly helped make up.

"I'll have to ditch the watermelon pinks and lemon-lime plaids, but it'll still be gorgeous. I'll just adjust my color palette. Tabitha and I have been poring over pictures of the house. I won't slavishly follow the old design, but I will use historically accurate touches and blend it with modern comfort and charm."

My anxiety began to melt away. It had taken a contest to get my mom on the right track, but I thought we were finally there. I pretended to hear about the contest for the first time. "That's awesome, Mom! You have a great chance of winning." Too bad it wasn't a real contest.

"I have one more trick up my sleeve." My mother's eyes danced and sparkled with hidden plans.

"Everything you just told me about the contest is great, Mom. Why don't you stick with that?"

"Nonsense! This is a surprise you'll *love*." She stuck her pencil back behind her ear, collected her fabric swatches, and whipped out of the room.

"Yoo-hoo, Jesse?" My mother headed down the hall and stuck her head into the rooms along the first floor.

I wished for the thousandth time that Doug had made the trip up with my mom.

I left her in her search and climbed to the second floor.

I opened the door to my temporary bedroom to find Jesse crouched with his body half in, half out of the wardrobe. He looked like a giant, tool-belted ostrich with its head in the sand.

"Um, what are you doing in there?"

He froze, then jumped up and hit his head on the shelf inside the wardrobe.

"Ouch! Oh, it's you, Mallory." He dropped his

voice and colored. "I'm, um, hiding from your mother."

I tried to tamp down my bemused smile, but a peal of laughter escaped.

Jesse backed out of the wardrobe and held his hands up in surrender.

"Relax. She's downstairs, but she is looking for you. I bet you have five minutes."

Jesse took off his Penguins hat and twisted it around in his large hands. "I wanted to ask you a favor. I'm not good at this kind of thing, and—" He stopped and craned his head.

Snick, snack. Snick, snack.

We both froze and stared at each other. The knitting needles had returned.

"Do you hear . . ."

"Yes!" Jesse's high voice was even higher and thinner than usual. He scrabbled to get out and slipped on the wool rug, landing in a heap in the hall.

We weren't alone. The rest of the contractors appeared in the hallway after their trek from the third floor, and from the looks on their panic-stricken faces, they had also experienced paranormal phenomena.

"It's the moaning again—"

"There's phantom water splashing in the bathroom—"

"*I quit!*"

I turned to Jesse with a look of panic. "You have bigger issues than my mom. The contractors are mutinying."

We rushed out into the hallway and down the

grand front staircase in time to see all five contractors beating a path to the front door.

"You couldn't pay me a million dollars to stay here."

Jesse turned to me, his eyes round and stricken. "Call Hunter."

"I can't believe I missed it." Hunter sagged against the door, as deflated as a kicked-in pumpkin the day after Halloween. He fiddled with his EMF meter, which was still, the digital display calm and silent. "I didn't leave any recorders in the room either, since you're staying there, Mallory. I would give anything to have heard the knitting needles." He gazed wistfully up the stairs.

"I'm going to stay and see this project through." Jesse jutted out his chin. "But I don't blame them for getting out of Dodge."

Ezra rolled his gray eyes and jammed his hands in his pockets. "I'm used to the supernatural because of my brother." He nodded at Hunter. "But that was scary, even to me."

"Hello, sweetie. You just missed the fireworks." Rachel descended the stairs in a clingy scarlet sweater dress and calfskin boots.

Her face was carefully and tastefully made up to impress. She made a beeline for Hunter and planted a big wet one on him. He returned her kiss in front of everyone with no compunction. Rachel leaned back when they separated and touched his chin dimple, an adoring look making her features soft.

Ezra stepped back from her and blinked fast. "I'm going to grab some lunch." His voice was gruff but didn't hide the pain underneath.

Rachel, oblivious, wrapped her arms around Hunter and gaily called out, "There're some leftovers in the fridge. Help yourself!"

"I'm not so sure it's ghosts." I frowned and gestured to the second floor.

"Mallory! Just because you don't believe—" Rachel was more indignant than Hunter.

"Now hold on." I held my hand out in front of me like a cop directing traffic. "There are two explanations here. One, there are ghosts in this house, who are mad we're renovating. Or, two, there's someone playing a prank."

Jesse shook his head. "We've searched in the walls for speakers, Mallory. We can't find anything."

We all fell silent for a moment.

"I'm not sure if we can finish in time." Jesse's voice barely rose above a whisper. "With just Ezra and me left, we can make a go of it, but it won't likely happen. Everyone else just quit."

A bath of icy cold water seemed to drench my veins. I couldn't let ghosts ruin Whitney's wedding.

"We have to figure out something." I couldn't keep the panic from my voice, which was an octave higher than usual.

"Rome wasn't built in a nanosecond, Mallory." Jesse held up his hands in mock surrender. "I'm doing everything I can."

"I know the guys at the Senator just finished up a

big project," Hunter broke in, rubbing his hands together. "They redid the recreation area in the hotel, and I don't think they have a new project yet."

Jesse perked back up. "Calvin Cook's guys?"

"That's them. I can call Cal if you like."

Jesse's face relaxed, and he broke out into a smile, newly invigorated. "I'll call him. Mallory, if we can hire them, we might pull this off." He bounded down the hall, cell in hand.

My mother emerged from the outside.

"Have you seen Jesse? Why did all of the contractors get into their trucks and drive away? I've never seen grown men run so fast." Her face clouded with concern under her new hairdo.

I shook my head over Rachel's shoulder, and she cottoned on.

My sister deflected my mom. "C'mon, Mom, let's grab some lunch, and I'll explain."

I was left in the hall with Hunter.

"I hope the contractors from the hotel can work here. You may have just saved the day."

Hunter offered me an easy smile, and I could see why Rachel was so smitten. He was boyish and friendly and helpful. And ghost hunting was pretty interesting, even if you didn't quite believe.

"I need to get back to work at the hotel. But if you hear anything, give me a call." He placed his hand on my arm and jutted out his chin dimple to go with his hero's promise.

"I do have a few questions about Lois."

Hunter paused. "What would you like to know?" He appeared slightly more guarded, as if he maybe regretted complaining about her the other day.

"You said she had a lot of enemies among the employees since she spied on them?"

Hunter sighed and relaxed. "Like I said, she was like the secret police. She was persnickety and acted like just because her family worked there for years that it was *her* hotel. She fired someone for running their candle business on company time. That's legit, but she'd also dig into personal business that had nothing to do with work. Lois used her role in HR to act as a de facto private investigator for her employer." He ran a hand through his thick hair. "She skulked about with her terriers like they were bloodhounds. She'd sneak up on people, but the dogs gave her away. She got mad when I was updating the Facebook paranormal page, then admitted it was my lunch break. She was furious when anyone dared to eat seafood around her. Just last week, Lois flipped out when someone brought in shrimp ceviche for a going-away-party appetizer and left it in the break room."

"Did you ever hear her ask people for a bribe?"

Hunter frowned and looked surprised. "A bribe for what?"

"Never mind. Thanks, Hunter."

He left with a friendly wave, and I made my way to the kitchen to fix lunch. Ezra was gone, but my mom and Rachel bustled around, making sandwiches.

My mother frowned and reached out to Rachel. "Hunter is so handsome, and he's very nice, dear. I just wonder . . ."

Rachel gave Mom a dubious glare. "Say what's on your mind, Mom."

"If you're moving too fast. I wouldn't want to see you get hurt."

"I can take care of myself." Rachel swallowed hard and shook her head.

My mom took a deep breath. "Just don't give the milk away for free."

Rachel dropped her sandwich and wheeled around. "Like you did with Jesse?"

"How dare you!" Mom quivered in her moccasins, then tucked in her chin. She grabbed her sandwich and minced up the back stairs in a huff.

It was going to be a long afternoon.

Chapter Eleven

I left my mom and Rachel on opposite sides of the house and set out to meet with the florist and chocolatier. Whitney was accompanying Porter to one of his many medical appointments, and I was going to see if I could create Whitney's vision in record time. And while I was at it, maybe I could follow Bev's tips and find out whether Lois had solicited bribes from them. I could mix a little sleuthing with wedding planning. I pictured Truman's heavy frown in my head and pushed the image away. I liked to snoop a little bit. *Okay, a lot.*

"Welcome!" The florist, Lucy Sattler, emerged from the back of her shop and hustled forward to shake hands. She was about my age, with a wild tangle of dark curls held back from her heart-shaped face with a glittery gold headband. She'd dressed her curvy short frame in a pretty red plaid shirt and jeans and topped her ensemble with a robin's-egg-blue apron bearing the name of her store, The Bloomery, in silver embroidery script.

I breathed in the heady scent of hundreds of

flowers. Lucy's store was outfitted for October.
Heavy harvest wreaths fashioned from sunset-
colored leaves and crimson berries lined the windows. Terra cotta vases held clusters of cheery
sunflowers. Rustic arrangements of pinecones,
gourds, and gold and amber ribbon wound their
way around the store.

"Let's see what we can do for Whitney." Lucy
rubbed her hands together in anticipation and got
down to business.

"Whitney loved the idea of a river of mums,
which is good, since you can definitely supply them,
right?"

Lucy nodded eagerly and stood to wheel over a
cart with a few more varieties of mums. "That's all
we can get on such short notice in the volume she
wants. It'll be a mum explosion, which will transform them from a standard fall flower into something special, just by virtue of how many we place
down the banquet tables. And we can add some
special varietals that I'm able to get in stock."

Lucy set out a lush flower that looked like the
inside of a juicy pomegranate, the petals compact
and beaded purple in the middle of the bloom, fanning out to intricate curved edges of mauve tinged
with a soft pink.

"This is a candid mum, and this one is a moira."
The second flower was a tight starburst, a mass of
delicate petals, all in a dreamy lilac.

"They're gorgeous." I couldn't resist running my
fingertips over the velvety flowers. "And perfect.
Whitney can't get enough purple, in every shade."

I approved the rust, plum, burnt orange, and
cream mums that would form the bulk of the

arrangements on Whitney's behalf, as well as the ribbons in chocolate, satin, and café au lait organza that would be wound around the flowerpots.

We hashed out the number of potted blooms we would need for each long table and moved on to Whitney's bouquet.

"She sent me pictures." Lucy grabbed her iPad and zipped her finger across the screen to show three photographs of elaborate bouquets. "I'll be able to create something stunning based on what she likes."

"Thank you for working with us on such ridiculously short notice." I glanced around at The Bloomery, with its buckets of arrangements, ranging from cheerful ten-dollar bouquets of Gerbera daisies in primary colors to lush groupings that seemed more like sculpture than flowers.

"Anything to help out a fellow new business owner. I want to help make your venture as successful as mine has been."

"There are so many things to do still to get off the ground," I lamented carefully. "My house still hasn't been rezoned to accommodate a business, though I do have all of my permits to renovate. You'd think if one were approved, the other would automatically follow."

Lucy rolled her big violet eyes heavenward. "Tell me about it. That was the hardest thing of all, cutting through the red tape in this town to start my business." For the first time, I detected a bit of a twangy lilt to Lucy's words. "I'm from West Virginia and moved here to be with my boyfriend. I was surprised they made it so hard to open a shop. You'd think they'd want to revitalize downtown."

She glanced around her store to see if anyone else was listening in, but so far there was only one customer on the other side of the flower shop.

"Before she passed away," I began carefully, "Lois Scanlon made a strange comment to me about getting rezoned. I could have been mistaken, but—"

"Let me guess," Lucy held up her hand with neatly trimmed nails and a few red prick marks. "She solicited a bribe from you, didn't she?" Lucy's mouth turned with a heavy frown like a marionette whose strings had been pulled down.

I brought my hand up to my mouth with careful mock surprise, though I'd guessed what was coming. "She did." I waited for Lucy to continue.

"And you didn't take her up on her offer?"

"Of course not!" I didn't mention that Lois expired from this earth less than a minute after she made her pitch.

"Well, I didn't, either." Lucy balled up her fists and buried them in her apron. "I was shocked, and I let Lois know it. She said this was prime corner real estate, and all of the plants filling the tables might be a fire hazard." The shop was crowded with blooms and a long table where Lucy's assistant worked assembling bouquets and ringing up the lone customer, but the effect was to make it a little wild and luxuriantly green, not hazardous.

"This Victorian started off residential, and Lois cautioned it should probably remain an apartment building, rather than be rezoned a shop. Then she mentioned she could approve the permits for the shop anyway, if I made it worth her while. She was bluffing, and I called her on it. I told her that soliciting bribes as an official for the city was illegal.

She just laughed it off! My permits were approved the next day. But I know what I heard. She was *not* joking."

Lucy filled me in on the rest of her process of getting her business up and ready, and after chatting for a few more minutes, I stood to go.

"It doesn't shock me that Lois was murdered." Lucy walked me to the door. "I can't imagine we're the only ones she tried to shake down for money."

I headed west on foot to the corner of Maple and Laurel to meet with another new Port Quincy business owner, Penelope Jelinek. Penelope's store, Mellow Cocoa, had beckoned me before, but I'd resisted the luscious smell of truffles and fudge for weeks. I was excited to try some chocolate and bring it back to Whitney in the name of wedding planning. I stopped before the elaborate Halloween wonderland window display. A milk chocolate witch on a pretzel broom flew against a giant white chocolate moon. Tawny owls fashioned from light and dark truffles joined the witch in her flight. They hovered over gingerbread houses decked out for autumn with miniature marzipan pumpkins and piles of candied leaves.

"Come in, come in." Penelope was short and stout and jolly, a bit like Mrs. Claus with her red apron, tidy cap of white curls, and delicate, clear half-moon glasses.

"I've died and gone to heaven!" The air was scented with cinnamon, nutmeg, and allspice. Different scents of chocolate wafted over me, and I didn't know which one I wanted to try first.

"Whitney is a chocoholic, yes?" Penelope set a small covered dish on the table between us.

"She is a self-professed chocolate addict," I agreed.

"Let's bring some of these back to her and see what she thinks. I designed three savory chocolates as favors for her guests." She whipped off the silver cover, and there lay three kinds of truffles, two gleaming like chestnuts and one sparkling with sugar crystals and cocoa on a deep red napkin. "There's cayenne, rosemary sea salt, and tarragon."

I tried to hide my shock, and Penelope laughed, a pleasant warm trill escaping her lips.

"Most people don't think of marrying savory spices and herbs with chocolate, but you'll find them to be quite complementary." Her bright blue eyes twinkled behind the half-moon glasses, and she waited expectantly for my reaction.

I bit into the first one.

"That's the cayenne."

A slow burst of heat joined the velvety dark chocolate, enough to warm up my tongue but not burn it. A subtle hint of cinnamon completed the truffle.

"This will be amazing on a cool November day." My eyes fluttered open, and I swallowed the warm dark chocolate goodness.

"And this is the tarragon."

I bit into the second truffle, and a delicate top note of anise melted with the chocolate. It was surprising and sophisticated.

"And now for the rosemary sea salt." Penelope had saved the best for last. The rosemary complemented the milk chocolate in a burst of piney, sharp flavor before my taste buds picked up the slight bite of sea salt.

"These are decadent and delicious! Whitney will

be delighted." I dabbed at my mouth with a napkin and eyed the rest of the chocolates.

Penelope actually clapped her hands together. "I love my job. Dreaming up new truffles and chocolates—this has been my wish for years, and now it's coming true."

I didn't want to ruin the warm fuzzies we'd exchanged, but I had to know if Lois had offered Penelope a bribe too.

"You must need a lot of paperwork to get a store like this up and running. I know I'm drowning in it at the moment with my wedding-planning business."

Penelope's eyes lost a degree of their twinkle and became guarded and narrow. "Yes, there was a mountain of paperwork and red tape too to open Mellow Cocoa."

"The thing that surprised me the most," I went on, not wanting to beat around the bush, "was this crazy request from Lois Scanlon. I swear I heard her offer to move my rezoning issues along if I'd just pay her to make it happen."

The rosy glow drained from the two spots on Penelope's papery cheekbones as if she'd wiped them with a napkin. She pushed her chair back slowly and rose from the table.

"She did it to you too?" She picked up a rag from behind the counter and began wiping down the glass cases that flanked the cash register, which held truffles of every flavor and shape laid out like jewels.

I nodded and waited for her to spill the beans.

"I can't say I wasn't a little relieved when I heard about Lois's death." Penelope quivered and put down the cloth. "She wouldn't leave me be!" She glanced around the empty store. "Lois hinted at a bribe to grant my permits to renovate this space from a hair dresser to a chocolatier. Instead of telling her to buzz off, I got scared. So she dropped by nearly every day until I caved. She claimed to have seen a rat on the premises. A rat! Of course, there were none. She was just threatening to tell the board of health to ensure I paid her."

"How much did she want?"

Penelope looked at her apron and wouldn't meet my eyes. "A thousand dollars."

"One thousand dollars?" My voice ended in an unladylike squeak. Not enough to build up her supposed fortune, but not chump change, either.

Especially when someone was opening a new business and needed every penny they could get. Lucy had shut Lois down fast, and Lois never approached her again. Penelope had waffled and ended up paying a bribe.

"I had to!" Penelope's eyes pleaded with me to understand. "She was dogging my every step. I started to think of her as my stalker in tweed. After I paid her, in a stack of twenties, she left me alone. That vile, terrible woman! I managed to avoid her until a week ago, at the chocolate convention at the Senator Hotel."

I jerked my head up. "She was there?"

"Yes. Scolding the hotel cook when she caught wind of the luncheon menu, which included a crab-cake sandwich. Lois went ballistic. She dressed the poor man down as if he were a child and claimed he was trying to kill her."

"How many people witnessed this?"

Penelope brought up her hands and raised them in a shrug. "The convention room was packed. There were candy makers and people from Port Quincy tasting and sampling chocolate."

Interesting. The chocolate convention had brought many people to town, and they had all witnessed Lois revealing the perfect way to kill her.

"Did Lois spend a lot of time at the convention?"

"She sure did, and she made something of a spectacle of herself in other ways. She chastised an employee for not wearing the proper attire. The poor woman's skirt was rather short, but it wasn't the time or place to embarrass her, with all the conventioneers milling around. She left her belongings and her dogs to run after the girl, muttering about embarrassing the hotel, but she was really embarrassing herself." Penelope sniffed in disdain and took a bite of a rosemary truffle.

"She left her things unattended? Like her bag?" I was stunned. That meant an untold number of people, the general public and hotel staff alike, had had access to her mints and bag. All while she drew attention away from it.

Penelope furrowed her white brows. It was as if I could see the wheels spinning in her head. "Anyone had access to her purse! She came back about fifteen minutes later, all red-faced, to get it and the dogs. Her purse was just sitting out in a booth until she got back. It could have been stolen or tampered with."

Did Truman and Faith know this?

"Do you know of anyone who would want Lois dead?" Hundreds of people at the chocolate convention had access to Lois's purse, but it only took one person to lace her Altoids with clam-infused Bloody Mary mix.

Penelope shrank back. "I detested Lois for soliciting a bribe, and I'm angry with myself for paying her, but that's a far cry from wanting her dead. Although," she propped her hand on her chin and stared out the front window, "if Lois was willing to solicit bribes, what else was she capable of doing?"

"What indeed." My thoughts strayed to Vanessa Scanlon, and we munched on truffles in heavy silence.

The next day, Whitney bit into a rosemary sea salt truffle, and her eyes went wide. "Where has this been all my life? This will make the perfect favor."

I grinned, but my smile faded when I recalled Whit's aunt shaking the jolly chocolatier down for dough. How would Whitney feel if she knew some of her inheritance had been earned from kickbacks from new business owners? I left Whitney on the sidewalk to take a phone call from her fiancé, Ian. I pushed thoughts of Lois's bad deeds out of my head and entered Fournier's Jewelry Store.

Of all the gin joints, in all the towns, in all the world.

Keith and Becca hovered over a case. Becca ogled the rings. She linked her arm around Keith's and pulled him closer. "That one! I'm sure of it." She licked her lips and waited for the clerk to bring up a heavy band of princess-cut diamonds. She pushed it down her ring finger and held out her hand to admire the prisms of flashing light.

A clerk approached Keith and motioned him over.

"I just wanted to let you know we haven't been able to sell . . . it. It's very large, and most people don't want a piece that was purchased for an engagement before. We could break the ring down and sell the diamond separately."

Keith raised his eyes, and they flicked over to me for a barely perceptible second.

Trying to sell my engagement ring? Good riddance!

I'd last seen the shiny bauble seconds before I'd thrown it down the street. Keith had scrambled after it, and I often wondered if he'd found it in the gutter. I had my answer now.

"Keep trying," he muttered testily. "Now, if you'll excuse me." He returned to his fiancée's side, ignoring the clerk.

A cool breeze from the open door told me another customer had entered the store, and I turned, expecting Whitney. But it wasn't Whitney. It was Keith's mother, Helene. She was dressed in her usual nineteen eighties finery, a boxy electric blue suit, pantyhose, and heels. Her shoulder pads were in full effect, and her pageboy was teased out in dramatic puffs like an old-time nun's wimple. She gave me a regal nod and made her way over to her son and future daughter-in-law.

She flicked her icy eyes over the platinum ring selection before Becca and shook her head.

"No, no, no!" Her mouth twisted down in a mean pucker. "You should get a yellow gold band. It goes with everything, Becca."

Keith looked caught between his mother and his fiancée, but he didn't rush to Becca's aid.

"But it won't match my engagement ring," Becca began tentatively looking at Keith for backup.

He demurred, stepping back to lean against the window, and Becca started a heated discussion with Helene. Before long, the tinkling door of the jewelry shop sounded.

Whitney joined me in the store and sent Becca a happy wave, and we made our way to the counter. I was happy to abandon Keith and Becca's troubles to help Whitney plan her wedding.

"What can I help you ladies with?" The jeweler, whom I recognized as Mr. Fournier from his billboards around town, leaped up to assist us.

"My wedding rings were stolen." Whitney bit her lip and shook away the memory. "My father gave me a band that belonged to my late mother, and I plan to use that as my wedding ring."

"A lovely gesture." Mr. Fournier folded his hands together and leaned expectantly over the glass case. His old-fashioned pompadour quivered.

"But the ring's too big. Could you resize it? I'm getting married the first day of November." Whitney produced the heavy, scrolled diamond and emerald band and laid it in Mr. Fournier's outstretched palm.

He raised the loupe from the chain around his neck and squinted at the ring, rubbing his mustache. Then he dropped the ring as if it had nipped him. The heavy piece spun in a dizzying circle on the counter, like an out-of-control top. Mr. Fournier clapped his hand on top of it with a loud slap and trembled. He picked up the ring with shaking hands and dropped it on the floor with a nervous bumble.

Whitney gasped at how the ring was being man-handled.

"I'm sorry. I just never expected to see this ring again." Mr. Fournier retrieved the ring from the floor and carefully laid it on the counter. "I'm afraid I'll have to turn this over to the police, Ms. . . ."

"Ms. Scanlon, and I beg your pardon, but you will do no such thing!"

Whitney reached across the counter for her ring, but Mr. Fournier was too quick. He snatched the glittering metal and stone and deposited it under the counter. His demeanor changed, and he snapped himself up into a straight line.

"This ring was stolen in the nineteen nineties, and its owner has been missing it ever since. This is a very unusual piece of jewelry, I'd know it any-where. We'll let the police sort this out, Ms. Scan-lon." His dark eyes flashed with annoyance, and he eyed Whitney as if she were a criminal who had at-tempted to put one over on him. Helene, Becca, and Keith stopped their perusal of rings to watch Whitney with interest.

Whitney stood with her hands on her hips, ready to do battle. "This ring was my mother's. I don't have much from her, and she's gone." Her lower lip quivered, but she steeled herself. "If it was my mother's ring, it wasn't stolen. Now hand it back."

The jeweler sneered and became even more righteous in his stance. "Scanlon, eh?" A look of recognition washed over his sharp features. "You must be Vanessa's daughter." He gathered himself to his full height and hissed out his opinion of her in a loud whisper. "I suspect, though it was never proven, that your mother was a highly skilled jewelry thief." Mr. Fournier rocked back on his dress shoes and dared Whitney to refute him.

Whitney's face registered shock, then anger, and finally dismay. "My mother was manager of the housekeepers at the Senator Hotel. She was kind and truthful and honest. How *dare* you!" She gathered up her plum purse and backed out of the store.

I turned to see her flee down the street, sobbing. I caught up with her after a minute and gave her a swift hug.

"I need some time to process what that horrible man said. My father will be so upset he kept Mom's ring. I'm just going to take a little walk and collect myself."

I left Whitney with a travel package of tissues and made my way back to the jewelry store, which Keith, Becca, and Helene had mercifully left.

"That was uncalled for!" I stared down the jeweler with petulant eyes.

"I should have said something about Vanessa Scanlon when she disappeared all of those years ago, but I couldn't prove it. I didn't feel right speaking ill of the dead, but now enough time has passed." Mr. Fournier was agitated, haughty, and unapologetic.

"What makes you think she was a jewelry thief?" This was the first mention I'd heard of such a possibility.

"Vanessa bought many things from this store, and she had the money from her family to indulge in her jewelry collecting. But about a year before she disappeared, she started selling me things in addition to buying. She had some unusual and expensive pieces, and she was very evasive about where she had acquired them. This ring"—he brought the heavy band of winking diamonds and emeralds up from its hiding place below the counter, but held it just out of my reach—"is what convinced me. She tried to sell it to me, only a little before she disappeared. She didn't think the price I offered was fair. She seemed a little desperate for money, quite frankly. I wouldn't budge, and she left in a huff. A few days later a woman came in, distraught, and told me a ring matching this one's description had been stolen and to be on the lookout for someone trying to fence it."

Vanessa Scanlon a jewel thief?

"I knew I'd seen the ring before and realized Vanessa had brought it in. But by that time, she'd disappeared."

"Why didn't you go to the police?"

The jeweler shrugged. "They didn't ask me, so why would I go to them? Besides, by then Vanessa was missing. It was presumed she'd run off. I'd bought several pieces of jewelry from her, and I was worried they had been stolen too."

This man was clearly more interested in self-preservation than justice or helping find a missing woman.

"This ring matches the description of the ring that was stolen. I knew at once when its owner described it that it was the ring Vanessa tried to sell me. I'll contact the police about it now." He turned his back to me and picked up the phone.

"Better late than never," I muttered as I let the door to the store swing closed behind me.

Whitney and I drove to her father's apartment in tense silence. I didn't rehash the jeweler's suspicions about her mother, and she didn't bring it up. A tiny sob escaped her lips every few minutes, and I reached over and patted her hand.

"Why would my mother have a stolen piece of jewelry? She loved collecting it, and she had a lot, if I'm remembering right. We used to play dress-up together. She inherited quite a bit from her mother. She never would have needed to steal something."

"Maybe he misremembered or misunderstood. The police will sort it out." There were probably a lot of things Whitney didn't know about her mother, despite sitting through Eugene's trial. "And maybe it's time you talked to your dad about this," I gently prodded. "Especially the notes you've been getting."

Whitney drew in a rattled breath. "I don't want to bother him, but I think you're right."

We reached a high tower of an apartment building on the grounds of the Whispering Brook retirement and nursing home complex. I hadn't been back here since I last visited Keith's grandmother. She had been in the nursing-home portion of the large campus, but Whitney's father was in the independent-living building. We entered a tasteful lobby done up in shades of olive and gray, designed to look like a swanky hotel. Seniors chatted in a great room off to the left, where a game of bingo was being held. Laughter poured out of a room labeled "Movie Theater," and groups of residents gathered at the sliding glass doors with dogs on leashes, ready for a walk. It was a bustling place, more akin to a college rec center than what I'd envisioned for a retirement home.

"Dad loves living here. He's getting worse, though. It won't be long before his nurse isn't able to take care of him in his own apartment. He's dreading moving to the nursing-home portion of the grounds."

We entered a sleek elevator, and at the last second, a man threw his hand between the closing doors to make them jump and slide open.

"Sorry about that. Darn things will chomp your hands off if you're not careful." The man shuffled in and gave us both a warm smile, but he froze when he saw Whitney. "Ms. Scanlon, right?"

Whitney stiffened next to me. She was wiping at her still-red eyes, probably trying to eradicate any puffiness before she saw her father.

"Yes?" she said warily. She cocked her head and seemed to be trying to place the man.

"Tell your dad Rusty says hello."

Rusty? Gears clicked in my head.

Whitney relaxed, and we stepped off the elevator at the fifth floor. "I sure will."

I stayed with Whitney and Porter for a few minutes, and we chitchatted, carefully avoiding the subject of the stolen ring. I figured it was Whitney's business to tell her father and maybe hear some things about her mother that she wouldn't be comfortable with. I ducked out after a few minutes and made my way back to the busy lobby. The man who had spoken with us in the elevator was sitting on a comfy-looking chair, reading a dog-eared Agatha Christie mystery.

I hesitated, then sat next to him. "Excuse me, are you the Rusty who was in charge of Vanessa Scanlon's police investigation?" I recalled Truman and Garrett's argument right after Lois had expired at the wedding tasting.

The man put down his book and assessed me. "Yes, I am. Rusty Dalton, former chief of police. That's how I knew Whitney. I thought she'd remember me, but I'm ill, and I've changed quite a bit since the trial." The man did indeed look unwell, with sallow skin, clothes that hung awkwardly from his medium frame, and shaking hands.

"It's a case that won't seem to go away," I blurted out. "I'm planning Whitney's wedding while she's in town, and things keep popping up related to Eugene Newton and Vanessa Scanlon."

He put down his mystery and eagerly turned to face me. "Like what?"

Oops.

"It's nothing. I shouldn't be—"

"Look, I don't think we handled the case correctly." Rusty shook his head and glanced at me. "If new things are coming to light, that's a good thing."

"What are you saying?" I cocked my eyebrow and held my breath.

Rusty tented his hands together, his fingers yellow and shaking. He sheepishly tucked his hands under his legs. "I'm not so sure, twenty years later, that we got the right guy."

Chapter Twelve

Rusty and I moved to his apartment, where I settled on a comfortable plaid couch and he served chamomile tea and Chips Ahoy cookies. Pictures of grandchildren were scattered around the neat apartment, as well as regalia from his time as chief of police.

"I almost died when my doctor told me I couldn't have coffee anymore because of my heart." He offered me a wry smile. "I've really come to enjoy herbal tea, but what I wouldn't give for a cup of joe." He picked up a pipe, and my eyes went wide with surprise. Most apartments like these wouldn't allow smoking.

"And this is a prop." He turned the pipe in his hands. "Something to keep me busy. My physical therapist suggested I take up knitting, but can you picture me making a sweater?" He chuckled, a low rattle accompanying his laugh deep in his throat.

I shivered, thinking of Mrs. McGavitt's phantom knitting needles. But I'd rather watch the former police chief knit than hear it in my bedroom with the lights out.

"If Eugene Newton isn't the right guy, who is?" I set down my chocolate-chip cookie.

Rusty's eyes grew as sad and heavy as a basset hound's. "If I knew, I'd share my thoughts with Truman Davies. I'm not too proud to admit we didn't handle the investigation the way we should've. But the buck stopped with me. I was chief, and I personally took on the case, both when Vanessa first went missing and we weren't sure if it was a case of her leaving her family and cutting town or a legitimate kidnapping, and when we found her body ten years later on Eugene's property." He moved the still-empty pipe to his mouth, and he chewed on the end like Maisie the Westie with an expensive shoe.

I shook my head, confused. "If you don't know who really killed Vanessa Scanlon, what makes you think you didn't get the right guy?"

Rusty put down his pipe and stared hard into my eyes for a brief second, flinched, and looked at his hands. "What the heck. I won't be around on this earth much longer." He rubbed his knee and closed his eyes. "I know because we planted some evidence to ensure Eugene's conviction."

A pin dropping on the Berber carpet could have been heard. I stared at Rusty for a full minute.

He lifted his head and defiantly stared back. "I wanted to bring the family some closure. It had been ten years since Vanessa disappeared, and then her body was found in the woods of her lover? The only way I can live with myself is knowing that, at the time, I truly believed Eugene was guilty."

I tried to keep my hands from shaking, but I did a poor job of it. I put my tea on the small tile-topped coffee table to keep from spilling it. "You need to tell someone this."

"I've tried." The former chief shrugged. "I talked to the former and current prosecutor, and they think the other evidence was enough to convict Eugene. And it was, on its face. They're too embarrassed to reopen the case."

"What evidence did you plant?" I asked as casually as I could manage. A man had been in prison for over a decade for something he might not have done.

Rusty pondered my question for a moment. "I took a single item from the woods and put it in Eugene's shed."

"The murder weapon?!"

Rusty blushed and nodded, moving the pipe nervously from hand to hand. "I was certain Eugene was to blame, so I thought I'd help things along and make it a slam dunk. I responded to the call. I secured the scene." His voice dropped to barely whisper level. "His neighbor's new dog had wandered onto his property and dug up part of the body. The hammer was ten feet away, buried, and I was the one to find it. I waited until that evening and planted it in the shed. There were no prints on it, but that didn't mean it wasn't Eugene's."

His audacity struck me dumb. I thought of Garrett and how he wished he could do the case all over again. He hadn't known evidence was manipulated to ensure a conviction.

"I wanted to bring the Scanlon family some peace," Rusty whined, leaning forward and resting his elbows on his knees. "I was about to retire, and it was my last chance for closure."

"And why don't you think it was Eugene? It still could have been his hammer."

Rusty flicked his eyes upward. "I just know in my gut that it's not. He wouldn't be dumb enough to leave the body in his woods. It was a setup."

"Then who *do* you think killed Vanessa Scanlon?"

Rusty blew out an imaginary lungful of tobacco and stood on creaking and popping knees. "It could have been anyone. The pharmacist across the street from the Senator Hotel was infatuated with her. He wore a white coat to work. Her husband had recently found out about her affair. As had her sister-in-law, Lois, who argued with her about it a few days before she went missing."

"Lois isn't around anymore. How convenient." *Could Lois have tried to blackmail her sister-in-law about her affair?*

Rusty slowly shook his head. "Lois's death could be connected to Vanessa's death, but I can't figure it out. I didn't have a bad feeling about Lois then, and I don't now." He waved away my suspicion with a weary hand. "I think it's just a coincidence."

"What did they argue about?" My money was suddenly on Lois, despite Rusty's feelings.

Rusty shifted uneasily in his chair. "Lois denied arguing with Vanessa, and then when she couldn't refute it, she said it was about Tupperware." He barked out a phlegmy laugh. "I think they were arguing about her affair with Eugene." A note of doubt swept across his face.

Exactly. Lois could have tried to blackmail her sister-in-law to keep her affair quiet, then killed her.

"But I believe Whitney. She was five when it happened, and her mother disappeared from the house. She was awoken from her nap and testified she heard arguing. And she saw someone leaving the house wearing white. Her mother had worn red that day and, indeed, was wearing a red dress when we found her body ten years later."

"So the pharmacist is a likely candidate."

"And Porter. He was a dentist before he retired and wore white as well. But they both had alibis. Lois did not—she could never remember what she'd been doing."

I told him about the incident at Fournier's Jewelry Store. "Could her jewelry fencing have anything to do with her death?"

A slow wave of recognition rolled over Rusty. "Jewelry thief, huh? That fits. It's possible it could have led to her death. And it opens the door for more people with a reason to kill Vanessa Scanlon."

"I knew it." Garrett paced in a circle around his backyard. "That bastard!" He kicked a clump of brilliant red leaves he'd just raked into a tidy pile and sent them flying like an overturned apple cart.

I didn't point out that the former police chief moving some evidence did not mean that Garrett's former client was automatically exonerated. Eugene could still be guilty, his conviction just assured that much more by moving the murder weapon from near the body to inside his shed. Still, it was a damning detail.

"Why would he do it?" Garrett ran a hand through

his near-black hair and picked up the rake, combing the leaves back into a neat pile.

"He resurrected a ten-year-old cold case, determined to close it at all costs because he was retiring. He wanted to bring peace to the Scanlons. At the expense of Eugene's life and freedom," I added.

I shared with him the other viable suspects that Rusty and I had brainstormed.

"And that was my whole case." Garrett ticked suspects off on his fingers one by one. "Porter, as the jealous husband. The pharmacist, as the lovesick stalker. Lois, the angry sister-in-law, who we now know liked to dabble in blackmail. The jury didn't buy any of it, all because it was a slam dunk, what with the murder weapon magically finding its way into Eugene's shed. Anyone could have killed Vanessa and left her in his woods."

"There is one wrinkle." I told him about Vanessa's short career as a jewelry thief.

"Hmm. That complicates things." He stopped pacing and sat on an old swing set, the seat too low for him. He dragged his leather shoes through the sand below and gave a few practice swings.

"Vanessa didn't lack money. Why would she want to steal, for kicks?"

"Dad, you're too big for that!"

Summer bounded around to the backyard, still wearing her backpack from school.

"Hi, Mallory." She gave me a big hug and settled onto the other swing, too small for her lanky frame as well.

"Have you decided on a Halloween costume? You're running out of time." Garrett continued to swing, sweeping his long legs out each time they threatened to dig though the soft oval of sand below.

"I'd still like to be a zombie." Summer pumped her legs furiously, and the rusty swing set shuddered and groaned.

"I think that's fine." Garrett turned to face his daughter and abruptly stopped swinging.

"*Really?!*" Summer hopped off her swing with a graceful leap and landed on her feet.

"But I don't think Grandma is on board. I doubt she'll help you make your costume."

Summer's face fell. "I can make my own, I suppose."

"I can help you this weekend when I have a little time," Garrett offered.

"Oh, sweetie, I'd help you too, but I'm so busy with the B and B. We can practice applying zombie makeup, though, and maybe we can tear up some of your clothes for the rest of the costume."

Summer's face lit up briefly.

"And you could always wear Natalie's Glinda costume," Garrett added. "As I recall, that was some getup."

This earned a glare from both me and Summer.

Summer's pretty face twisted in a frown. "Thanks, Dad, but I don't want to be a good witch. I'll figure it out."

"What if you compromised?" I asked slowly. I could see it.

"What do you mean?" Summer sat back down on the swing and turned to me with interest.

"What if you zombie-fied the Glinda costume and you were a zombie princess? Grandma Lorraine might be on board with that, and it'd be unique and even beautiful."

Summer cocked her head to the left. A slow smile spread across her face.

"Ooh, let's do it!" Summer jumped off the swing and started brainstorming. "I can slash the dress and tear the sleeves. I'll spill red paint on it to make it look like blood—"

"Now wait a minute, young lady." Garrett held up his hand. "I'm not so sure Natalie will go for that. You need to tell her your plans before you do that to her costume."

"Of course I will," Summer exclaimed. She was already up and bounding off for the house. "I've got to call Jocelyn and Phoebe! Thanks, Mallory!"

"What have I done?" I hung my head and sunk onto a worn wooden seesaw.

Garrett laughed. "I'm not sure if this will please my mom, or Natalie, but it will be one heck of a costume."

"It looks like you can ask her yourself." I jerked my chin toward the driveway.

A lemon-yellow Beetle with a little flower attached to the antenna pulled in. The costume in question hung in the car. The poufy pink dress filled the entire backseat, little sequins and mirrors winking on the netting and bodice.

"Hello!" Natalie waved like a maniac from the driveway and tried to wrestle the gown out of her car. "Garrett, be a dear and help me, please." She batted her ginger-colored lashes coquettishly and offered him a gentle smile.

Garrett was already on his way and carefully leaned over to help her hoist the costume out of the backseat. Natalie didn't move and crowded him beside her car. They laughed as they carried the dress up the wet walkway, standing close to make sure the fabric didn't touch the ground.

I followed them wordlessly to the front door, five paces behind. It clicked shut after Natalie, and I tried to suppress rolling my eyes as Summer opened it for me.

"Thank you for the costume, Natalie." Summer was all politeness and solicitude. "I was just telling Dad and Mallory I'd like to wear it after all."

Natalie flashed a sunny smile and helped Garrett lay the voluminous dress on the couch. It was so stiff and big, it looked like there was a person already in it.

"I knew once you got a look at it that you'd want to wear it, sweetie." Natalie spoke to Summer but her eyes were on Garrett.

Summer winced at the term of endearment but quickly recovered.

"I'll return it after Halloween." She stared glumly at the dress, consigned to her fate of being a good witch. Her dream of being a zombie with her friends seemed to be slipping away. There was no way Natalie would let her modify the dress.

"I go all out each Halloween, and I never re-wear a costume," Natalie gushed. "Tell you what, you keep it, my treat."

A glimmer of hope lit up Summer's big hazel eyes. "Do you mind if I alter the dress?"

Natalie's big grin dimmed a few watts. "I suppose," she mused. "It is your dress now to do with as you like. Even that preposterous idea to be a zombie." Natalie winced.

"Great!" Summer picked up the heavy gown and examined it, no doubt planning her makeover with scissors and red paint.

"I'm going to try it on right now." She heaved the heavy dress over her shoulder and dragged it back to her bedroom.

"Have a seat, Nat."

Natalie flashed a flirty smile and joined Garrett on the couch, where she crossed her legs and scooted a bit closer to him.

"I know you weren't a coroner when the Vanessa Scanlon case went down, but can you do me a favor?"

Natalie sharply inhaled and leaned in closer to Garrett. "Anything for you."

"Can you look into the case file for anything . . . unusual? Any sign that evidence was tampered with on the coroner's end?"

Natalie frowned. "I've heard some rumors over the years about that case, but I don't believe the coroner's office would be involved. My predecessor was old-fashioned, but he was a straight shooter. Still, for you, I'll look." Again with the megawatt smile. "I'll see if something was overlooked."

"Thanks, Nat. It means a lot to me."

"Natalie!" Lorraine opened the door laden with grocery bags, and Garrett jumped up to help his mother. "What a lovely surprise."

"Good news, Lorraine! Summer is going to wear my Glinda costume for Halloween!"

"That's just wonderful." Lorraine set down a bag of veggies and clasped her hands together. "You worked some magic on that girl."

Natalie bid Garrett good-bye with a quick hug,

taking him by surprise, and a longer one for Lorraine. She nearly skipped down the front path. Garrett and Lorraine walked Natalie to her car and began to unload groceries.

"Is she gone?" Summer peeked her head out of her bedroom and called down the hall.

"The coast is clear. Natalie's getting into her car."

Summer breathed a long sigh and joined me in the kitchen.

"I can't stand Natalie." Her eyes were the picture of melancholy. "She doesn't like me," she said softly, pushing a lock of short blond hair behind her ear. "I hope Dad picks you, and not her. Dad and me, we're a package deal. Natalie doesn't get that."

"Oh, honey, I bet Natalie didn't mean anything." But I wasn't sure. Summer was pretty perceptive.

"She was always trying to change me. She tried to make me more like her. When she and Dad were going out, she got me pink sweaters and girly perfume and wanted me to be more cheerful." She stared up at me through her short blond bangs, tears gathering at the corners of her elfin eyes. "I'm plenty cheerful!"

"You never told me this." Garrett appeared in the doorway with his hands weighed down with heavy grocery bags. He set them on the floor and crossed the small kitchen in three steps. "Sweetie, I wish you would've said something." He scooped his lanky daughter up in a bear hug.

"So you're not getting back together with Natalie?"

Garrett raised his eyebrows at me over Summer's

head. "No, I'm not." He seemed to be saying it for my effect as much as hers.

Summer relaxed and broke the hug. She started to put away groceries, and her smile was so big it revealed all of her magenta braces. I had to stifle my smile and pitched in with the unpacking. We finished, and I stayed to help Lorraine make dinner while Garrett helped Summer with her homework. We ate without Truman, who was held up at work.

Garrett walked me to the Butterscotch Monster and gave me a gentle kiss.

"Break it up, you two," Truman said, all affability and weary smiles. He stepped out of his police car and ambled over. Garrett's face turned to steel, and he broke our embrace.

"What do you know about tampering with evidence in Eugene Newton's case?"

A look of confusion was followed by a flash of anger. "That's a fine way to greet your father," Truman grumbled.

"Mallory spoke with Rusty today. He admitted it."

"What were you doing talking to Rusty, Mallory?"

"You had to have known, Dad."

Truman focused his laser beam of anger on Garrett instead of me. "You're lying. Rusty is a man of integrity. He would never have been anything but ethical with an investigation, especially for murder."

I shook my head sadly. "He moved the murder weapon from the woods to Eugene's shed."

Truman backed up as if he'd been struck in the face. He looked horrified for a single second. And even more alarming, his expression turned to one of recognition.

Chapter Thirteen

"Just look at the potential customers!" My sister took in the Senator Hotel ballroom and plastered on a winsome smile. A woman and her daughter stopped to take a brochure and a miniature scone. Today was the Port Quincy Hospitality Expo. The event featured every hotel, inn, and restaurant in town showing off their services. Denizens and businesses from Port Quincy and nearby towns drifted from booth to booth and perused venues for weddings, parties, meetings, and out-of-town guests. We'd scored a prime location, as our booth was one of the first ones a visitor would encounter upon entering the busy room. The expo had begun fifteen minutes ago, and we'd already gone through a tray of treats and a stack of brochures featuring pictures of the finished exterior of the B and B, the yellow bedroom, and a table set for tea. I was glad the expo was this weekend. I could push thoughts of Rusty and Truman's reaction to the news that he'd rigged the investigation out of my mind.

"Oh no . . ." A prickle ran down my back, and I gazed up at Ingrid Phelan.

She had arrived late and paused from hurriedly setting up her booth. Her display consisted of a stack of black-and-white fliers advertising the Mountain Laurel Inn, and her sour face glared at yours truly.

"Who peed in her Cheerios?" Rachel hefted up another tray of food and placed it at an enticing angle at the edge of our booth. This one held cupcakes iced like tiny tuxedos, with a rim of matching white chocolate strawberries. I hauled up a giant carafe of tea and another of coffee to give to inquiring customers. Ingrid was barely listening to the young couple who peppered her with questions and instead seemed more focused on giving my sister and me the stink eye.

"She's just mad she has such a lackluster booth." I kept my face impassive. I didn't want to give Ingrid any ammunition for her husband, Troy, to deny my rezoning application.

As another couple left our booth with a treat and a paper cup filled with steaming tea, Ingrid yelped and swiftly marched over. She waited with barely suppressed ire for the representative from Quincy College to finish speaking to us. As soon as he was gone, she descended upon us like a flying monkey.

"What do we have here?" She picked up a strawberry and held it in front of her as if it were rotten. "The rules for the expo stipulate purveyors are not to give out food and drink." She jutted out her chin in a haughty puff and deposited the strawberry on the tray.

"There's nothing about that in the rules, and you

know it." I gestured to several booths to our right. "There are several restaurants giving out food."

"The guidelines stipulate that *restaurants* can give out food, but it doesn't say anything about B and Bs." Ingrid pointed her nose skyward with a superior air and didn't seem to notice that a few people were gathering to listen to her complaints.

"Gimme a break." Rachel tapped her sparkly nails on our booth in annoyance. "It doesn't say we can't. You're just jealous more people are visiting our booth and that you didn't think to offer food."

Ingrid's eyes went wide, and her mouth opened and closed like a fish.

"You impertinent girl!" She lost any semblance of dignity, and her cries echoed around the ballroom. "My inn has been around for fifty years, and it won't be driven out by the likes of you two imposters!" Her reedy voice screeched like an incensed barn owl, and her lacey brown shawl flapped around her shoulders like a pair of tattered wings.

"Is that what this is about?" I sighed and handed her a brochure. "Ingrid, we're not trying to run you out of business. We'll have different guests and different functions. For instance, we're holding weddings at our B and B, in addition to visitors. I think we can peaceably coexist."

Ingrid's face broke into a slow smile. "The Mountain Laurel is now hosting weddings as well."

I tried to stop my eyes from growing wide, but I was taken off guard too fast. "But—"

"But you're too small!" Rachel sputtered.

"I'm putting on an addition this spring that will

double my square footage and allow for weddings seating up to one hundred people." She glared at the two of us and raised her voice for the rubberneckers. "And unlike you, this isn't my first rodeo. We're rated Port Quincy's best bed-and-breakfast."

"That's because you've been Port Quincy's *only* bed-and-breakfast," Rachel piped up.

"You've got that right, Miss Shepard." Ingrid put on a hard smile. "And after the Planning Commission denies your request, the Mountain Laurel will remain the only B and B."

"Excuse me, *ladies.*" A portly man in a herringbone vest emphasized the last word, letting us know he thought we were anything but. "Is there a problem here?" It was Randolph Wayne, the manager of the Senator Hotel. He could have been an NFL referee breaking up a scuffle between players instead of a hotel employee reminding two B and B purveyors to mind their manners.

I smoothed the front of my shirt, and my face warmed. "There's no problem."

Ingrid scurried back to her booth and shuffled her stack of fliers. Duly chastened, we carried on with the rest of the morning, talking up the B and B and handing out treats. Ingrid hightailed it out of the ballroom the second the expo was over, but Rachel and I lingered, chatting with other restaurateurs and hoteliers.

"Thank you for keeping your cool." Mr. Wayne appeared at my side, looking officious with a clipboard and walkie-talkie. He accompanied Rachel and me as we left the ballroom and headed for the elevators.

"No problem." I hesitated as the elevator doors

slid open with a metallic clang. "I know Lois Scanlon worked here for years in HR. I wanted to express my condolences."

Mr. Wayne's bushy eyebrows shot up above his round tortoiseshell glasses. "We're still reeling from Lois's passing." The elevator closed, trapping Rachel and me with Mr. Wayne.

"I have an odd question." I bit my lip and took a chance as my sister pressed the button for the ground level. "Years ago, were there any problems with jewelry here at the Senator?" I let the air whoosh out of my lungs and pushed away thoughts of Truman's disapproval.

Mr. Wayne gave me an odd stare. "When would that have been?"

"The nineteen nineties." The door slid open on the ground floor, and guests waited impatiently for us to leave the elevator.

"Miss Shepard, you'd better come with me." Mr. Wayne's ruddy round face took on an odd yellow cast.

Rachel left with the keys to the Butterscotch Monster, and I rode the elevator up to the seventh floor and followed Randolph Wayne to his office.

"Have a seat."

I settled into a plush chair and took in the photos flanking Mr. Wayne's desk. There were pictures of politicians and dignitaries dining and attending events at the Senator. There was a photo of JFK standing on the steps of the hotel, and of Jimmy Carter shaking hands with a young and befuddled Mr. Wayne. Mr. Wayne seemed to be rooted in the past goings-on at the hotel, and I hoped he could remember what had happened when Vanessa was an employee.

"I've worked here for forty years, moving from bellhop to general manager of this hotel. I consider myself to be something of a historian for the Senator." He glowed with pride and straightened his vest. "And yes, your question about thefts in the nineties does ring a bell. I was assistant manager then, and we had a little problem with guests' wallets and jewelry walking off." His shoulders drooped in embarrassment, and he sat back in his chair.

I cleared my throat. "Er, I'll just get to it. I've been looking into the whereabouts of Vanessa Scanlon back then and think she was fencing jewelry."

Mr. Wayne's eyes stretched to the size of saucers behind his magnifying glasses, and he sputtered, "It all makes sense now. No one would have believed it until she disappeared. She was so sweet. But she ran the housekeeping unit and had access to all of the guests' rooms." He shook his head and hid his face in his hands. "Come to think of it, the thefts stopped after she disappeared. I didn't realize it at the time."

"Did you ever say anything to the police?"

Mr. Wayne bristled and drew himself up in his chair. "They never asked!"

I stifled a groan.

Mr. Wayne grimaced. "It was awful when she disappeared." His eyes narrowed. "And why are you so interested in the Scanlons?"

Good question.

"Because Lois died right in front of me," I stammered. "And Vanessa's daughter, Whitney, is marrying at my B and B in a little over a week. And because I don't think Eugene Newton is guilty of Vanessa's death."

Mr. Wayne's eyes went wide again. "You don't think Lois's death had anything to do with the Senator Hotel and Vanessa, do you?"

"That's what I'm trying to find out. Someone placed Bloody Mary mix with clam juice on Lois's mints. She spent the day before at the chocolate convention, right here in the hotel." Where there were plenty of people who held a grudge against her. Including one Penelope Jelinek, who had been forced to pay Lois a bribe. "She left her bag with the mints alone in a convention booth for fifteen minutes while she harangued some poor employee."

"Oh no." Mr. Wayne hid his head in his hands. "I can't have Lois's death tied back to the Senator Hotel."

"I haven't slept in days." The Truman Davies who sat across from me was different from the one I usually encountered. He was nervous, shifting about in his chair, his usual monolithic confidence and presence diminished to a spark of his former self.

We sat at a table for two at Pellegrino's, in the back, away from the other patrons and their tinkling laughs, smiles, and warm greetings. Soft instrumental music layered over chitchat from other tables gave us some auditory cover, and dim lighting hid Truman's anguish from the well-wishers who waved and stopped by.

"I had my suspicions about Chief Rusty." Truman's

face crumpled into a miserable mask. "But I couldn't believe my mentor would tamper with an investigation. He taught me everything."

"I can't figure out why he admitted it," I murmured, taking a sip of my red wine.

"He's dying." Truman looked like he was getting choked up for a moment, but he steeled himself. "Told me today. He admitted hiding the hammer in Eugene's shed." Truman looked utterly shell-shocked.

"The worst part is," he continued, "I can remember thinking it was all too good to be true. I thought that finding the killer on the ten-year anniversary, right on the eve of Rusty retiring, was too coincidental, but I pushed those thoughts out of my head. I didn't trust my *own* instincts or have the cojones to question my mentor. He had a perfect clearance rate, and I guess he couldn't go out with the Scanlon case unsolved on his plate."

"But it isn't your fault, Truman." I patted his hand. "You may have had your suspicions, but you wouldn't have been able to challenge him."

Truman grunted. "The police bungled Vanessa's kidnapping and murder. Not too many around here, until you came to town," he added drily. "We had little experience." Truman was admitting mistakes?

"You two look like you're discussing something serious." Angela bustled over to our table with a fragrant dish of olives, cheese, and meat. "A special antipasto dish, on the house."

"Thank you, Angela." Truman didn't even look up.

Angela raised her eyebrows at me, and I shrugged in apology. He finally looked up with a tight smile that barely lifted his jowls.

"Is there anything else I can get you?" She waited with a hovering stance and didn't seem to read Truman's body language, which screamed, *Go away.*

"We're doing great, Angela. Thanks for checking. I think we're all set with our server."

"Mrs. Pellegrino, we have a problem in the kitchen." Another server sidled up to Angela, and she excused herself to bustle after him, her bun bouncing behind her like a cropped horse's tail.

"I thought she'd never leave."

"So, back to the subject at hand, Eugene Newton's possible innocence."

Truman tore into a piece of salami.

"And we need to figure out who really killed Vanessa."

"Whoa, whoa, whoa there, girl detective." Truman held up his hand and regained some of his old composure. "There is no *we* here. Leave this to the police and the new district attorney."

"I would leave it to them if they'd gotten it right the first time!" I dug into my salad and speared a piece of spinach. "Your son, whom I hope you're now speaking to, is convinced of Eugene's innocence. Rusty's confession really bolsters that claim."

"It could still be Eugene, and I think it is." Truman didn't sound as sure of himself. "But this definitely opens the door for other suspects."

"Like . . ."

"The pharmacist, who was obsessed with Vanessa. He owned the store across from the Senator. He passed away two years ago, but I still don't think he did it."

"What about Lois?"

Truman snorted and polished off a roll. "Lois

was harmless. A little eccentric, but she'd never hurt a fly."

I cleared my throat and studied Truman with nonchalant eyes.

Truman sighed and put down his third roll. "Spill it, Mallory."

"I think she wanted a bribe to get the B and B rezoned to commercial status."

Truman's face went white. "And you didn't tell me?"

"I told Garrett," I offered meekly.

Truman exhaled, and I felt marginally better. I didn't want to be subject to his ire, but at least he was acting more like himself. "As you know, I haven't exactly been speaking to my son."

"Yes, I noticed," I said wryly.

"It's not good for Summer," Truman admitted, hanging his head.

"There's something else I want to tell you." I spilled the beans about Vanessa's suspected jewelry thievery.

"Fournier called it in. Promise me this." He leaned forward over his plate and stared me down. "Stay out of my investigation."

"Evening, Mallory, Truman."

Whitney sidled up at our table, with Angela and Porter in tow. I tossed a grateful look at Whitney, and Truman sat back, his expression neutral.

"I'll take Porter home," Angela volunteered, helping her brother get his coat on over his shoulders. "Mallory, would you mind driving Whit to Keith and Becca's?" Angela looked at me expectantly.

"I don't mind at all."

Whitney joined us, and Truman and I continued our meals. I wondered whether Whitney had finally told her father about the anonymous letters during dinner.

"It was the right thing." Whitney settled back into the passenger seat. "I should have told my dad about the notes much earlier. But I didn't want to alarm him."

I breathed a sigh of relief and squinted in the night.

"I thought coming home would be a relaxing time with my dad and we could catch up."

She slowly undid and re-snapped the catch of her purple purse. "Instead, I feel like Mom's life is on trial all over again."

Lucy Sattler's robin's-egg-blue florist delivery van was perched at the entrance to Windsor Meadows as I slowed down to turn. She recognized me right before she exited and gave me a friendly wave. Her van drove off into the night, THE BLOOMERY emblazoned on the side in cursive silver script.

We pulled up in front of Keith's cubist nightmare of a house, and Whitney stepped out. "Thanks again, Mallory."

"Do you want me to wait for you to get safely inside?"

"Don't worry. What could go wrong now?"

A chill ran through me, and I decided I really didn't want to test the fates with that question. Whitney hurried up the path, clutching her wool coat around her thin frame and against the crisp

October night. She opened the door and gave me a friendly wave.

I sat outside the house for a moment, savoring the cool night air. I turned the key in the ignition, and the loud start of the station wagon was drowned out by Whitney's scream.

Chapter Fourteen

I ran up the front path and into the house. Whitney looked up with a second's worth of relief before panic took over again, making her delicate features sharp and anguished.

"Mallory, call nine one one." Whitney hovered over a prostrate Becca, crumpled at the base of the kitchen island. Maisie stood nearby and paced in front of the stove, whining softly. Whitney gently slipped her arm under Becca and rolled her onto her back.

I jabbed at my cell phone with shaking fingers and explained the situation to the operator. "The ambulance should be here soon. Does she have a pulse?"

Whitney nodded and spoke to her cousin in low, calm tones. "She's flickering her eyes open. She's conscious, but just barely."

I slipped a pillow from the couch under Becca's head, and she let out a distant moan.

"Wasn't supposed to be here," she croaked out. Her eyes rolled back so only the whites showed, and Whitney renewed her intense questions, trying to keep Becca awake and lucid. I'd never been so happy to hear the sound of an ambulance roaring up the circular drive. The team of EMTs loaded Becca onto a stretcher and carted her off, leaving Whitney and me to ponder her fate.

"I'll need you two to step away from the crime scene." Faith Hendricks strode into the room and frowned at Maisie, who was sniffing the pool of blood where Becca had been.

Whitney scooped up the white dog and explained what she'd seen when she got home. Maisie left a bright red paw print on Whitney's cream-colored coat, like a sprig of cherries on snow. Fiona crawled out from beneath a peach loveseat, her white fur shaking. I scooped her up and gave her a cuddle.

"Where's Bruce?" I called his name several times, but the dog didn't respond.

"Oh, no! The back door was open when I came in. I shut it before I saw Becca." Whitney rubbed her arms.

The room was freezing; I'd just chalked up the cold feeling to shock.

"I bet Bruce ran out. He's always darting off if he's not leashed." She clutched Maisie harder to her, and the little white pooch gave her an affectionate doggie kiss on the nose.

"You shut the door?" Truman was back in his official uniform. He must've changed in a hurry when he heard the call about Becca. His eyes swept the scene, and he ordered that fingerprints be taken of the glass back doors.

"I'm sorry," Whitney stammered, sinking into an ivory suede couch.

"It's fine, Whitney. You got here at just the right time. You probably saved your cousin. Now, who would want to attack her?"

"That's just it—she didn't have an enemy in the world." Whitney stared at the spot where we'd found Becca and began to shake.

Truman's gaze swept over to me.

"Don't look at me! She's no enemy of mine."

"I'm not sure what she was doing here. She's usually at the gym Sunday evenings, or running errands with Keith." Whitney swallowed. "Do you think her attacker was looking for me?"

We were all silent for a moment. Truman filled the silence with questions and more questions. We sat for what felt like hours. Keith called to say he'd joined Becca at the hospital.

"Is there anything missing from the house, Whitney? Officers are checking it out as we speak." We took a slow walk around the first floor while Whitney looked for changes.

"There are a few petals here. Mallory and I saw the florist, Lucy Sattler, leaving the development as we drove in." She pointed to a smattering of silky yellow rose petals lying in a barely perceptible layer of dust on a small curio. "But there's no bouquet."

I bent down and snatched up a slip of paper peeking out from under the curio. "Becca," I read, "I guess the third time wasn't the charm. I'm sorry you didn't pass the bar. Better luck next time. Love, Mom."

"The missing vase of flowers could be the object used to conk Ms. Cunningham on the head," Truman grunted. "I'll need to get in touch with Lucy. She might have seen someone."

There wouldn't have been much time between Lucy dropping off a delivery and Becca's attack. Lucy might have unknowingly passed the assailant on her way out.

Unless Lucy attacked Becca? But why?

We followed Whitney through the house, and nothing else was touched, to her knowledge, until we reached her guest room.

"Oh no, not again." The room had been up-ended, her drawers opened, and the contents spilled to the floor. The mattress hung cattywampus off the bed, and papers on a little writing desk were scattered.

"I don't think anything was taken." Whitney slowly turned around the room but didn't touch anything.

"But what were they looking for?" I squinted and tried to discern a pattern, but the room was thoroughly ransacked, with no apparent rhyme or reason.

"I'm sure you have a good idea." Whitney, Truman, and I turned around to face Keith, standing in the doorway.

"What did you do to her?" He took a step toward me.

"Hold it right there, Keith." Truman held up his arm and stopped Keith in his tracks. "Mallory was having dinner with me when this all went down. She dropped Whitney off, and they found Becca."

Keith shook his head and let Truman's arm fall to his side.

"Is Becca alright?" I stared defiantly at Keith for

daring to think I was involved with the attack on his fiancée.

A wave of tiredness seemed to wash over him, and he sank against the wall.

"She has a concussion, but she was discharged from the ER. She's resting downstairs. She's lucky." His breath caught and he took a moment to compose himself. "She'll be alright, but she'll have a nasty headache. And her engagement ring is gone." I hadn't noticed the monumental diamond's absence from Becca's finger while Whitney and I waited for the ambulance.

We followed Keith down the stairs to find Becca convalescing on the couch, resting her head on a mammoth bag of peas. A gauze bandage covered half of her forehead, and she offered us a shaky smile. Her usual haughty demeanor was gone, replaced with fear, exhaustion, and pain.

"We're not safe here, babe. We're moving in with my mother." Keith sat on the couch next to her and gingerly picked up her now bare hand.

"No!" Becca sat up and groaned, grabbing her head. "I mean, the police said my attacker isn't here anymore, right?"

"I don't think you'll be able to rest well here tonight."

Becca lowered her head back to the pillow of peas with a slow, agonizing movement. "Maybe we can go back to Mallory's B and B?" She flickered her big blue gaze over to me and gave me a pleading look.

"That's the concussion talking. Stay right here. I'll pack your things." Keith tenderly stroked her forehead and then rose to get her belongings, while Becca shot me a desperate look.

"This Friday I found out I failed the bar exam. I've been in a funk and couldn't concentrate at the gym, so I came home early. Then I got attacked in my home, my ring's been stolen, and now we're staying with Helene? I didn't think this weekend could get any worse." She leaned back and closed her eyes.

"I should have done this a few weeks ago." Garrett gripped the steering wheel of his Accord. It was Monday morning, and we rocketed down the highway toward the supermax prison to speak with his former client, Eugene Newton. Whitney was to marry on Saturday.

"You've exhausted all his appeals over the years and had no idea the case would be stirred up again." I turned kind eyes on Garrett.

"People are getting hurt." He dared to glance at me. "If I'd gotten Eugene a not-guilty verdict ten years ago, Becca wouldn't have gotten attacked. Whitney wouldn't be getting anonymous letters."

We pulled into the parking lot in front of the State Correctional Institution.

"Leave your cell phone in the car. They don't allow them in here."

We made our way into a lobby and stated our business, showed our IDs, and read the list of rules for visitors. We sat at a bank of tan chairs and stared at portraits of officials from the department of corrections. Half an hour later we were summoned back to see Eugene.

"I shouldn't have worn an underwire." I cursed my decision to wear a bra with a metal component.

Garrett let out a laugh as I nervously shuffled my feet along the ground on my third attempt to not make the metal detector go off.

I wanted to believe in Eugene's innocence since Garrett was sure of it. Still, my heart beat as we were led to the visiting room. I didn't know what to expect, but it wasn't the frail, meek man in a striped shirt who rose to stand and face us on the other side of the glass.

"Garrett. So good to see you." His face split into a friendly grin, and I caught my breath. The years of confinement hadn't aged him so much as worn him down. He looked almost as young as he had in the newspaper pictures from the time of his conviction, just skinnier and paler. The lack of sunshine had been kind to his complexion, but his eyes were infinitely sad. He was a handsome man when he smiled, and I saw why Vanessa had been infatuated with him. I'd unconsciously been expecting Hannibal Lecter, not a genial man who looked like he should be outside enjoying the crisp fall weather instead of sitting behind a bank of glass, separated from the rest of the world by a life sentence.

"This is Mallory Shepard. She's an attorney as well. We have some questions for you." I squirmed in my chair when Garrett misrepresented me. I was still an attorney, but I wasn't here in that capacity.

"Shoot away." Eugene's eyes were open and calm and curious.

I decided to not beat around the bush. "Whitney Scanlon has been receiving anonymous letters stating you didn't kill her mother."

Eugene blinked and slowly rubbed his jaw with his left hand. His smile curved up again for a fraction then fell. "They're right. I didn't kill Vanessa." His voice was quiet but firm.

"Do you know who might be sending the letters?" Garrett leaned forward and tented his fingers in front of his mouth.

Eugene chuckled. "Before she died, you and my mother were the only two people left on this earth who knew I didn't do it. You never thought I did, and I appreciate that." He closed his eyes. "I have no idea who would be sending letters now. Do you?"

Garrett sighed and shook his head. "No. And other things are happening." He detailed the break-in at his office and Becca's attack, as well as the slashing of Whitney's dress.

Eugene whistled. "This is the last thing Vanessa wanted for her daughter." He hung his head sorrowfully and seemed to shrink in stature before our eyes.

"Who do you think killed Vanessa?" I blurted out.

"I've had a lot of time to think about it, and after ten years, I still don't know." He shook his head ruefully. "Believe me, if I did, I'd call Garrett in a heartbeat. Vanessa's marriage wasn't so great, even before we got together." He blushed. "Her sisters-in-law weren't her favorites. She complained about Lois and Angela and how they treated their brother like the baby of the family, but I can't imagine either one of them killing Vanessa. She didn't have an enemy in the world."

Garrett and I exchanged a silent glance, pregnant with meaning.

"Go on, tell him." Garrett nudged my shoe with his.

"We recently found out Vanessa may have been fencing jewelry she stole from guests at the Senator Hotel." I watched Eugene carefully.

He cocked his head in thought, then nodded.

He sank back into his chair. "There were things Vanessa didn't tell me. We were planning to run away together, and she was going to bring Whitney with her. I was a muralist, and I painted houses for extra cash, but there was no way I could finance the kind of living she was used to. She said she had it covered and there was a line of money she could tap into that her husband, Porter, didn't know about."

Garrett's hazel eyes burned with a flash of annoyance. "Why didn't you tell me?"

Eugene shrugged but looked embarrassed. "I did, just not phrased that way. I knew she had money from her family, and I assumed that was what she meant." Eugene turned to me. "Vanessa was secretive. If she was stealing jewelry from guests, it would have been for kicks, not because she needed it. She liked thrills, and I always wondered if she would have gone through with it. Running away with me." His face grew somber. "Sometimes I questioned whether she really loved me or was using our affair for some excitement in her life."

"This is important, Eugene. We've been over this a thousand times, but can you think of any way to prove you didn't kill Vanessa Scanlon? Anyone that could have seen you?"

Eugene exhaled loudly and pushed back from

the window in frustration. "You know the answer to
that. The minister at the First Presbyterian Church,
and he's dead. There's no record of me painting
that church mural the same day Vanessa disappeared, so it's my word against the police's."

Garrett and I glanced at each other again.

"Okay, you two, what else do I need to know?"
Eugene leaned forward hungrily until his boyish
face touched the thick glass.

"I don't want to get your hopes up. The prosecutor already thinks it's not enough. But—" Garrett
paused and turned to me.

"—Rusty Dalton, the former police chief, admitted he moved the murder weapon into your shed."
I finished for him.

"I knew it!" Eugene jumped up and crowed, causing a guard to hustle over to give him a stern word.
"Our other theory was the killer planted the hammer
in the shed, but it makes more sense that the police
planted it." His eyes glowed with hope, and I hated
to see him get excited about something that might
not come to fruition.

Garrett counseled that his appeal chances were
slim, even with the admission that the former chief
had rigged the evidence. Eugene's face fell.

"Don't get my hopes up, man. What I wouldn't
give to get out of here. I could paint again, and start
my life over."

"You said you were a muralist?" My thoughts
went back to the mess of a mural on the parlor ceiling at Thistle Park. "There aren't too many of you
around, and I sure need one now." I told him about
my predicament.

His grin returned. "Sylvia Pierce used to own that house. She hired me to restore her ceiling. I was supposed to begin a month after I was arrested and charged." His face fell.

Garrett frowned and turned the interview back to the murders. "You said Vanessa didn't always get along with her sisters-in-law. Lois found out about the affair and threatened Vanessa, right? Do you think she could have killed her?"

Eugene stared behind us at the wall. "Lois is a big woman. It's possible Whitney mistook her for a man. But I don't think she could kill Vanessa. It was more of an annoyance between them."

"Did Lois ever wear all white?"

Eugene shook his head. "I don't know. Why don't you ask her?"

"We can't. She's been murdered."

Eugene's eyes widened in shock. Before we could discuss it further, the guard returned to take him back to his cell.

Chapter Fifteen

"Whatever else may go wrong with this wedding, these chocolates almost make it worth it." Whitney took a delicate bite of a rosemary truffle and closed her eyes in bliss. I'd returned from my trip with Garrett and sat at the old oak table in the breakfast room, making favors for Whitney's reception. We sampled the chocolatier Penelope's wares as we tied up one of each kind of chocolate into a small box emblazoned with Whitney and Ian's initials and the date of her wedding. So far we'd eaten more than we'd boxed up.

"If I'm not careful, I won't fit into my mom's dress." Whitney giggled and took another bite, this time of a cayenne truffle.

"Just wait'll you try the cocktails." Rachel poked her head in from the kitchen, and a moment later, we heard the telltale sound of a martini shaker.

"Voilà." Rachel returned and set down a tray with three martini glasses and three glass mugs.

"That's a lot to sample." I eyed the pretty glasses. Would the drinks hinder our favor-making project?

"Just sip slowly. From the looks of it, we'll be here for a long time."

Rachel was right. There were mountains of truffles on trays waiting for us to sort, wrap, and box up. After we finished, we'd have to embellish each gold box with a satin, chocolate-colored ribbon.

I took a sip of smooth liquid and closed my eyes with a sigh. "This is heaven." The drink was a concoction of caramel and cream liqueurs over ice with a hint of cocoa. A sprinkling of salt dusted the rim of the glass and sparkled in the light.

"A salted caramel martini!" Whitney grinned and set down her glass.

"And this is traditional mulled wine for fall." Rachel gestured to the second set of drinks, and we each took a sip. A fruity explosion danced tête-à-tête with a chorus of spices. Sweet cinnamon, nutmeg, and cloves exploded on my tongue.

"It's like drinking the essence of fall." Whitney twirled the cinnamon stick in her glass.

Rachel breathed a sigh of relief and sat down to make favors.

"I'm glad you like them. It's all coming together." My sister clasped her hands together and gave me a satisfied smile.

I couldn't help grinning back. We were going to pull off the wedding. The house was starting to look like my vision for the B and B. Each day Jesse and the Senator Hotel contractors inched closer to completion, and I could see what the finished result was going to look like. It would be close, but I actually believed we had a prayer of finishing in time for Saturday's wedding.

Maisie emerged from the hallway and sat on her

haunches. Whitney hadn't let the dogs out of her
sight after Bruce disappeared. She lifted her front
paws up in the international canine sign for begging. Fiona lifted her head from her bed and
seemed to give a look of disapproval before yawn-
ing and returning to her nap.

"No chocolates for doggies," I admonished the
pup. I brought her a dog biscuit and she gobbled
it up.

She trotted over to Soda, the kitten, who was
curled up in a weak patch of autumn sunlight. The
kitten lifted her head and sniffed the Westie and
finally consented to lick her nose. Maisie sat with a
satisfied sigh and curled up next to the orange kitty.
Whiskey opened one eye from her perch on the
window seat and closed it again, curling up into an
even tighter calico ball.

"I can't believe we haven't found Bruce." Whitney sniffed and hurriedly looked at the ceiling,
seeming to stave off tears. "All I can think of is him
wandering around Port Quincy, scared, cold, and
alone." We'd put up flyers all around town, but no
one had called Whitney with information about the
Westie, and he hadn't turned up at any of the
animal shelters.

"And I'm starting to have doubts about my
mom's murder." Whit sat back and wilted like a
flower under the harsh scrutiny of the sun. "What
if the person sending the notes is right? What if
Eugene Newton didn't murder my mother?" She
set down a box of chocolates and got up from the
table, scraping the chair on the floor with a harsh,
quick jerk. She stared out the kitchen window for
a minute, then turned around, backlit by the waning

fall daylight. "I was only five. I told the cops everything I could remember that day my mom disappeared. What if I got it wrong? I *thought* I heard my mother arguing, and I *thought* I saw someone wearing white leave our house. But I can't really be sure."

"They based the case on other things," I said gently. "And the police investigated fully." *And the police chief tampered with a key piece of evidence.*

"But it's a lot of pressure. What if that man—Eugene—was wrongly convicted and spent a decade in prison based on the word of a five-year-old?" Whitney drifted back to the table and sank down onto her chair. She picked up a box and filled it with chocolate on autopilot, her gaze far away.

Rachel and I glanced at each other.

"I hid in the closet," Whitney whispered. "When she told me to go to my room and take a nap. The prosecution made a big deal out of that, that my mother recognized her killer and didn't want me to see him. But she did let him in, so she trusted him. That part I remember. And Mom was shouting and arguing with that man pretty quickly. That's when I got scared and ran into the closet." Whitney's eyes stared ahead as if in a trance, and she quietly continued her tale. "I heard something break in the family room, and I waited a few minutes to sneak out of the closet. He was heading to the driveway. He must have already gotten my mom in the car. He wore a cap, all white, and the rest of his outfit was white too. Or so I thought." She shook her head as if to clear it and set down the box with trembling hands. "And after that, I never saw my mother again."

Rachel downed her mulled wine in one swig. "I'm so sorry, Whitney."

We reached out to hold her hands, and she sniffed back some tears.

"I haven't told anyone that for years, besides Ian. And I had to recount it a million times at the trial, of course." Her face hardened, and she turned to me. "That's why I have such a strong reaction to Garrett, Mallory. It isn't his fault. But, for me, he's caught up in all of this."

I nodded and gave her hand a squeeze.

"What I don't understand is what Mom was doing with stolen jewelry. Faith got back to me, and Mr. Fournier was right. That ring was definitely stolen from a woman back in the nineteen nineties. She left it on the dresser at the Senator Hotel, and when she came back from a day of visiting her grandchildren, it was gone."

Rachel and I exchanged a surreptitious glance. I'd told my sister about Garrett's and my trip to see Eugene but hadn't broken the news to Whitney.

My cell took that moment to blast out a chipper ringtone, and my face heated as I took it off the table. Saved by the bell. The screen read **Truman Davies**. Okay, maybe not saved.

"I have to take this." I stepped into the hall and shut my eyes as I swiped to answer. "Hello?"

"I know you and my busybody son visited Eugene Newton in prison," A voice blared into my ear. "Garrett may have a reason to visit his client, but as for you, missy, get out of my investigation!"

I dropped the phone.

The doorbell rang. I thought of Whitney's mother

looking through the peephole and unwittingly letting in her killer.

"Thank goodness it's just you." I smiled up at Garrett as he stepped through the door, a worried expression marring the symmetry of his face.

"Recognize this?" He held up another note, identical to the ones Whitney had received, encased in a large plastic bag.

You know it's true. Eugene Newton is innocent. Get on it.

"It's the same stationery as Whitney's latest note." A faint border of helixes traced the edges of the paper, in shades of red and blue. A faint tickle of recognition ran through my brain, but I couldn't catch it before it left.

"Better call your dad." I told him about his call to me seconds before.

Garrett laughed. "I'm on my way to see him." He dropped a kiss on top of my head. "Be careful, Mallory." He got in his Accord and pulled out of the long driveway just as another car pulled in.

"You've come a long way, girls." A smile cut through the harsh cast of Angela's face as she took in Rachel and me, and I basked in its glow for a moment. "This is delicious." She set down her salted caramel martini and finished the last box of chocolate favors. "Whitney, dear, your wedding will be beautiful, and your father will be so thrilled to be here to witness it. To Whitney and Ian."

Rachel and I dutifully clinked our martini glasses to Angela's, and Whitney blushed.

"I'd give anything for Dad to get better, but at least I get to spend time with him now." She picked up her purse and took in the mountain of chocolate boxes. "Thanks again, Mallory and Rachel and Aunt Angela. I'm going to go have dinner with Dad." Whitney had declined the invitation to stay at Helene's house and was staying with her father until she married on Saturday. She leaned down, kissed her aunt good-bye, and slipped out of the breakfast room to let herself out.

"I've got to run to yoga, but it was good seeing you, Angela." Rachel was still taking classes from our neighbor, Charity, who had stayed quiet after her latest outburst. Rachel followed Whitney, and I was left with Angela at the table. She stood to go when I held up my hand.

"I have a few questions about Vanessa's death, and I didn't want to upset Whitney by asking her."

Angela stiffened and put down her purse with a clunk on the table. She cocked her eyebrow and remained standing but gave me a cool nod.

I momentarily regretted my decision to ask her questions but pressed on. "Was Vanessa involved in fencing jewelry?" I decided to be direct since Angela was already giving me the stink eye.

"She was no saint, since she was cavorting around on my brother, Porter, with that housepainter. You don't need to make her out to be a common thief as well." Angela seemed more distressed by the fact her sister-in-law had had her affair with a painter than that she was murdered.

"I'm sorry I brought it up. I just thought—"

"You just thought you'd get to the bottom of those notes? They're upsetting Whitney enough as it is. I don't think she'd be very pleased if she knew you were adding amateur sleuthing to your repertoire as a wedding planner." She stared down her nose at me and dared me to say something. "I must admit I overheard you talking to Chief Truman about it the other day at my restaurant."

I flashed back to Pellegrino's. Angela had hovered pretty closely while Truman and I talked about Rusty's admissions of moving the murder weapon.

Angela softened a millimeter and sat at the table with a sigh. "Mallory, I had to work around the clock for years to make Pellegrino's the most successful restaurant in Port Quincy. My late husband and I turned our idea into reality through hours of blood, sweat, and tears. You and Rachel have the beginnings of what could be a fabulously successful business. Focus on your career and stop meddling in my family's affairs."

I choked down the last swig of salted caramel martini and nodded. "I'll let the authorities handle it."

She nodded. "It isn't Whitney's fault her mother was kidnapped and murdered. She was involved in a lot of seedy things, in addition to that affair." She shook her head slowly. "Jewelry thief as well? I wouldn't put it past her. But this is supposed to be a happy time for Whitney, a time to spend with her father. So not a word of this to her. Am I understood?"

"Loud and clear," I whispered.

Chapter Sixteen

Three seconds after Angela left, Rachel blew into the breakfast room. She shook her head in anger, her hair swishing over her shoulders like Medusa's snakes. "I can't believe you're jeopardizing my mentorship with Angela to play detective."

"I thought you left for yoga," I said levelly and sat down at the table.

Rachel remained standing, her feet planted wide apart. "I forgot my mat and came back. Just in time to hear you interrogating Angela!"

"I asked Angela because I didn't want to upset Whitney. Someone is threatening Garrett and Whitney with anonymous notes. And they might be the same person who dismantled Garrett's office, trashed Whitney's dress, and clobbered Becca with a vase. Of course I'm concerned and looking into it."

"I don't recall your stint at the police academy. Why don't you just leave it to Truman and Faith?"

I ignored her logical reminder. "If Garrett thinks

Eugene is innocent, then he is. And you heard Whitney today. She isn't sure if she even saw what she thinks she saw."

"What's going on, girls?" My mother rushed into the room, her hair bouncing with each step. I was still getting used to her haircut.

"Nothing, Mom." Rachel sent me a withering look and picked up her yoga mat.

A knock on the back door startled the three of us. I crossed and peeked out into the now dusky backyard. A smiling Hunter waved on the other side of the glass. For once he carried no ghost-hunting equipment.

"Am I interrupting anything?" Hunter breezed into the room with a kiss for Rachel and a smile for my mom.

Rachel giggled and set down her mat, her yoga class temporarily forgotten.

"I have a great idea." Hunter turned around a kitchen chair and straddled it.

My mother raised a skeptical eyebrow. I shrugged and waited for Hunter.

"We should have a séance!" He spread his hands out and looked from me to Rachel to our mother.

"That's fantastic!" Rachel nearly bounced on the balls of her feet.

I did a double take. "The week of Whitney's wedding?"

Hunter's face fell. "But it's the most liminal time of the year. The ancient holiday of Samhain is this week. The ghosts will be at their most potent energies. This is a unique opportunity, since we know this house contains spirits—"

"We'll be running around setting up for the wedding this week. I doubt we'll have time." I softened my stance. "Where would you hold a séance?"

Hunter stroked the cleft in his chin. "Wherever would be out of your hair. We'll keep it short. Besides," he paused, "there's a producer who's interested in featuring the séance and your B and B."

"Oh, Hunter!" Rachel squealed and swooped down to give her beau a hug. "We'll be on TV!"

My antennae went up on high alert. "What show?" I wasn't sure if being featured on a ghost-hunting show would help or hurt the business.

"*Haunted Histories.* It's their special episode on historical buildings. I hope you don't mind. I sent them some pictures of the house, and they thought it would be a beautiful place to shoot. And with the genuine phenomena going on around here, they wouldn't want to miss it. We're wrapping up here, and now's the time to get them in."

Haunted Histories was a paranormal reality show. They would probably do a good job showcasing the house in a favorable light. If all went well, our renovations would just about be wrapped up the day before the wedding.

"This could be just the boost in recognition that we need." Rachel paced the floor in her excitement.

"It would be fun to be featured on television." Mom fluffed her hair, and I stared at her, incredulous. She was bitten by the same bug as Rachel. It was Rachel's dearest ambition, besides becoming a famous pastry chef, to be discovered. She'd been scheming and dreaming all summer of ways to get her cakes featured where someone in Hollywood would take notice. She'd love to have her own show making cakes and confections. And Hunter appeared to be the star she was going to hitch her wagon to.

"Let's do it." I was getting excited. "But we really will be scrambling to put together all of the pieces for Whitney's wedding."

Rachel brightened. "We'll work like crazy to do both!" Her eyes sparkled, and she impulsively grabbed Hunter's hand. "Let's scout out places to shoot on the third floor. That will be well away from Whitney's wedding. It's still unfinished, but the living room of the apartment is presentable."

They left, nearly skipping out of the kitchen, my mother in tow.

A minute later, Hunter bounded back down the back stairs, alone. "Mallory, I have another thought. Has Whitney ever mentioned feeling the presence of her mother? The producers would love to explore that angle."

"Not that I know of," I said guardedly. "And I wouldn't want to upset Whitney with that kind of questioning. She's had enough people interested in her only because of her mother's horrible death."

Hunter held up his hands. "Sorry. Just wondering. Sometimes people who usually don't see ghosts are able to in a place with such high spectral energy. Like a DNA connection or something." He sighed and took his inquiry off the table. "Of course, I won't bother her."

Something skittered across my mind. "What did you just say about DNA?"

Hunter looked at me like I was crazy. "I just meant Whitney might have felt her mother's presence in this particular house. Like they have a connection." With a shrug of his shoulders, he bounded up the back stairs to join Rachel and my mother.

"DNA," I whispered. "I know who sent those notes."

"I know where I saw that notepaper." I didn't even say a proper hello to Garrett when he answered his cell.

"I'm coming over." He was equally abrupt, and ten minutes later, Garrett returned to Thistle Park with a copy of the note sent to him professing Eugene's innocence. "I gave the original to my dad, and they'll dust for prints."

"You won't find any prints. He wouldn't leave any, not that it matters." I explained my epiphany.

"Hunter mentioned DNA, and it triggered my memory. I remember where I saw that pattern." I tapped the copy of the note at the bottom edge, where a delicate double-helix pattern laced across the page. "The same notepad was on the kitchen island at Rusty Dalton's apartment. It's from a pharmaceutical company. His place was filled with prescription medicine."

Garrett's eyes went wide. "The former chief of police?"

"The very one."

"Let's go." We nearly ran down the drive to Garrett's black Accord and drove as fast as we could to Whispering Brook.

* * *

"Well done." Rusty gestured to a plate of Oreo cookies and urged us to partake of his hospitality.

"No thank you." Garrett's eyes were cold, and he remained standing over the disgraced former police chief. "Do you have any idea how many people you've terrorized with your anonymous notes?"

Rusty hung his head and coughed. The phlegm rattled in his chest, and he hacked for a moment. Garrett stood unmoved.

"I deserve that. But the current prosecutor doesn't want to overturn a murder conviction, and he wouldn't listen to me. So I decided to go another route." His eyes were filmy and dull, and he looked more ill than the last time I'd seen him. My heart surged with pity until I reminded myself of all the trouble Rusty's notes had caused and how his tampering with evidence had helped to put away an innocent man.

"You really shook up Whitney," I said softly. "She didn't deserve that."

"I know. I'm dying. Just like Porter. I don't have much time, and I'm a selfish old man. I wanted to get it off my chest that I planted the hammer in Eugene's shed. I sent those letters to Eugene and to Whitney where she worked in Baltimore. Her father mentioned she'd come back to Port Quincy to get married, and I started sending them to her care of her aunt at Pellegrino's." His eyes brightened, and he seemed marginally less tired and frail. "And it worked!" he crowed. "Now you're actually doing something."

"We're going to turn you in." Garrett finally sat down.

"That sounds right, son." Rusty chanced a glance

at Garrett. "And I deserve whatever I get for it. But I won't be around long enough to be really punished. My maker will take care of that." He let out another rattling cough and sank back.

"Were you behind the break-in at my office too?" Garrett leaned forward intently.

"Your office?" Rusty's milky blue eyes clouded over. "I hadn't heard that. Definitely not me." He looked as sick as Porter, and it would be a stretch for him to break into Garrett's office, no less climb the three flights of stairs.

Then who broke in and stole Eugene's case files?

Chapter Seventeen

"So you think I can help you prove Eugene Newton's innocence?" Marcus Callender, the Presbyterian minister sat before me at his glossy desk and rested his chin on his plump hands. His office was awash in the gingery smell of Murphy's Oil Soap, and classical music gently played from a small stereo behind him. Marcus's face was pleasant and round, an even mask that gave nothing away. I couldn't read whether he thought I was crazy or if he was humoring me. I'd called him yesterday under the pretense of Whitney and Ian's wedding and set up this meeting. It was a last-ditch effort to prove Eugene's innocence before I turned full bore to Whitney's wedding. I segued into a line of sleuthing that would surely make Truman livid.

"Well, I spoke to a . . . former member of the police force." I wasn't going to give Rusty away. I stilled my nervous hands. "According to him, and to Eugene, Eugene was painting a mural here the day Vanessa Scanlon disappeared."

The minister nodded. "That was long before my

time." His voice was gentle, and he crossed the small office to look out his window. He plucked a picture from a shelf and handed it to me. "Pretty, isn't it?"

"It's gorgeous." The photo showed a large mural spanning the back section of the church. It featured a rising sun, with lambs in a meadow. It was startlingly lifelike, with an especially realistic sense of depth, perspective, and light.

"Eugene Newton painted this mural the summer Vanessa disappeared. No one knew at the time that they were having an affair. When her body was found ten years later on Eugene's property, he said he was here at the church the day she went missing, painting the mural. But he couldn't prove it. The mural was painted over the same week Eugene was charged with Vanessa's murder. The former minister didn't think it was right to keep it in the church. It's just a white wall now."

I nodded. I was to be married in this very church once upon a time, and I was familiar with it.

"My predecessor passed away before Eugene was even accused of murder, and no one could remember if Eugene was here or not."

I offered him a polite smile. "Thank you for considering my question. I didn't think there would be any evidence all these years later, but I thought I'd give it a shot."

"How is Whitney's wedding coming along? I'm looking forward to the ceremony." Marcus deftly changed the subject and peered at me over tented hands.

"Between ghosts, random accidents, and attacks, it's just dandy." I pressed my lips together.

He definitely thought I was crazy.

But Marcus's brows furrowed with concern. "I know about Lois's unfortunate passing. But what's this about ghosts?"

"Do you believe in them?" I asked the minister point-blank.

Marcus sat and rubbed his chin. He swiveled his chair around to study the late-October light and turned back around after a minute. "Not all is as it seems, Mallory. There are things in this world that can easily be viewed and understood. And there are things that are unseen. Beautiful things, like faith. And love that endures after death. So maybe," he cocked his head, "there are the kinds of presences you think of as ghosts." He chuckled. "Some think this very office is haunted by our former minister." A strange look lit up his face, and he cracked a crooked grin.

"On second thought, that reminds me. I may have something to help you after all."

I perked up and turned. He crossed the room to a small wooden curio. He withdrew a key ring hanging on a peg and extracted a tiny silver key.

The minister's eyes twinkled, and he knelt next to a filing cabinet. He produced a small, brown, leather-bound book.

"A diary?"

"Of a sort. This belonged to my predecessor, the Reverend Lawrence Rast. He was something of a detail man and wrote down what happened each day. Whom he met with, what sermons he was working on, and what community gatherings he'd attended. A carpenter found Rast's daybook wedged behind a shelf in this office a year ago."

I took the book from Marcus and flipped it open gingerly. The spine gave a groan and cracked down the middle. I cradled the small book to keep it from breaking apart and leafed through pages with neat, slanting blue ink filling every page. Each entry provided mundane details of the goings-on of the church.

"Have you looked at this?"

Marcus shook his head. "I've had no reason to. Lawrence was meticulous about his days, but there's nothing in there that would be of any use to me, and I do consider it to be private. But if it could prove a man's innocence, I have no qualms about you inspecting it."

I sank into the chair facing Marcus's desk and flipped through to the day in question.

My finger traced down the page to the entry for July eleventh, nineteen ninety-five.

"Spent the day in the pleasant company of one Eugene Newton, a young muralist," I read aloud. "He sketched the sheep and lambs in pencil, preparing to paint next week. Mr. Newton joined me for a lunch of lentil soup and ham sandwiches and packed up to leave at five."

I snapped the diary shut. "Whitney went running to a neighbor and told about her mother being kidnapped around two that day. Eugene would have been here painting the mural. An innocent man has been locked up for ten years." I held up the book. "May I keep this?"

"Certainly. Provided you use it to set that man free." He folded his hands carefully in front of him. "We need a little more forgiveness in this world. It would be wonderful to see Eugene get a new chance, a new beginning."

"He's really innocent." Whitney paced around the parlor and slipped her engagement ring on and off again and again. "To think he's spent the last ten years languishing in prison and the person who really killed my mother is still at large." She sat on the window seat with a huff. The upholsterer had removed almost every scrap of furniture from the first floor for my mother's makeover, and the window seat was the only place to sit. A little cloud of dust rose up around her. "Those creepy letters were right."

"If Rusty hadn't been so intent on retiring with a perfect record, he wouldn't have moved the murder weapon into his shed, and he might be free."

"And maybe they would've focused on finding the real killer." Whitney's eyes flashed.

"There was a lot of evidence that made it look like he did it. Your mother's body was found on his property. They were having an affair. Still, I don't think he did it."

"And neither do I. Tell Garrett I'll do anything I can to help get that man free and to find who really murdered my mother."

I took a deep breath and brought up something I'd been avoiding. "Whit, your aunt Lois was the only one in your family who knew your mother was seeing Eugene at the time of her disappearance." I let the statement hang in the air for what seemed like infinity.

"Aunt Lois did have a terrific temper." Whitney's voice was small and laden with misery.

I was surprised she readily took the bait.

"Lois and Angela helped my dad raise me. Angela was a little cold and distant. Lois was the warm and funny one. But she did fly off the handle. Nothing too bad," she quickly amended when she saw my alarmed expression, "but Angela is the type to use guilt to make you regret not living up to her expectations." She chuckled without mirth. "Whereas Lois would have a gut reaction. Her bark was worse than her bite, but still . . . I wonder if she confronted Mom. That isn't something my mom would have taken lightly. I didn't spend too many years with my mother, but she stood up for herself. She didn't let my aunts push her around."

Whitney paced over to the mantle and ran her hands over the newly finished decorative tiles, her ring sparkling off the peacock design, reflecting bits of indigo, violet, and azure. She shivered though the room was toasty and warm. "They could have been the ones fighting. Lois had a pretty deep voice. Maybe I was wrong. Maybe Lois confronted Mom."

"Did she ever wear white?" I reminded her of the key piece of evidence her five-year-old self had provided.

Whitney returned to the window seat in a daze. "It was before Labor Day. It's possible. She wore sundresses and linen jackets and light airy things back then to work; some of them must've been white. She always worked at the Senator, for as long as I can remember. Hotels are in our blood." She said this last bit fondly. "That's why I went into HR at the Ferris Hotel in Baltimore. Ian works in security there. That's how we met. And everyone in my family worked at the Senator when I was growing up, except Dad. Mom was manager of the housekeeping department. Lois worked her way up through HR, and Aunt Angela was the cook."

"I thought Angela worked at Pellegrino's with her husband for years."

· "Oh, no." Whit shook her head. "She was the cook at the Senator forever. She wanted her own restaurant more than anything, though. She started the restaurant when she married Mr. Pellegrino, my uncle, and he passed away about five years later. To tell you the truth, my dad was a little miffed I didn't have my wedding at the Senator. That's where he married my mom, of course. But I'm glad the way things are working out, despite all of the madness."

I offered her a small smile. "Me too, Whit."

That night I crawled into bed with trepidation, expecting to keep Evelyn McGavitt's ghost company while she knitted from the great beyond. But it was blessedly quiet. Whiskey curled up on an armchair and peered at me with one keen eye opened, and Soda hunted my toes beneath the comforter. I fell into a deep sleep in minutes. Unofficial sleuthing was hard work, especially since I expected Truman to find out at any moment.

CRASH.

I sat up and groped for the alarm clock on the bedside table and peered at it through slitted eyes. It was three in the morning. Had I imagined a noise? All was still, and I debated getting up to investigate.

Hunter and the Paranormal Society weren't here tonight. After the sun rose, they'd be setting up for the séance, but no one was supposed to be inside but Rachel, Mom, and me.

A clammy hand gripped my arm, and I screamed.

Rachel flicked on the light. Then I got a good look at her face and broke into a jagged laugh.

"I thought you were the ghost. Or a monster. What's on your face?"

Rachel gave me a sheepish shrug. "It's a Dead Sea salt mask." She gingerly touched her cheek, and a piece of green plaster-like material fell off and crumbled on the floor. "I forgot I was wearing it. Did a noise wake you?"

I nodded. "And look, the cats are acting weird."

Whiskey's soft calico fur stood on end all along her spine, and Soda's apricot tail was as puffy and full as a bottle brush. A low guttural growl coursed through the kitten. They were spooked.

"Let's investigate." I reached for my fluffy aqua robe and slid my feet into my slippers.

"I'm not going out there!" Rachel raised a hand to her temple, and more green flaked off.

I grabbed the poker from the fireplace set (purely decorative since Jesse had installed surprisingly lifelike, safe electric inserts) and handed Rachel the matching miniature shovel.

"This is so dumb," she muttered as we quietly tiptoed out into the hall.

The thick, flowered runner masked our footsteps as we tiptoed away from my room, our ears alert for the slightest sound. "If there's someone in the house, we should be barricaded behind the bedroom door, calling nine one one."

"There." I ignored my sister's sensible plea and pointed to the back stairs. "I heard a creak."

"The third floor, of course. Only the spookiest part of the house." Rachel hit my rear with the back of the shovel. "You first."

I cursed my trepidation and set one foot on the stair. It creaked loud enough to be heard three counties away. We crept up slowly and paused on the landing when we heard a shout just beyond us, behind the closed door. A full moon shone through the stained-glass window, overlaying my sister's green face with a kaleidoscope of jewel tones. We pressed our ears to the heavy door.

"I know you're in here somewhere. I'll just wait you out."

"That sounds like—" I reached for the doorknob.

"Ezra!" Rachel lifted up her shovel and held it in front of her like a lance.

Ezra took one look at her green visage and screamed.

"What are you doing here?" I half shouted, then toned it down, since there was a chance my mother was still sleeping.

"What's on your face?" Ezra stared at Rachel in horror.

"It's a beauty treatment." She jutted out her chin. "Care to tell us what you're doing here?"

"I thought you were the intruder." He shook his head in impatience. "He must've gone down the stairs while I was searching the rest of the third floor."

"What intruder?" I didn't lower my poker, but I didn't hold it out in front of me like a jousting stick, either.

Ezra ran his hands through his hair with quick, nervous movements. "I've been keeping an eye out here for the last week," he admitted, his eyes downcast then pleading.

"I don't recall the police tasking you with that." Rachel took a step toward him. "And you do have a key to the house. How do we know you aren't the person sabotaging the renovation?"

"This doesn't look good, Ezra." Rach was right. Ezra had access to the house whenever he wanted, and he knew his way around construction. He could have rigged any of the accidents.

"You have someone else in your house now." Ezra looked panicked and frustrated all at once. "If we hurry, maybe we can catch them on the front lawn." I willed my pulse to slow down.

"I don't believe you," Rachel's green eyes were filled with skepticism. "You just want a chance to escape."

Ezra shook his head. "I'm not lying! I wanted to protect you. I sat outside in my truck and saw him approach from the south end of the house. He disappeared around the back, and when I let myself in, I caught him on the main stairs." Ezra was convincing, but he'd been stalking this house for weeks and we'd been none the wiser, so maybe he was just a good actor.

"Likely story," Rachel tossed her head and an avalanche of Dead Sea Scrub flaked off and landed at her feet.

"Where is this person now?" I wanted to believe him, but I was seriously creeped out.

"I told you, he must've slipped out. I followed him to the third floor, then it got utterly quiet. I searched every room, but he must've been hiding in one and doubled back." He frowned. "I don't have to take this." Ezra sniffed and wiped at his eyes in a rough motion. "I was just trying to protect you."

"Call the police." Rachel slowly lowered the shovel and burst into tears.

"He's fired." Jesse took off his Penguins cap and rubbed his head, his face a sad cast. "You think you know someone, but Ezra turned out to be a rotten egg. And no amount of rotten eggs will make an omelet."

His quintessential malaprop couldn't even make me smile. Truman and Faith had arrived as Ezra was getting into his truck, and it hadn't been pretty. He couldn't deny being on the premises, and his story didn't hold much weight. He was charged with trespassing and released, and Jesse had also released him from his employment.

"I feel double-crossed. I trusted him." Jesse cursed and clapped his hat back on his head. "And he was a darn architectural genius. I probably didn't give him enough credit. Lots of the ideas for this place were his."

I gave Jesse a sympathetic glance. "You gave Ezra credit. And we do need him. We're running out of time and could use every single hand. But not if he's going to be skulking around here after hours, possibly undoing everyone's hard work."

"*Possibly?*" Rachel's eyes were filled with disbelief. "Accept the most logical explanation, Mallory. Ezra sabotaged this renovation to get attention. He was jealous of Hunter and me, and he tore this place apart to distract us."

"Then there are no ghosts here, and Ezra must have been behind the hauntings. Now that we figured that out, Ezra's probably been sabotaging things, so we should cancel the séance."

"No!" Rachel toned down her voice and looked sheepish. "Just because Ezra was sabotaging things doesn't mean there aren't ghosts."

You just don't want to cancel your chance at being on TV.

I glanced around. The B and B was nearly finished, but a conservative estimate told me there was a whole week in store of painting and laying down tile and buffing and refinishing hardwood floors. The furniture wasn't back yet. My voice echoed through the empty shell of a room. And we had three days, counting this one, until Whitney's wedding.

"It'll be okay." Jesse had picked up on my worried vibes, and his already high voice reached almost falsetto range. "Let's start now."

We cracked open cans of paint in a gorgeous pistachio color. "Historically accurate and everything," I chirped, trying to sound cheerful and encouraging. "Let's see how much we can paint before the TV crew gets here."

Jesse groaned. "I can't believe you're going through with that. All I ask is that they stay out of our way."

Jesse, Rachel, Mom, and the new crew from the Senator painted and painted and painted, stopping for a quick lunch break around one. We'd barely made a dent when four vans emblazoned with HAUNTED HISTORIES rolled down the drive.

"Eeek! They're here!" Rachel dropped her roller brush with a splat, and creamy-yellow paint for the library spread out in a circle on the floor. She wiped her hands on her parachute cargo pants.

"How do I look?" She flashed us a grin.

"Like you should keep painting," Jesse drolly reminded her as he cleaned up her mess.

"Be right back." She skipped out of the room. Rachel was waiting to be discovered and thought if she played her cards right, she could finagle a pastry reality show out of this TV crew visit.

"Mallory, thanks again." Hunter strode into the room with an attitude of unadorned pride, and with Rachel and a man in tow.

"I'm Xavier Morris," the man said smoothly. He was tall and thin, his angular cheeks highlighted by a gorgeous honey tan too perfect in October not to have been gained on some tropical vacation or more likely a tanning bed. His teeth were blindingly white, and his gray hair stood in gelled spikes. "Thank you for having *Haunted Histories* in your home. This is some house." He blinked and took in the library, which was impressive with its two fireplaces and tin ceiling.

"Thank you." I wiped some paint off my hand to give his a hearty shake.

"This could be perfect," he mused, walking around the room and stopping to peer out the window at the vivid foliage. "Do you get a lot of snow?"

"Does a bear poop in the pot?" Jesse rolled his eyes. "Of course we do."

Xavier stared at the giant man for a moment, then turned back to me.

"Dakota Craig is getting married this winter, and we're scouting locations for her. For *I Do*."

A tiny bubble of excitement percolated in my chest.

"*The I Do*?" *I Do* was a reality show based on D-listers' weddings. It was unintentionally hilarious and had a great following. The fallen stars and starlets always married in gorgeous resorts, and though the show was more about prefabricated drama than wedding venues, the locations were featured well. I was sure the B and B and our wedding business would get a boost if we were on the show.

"The very one." His teeth came back out and nearly knocked me out with their gleaming pearlescence.

My sunglasses were in my purse or I'd have put them on to protect my eyes.

"And *the* Dakota Craig?!" I tried to hide my excitement. *Play it cool.*

Dakota was the washed-up but endearing former teen actress from *Silverlake High*, a mean girls teen soap opera from my youth. She'd been making a comeback and last year played a small but critical part in a highly praised indie film, *Roberta's Bastard*. There was Oscar buzz about her role, and she was the hottest thing at the moment: a teen starlet who'd fallen on hard times and risen from the ashes, phoenix-like in her late twenties, to recreate her career.

"Dakota was born here in Port Quincy, but her mother moved her to LA to star in commercials when she was three. I think this place has potential, and I can tell it'll film well. I'll run it by Dakota and Beau tonight."

My heart did a loop-de-loop. Beau Wright was one of the most popular country music stars and engaged to Dakota Craig.

"That would be great," I croaked. *That's smooth.* "I mean, I'd love it if Dakota and Beau picked Thistle Park and took us up on our wedding-planning services for *I Do.*"

Xavier's lips parted, and his teeth made another appearance, and he was gone, back with the crew in the van to set up for the séance.

"Ohmigodohmigodohmigod!" Rachel clasped my forearms, and the two of us jumped up and squealed.

"Can you believe it?! We might be featured on *I Do.*" All of Rachel's excitement over a bit appearance on *Haunted Histories* vanished at the prospect of a longer, bigger feature on *I Do.*

Jesse shook his head and stared at our roller brushes, willing us to pick them up and start painting again.

Three hours later we were showered and in fresh clothes for filming the séance. Xavier had already ticked off Rachel by suggesting she change into something a bit more "low key," and she'd hid her irritation until his back was turned, then flounced out in her glittery halter top and returned in a more sedate, if low-cut, scoop-necked T-shirt.

"I'm not so sure about Xavier." Rachel settled into a worn-down chair.

We were all ensconced on the third floor in the living room of what was to be our apartment, next to the hallway nearest to the widow's walk. It was a mess, and I was wistful we weren't filming in one of the completed bedrooms, but *Haunted Histories* hadn't been impressed with my knitting-needle paranormal experiences. At least the floor had been replaced in the third story.

"I've gotten my strongest readings here," Hunter said to the host, Nigel Stone.

Nigel nodded and looked around the room. "The bedrooms downstairs are too small for the séance, but we'll get some good shots here. Provided the ghosts show." His clipped British accent expressed some skepticism, but Hunter seemed unfazed.

"This house has the clearest manifestations of ghosts I've ever encountered, and they're ticked off about the renovations."

I shivered at his confidence in the reason for the hauntings and hoped he wouldn't be mad when he figured out I was trying to debunk them. Jesse had stayed to paint and was going to help me in my last-ditch effort to prove whether there were truly spirits here at Thistle Park, or if we were just victims of a cruel joke. Ezra was a skilled contractor who knew his way around electrical work and could have perpetrated the whole thing. Truman was concealed a few houses down the street in an unmarked car and was watching to make sure no one approached from the front of the house. Delilah was grumpily stationed in the doorway between the living room and the widow's walk, and Hunter had given her his night-vision goggles. He didn't know she was a double agent and thought she just wanted to catch some ghosts. Her role in debunking her idol, Hunter, hadn't stopped Delilah from dressing up for the show. Jesse and the Senator Hotel contractors carried her and her scooter up to the third floor, and she wheeled into the room wearing an electric-blue, sequined dinner jacket, her inky hair piled atop her head in a dramatic bun. This séance had more glitter and razzmatazz than a beauty pageant.

"It's go time, people!" Xavier clapped his hands, and the camera crew got into place.

"This is so fun!" Mom giggled and settled into her chair. She turned to Hunter expectantly, as Xavier called, "Action!"

Hunter sat on a tall wingback chair, wearing his white Port Quincy Paranormal Society T-shirt. He clasped hands with his fellow ghost hunters. My sister settled with a pout in a chair five spaces away in the circle. She'd wanted to sit next to him to get into the shot, but Xavier wanted Hunter flanked by his fellow ghost hunters.

Dozens of candles flickered en masse on the battered coffee table in front of Hunter and threw long, dancing shadows up and down the walls and on the ghost hunters' faces. Hunter touched several articles resting on a black felt cloth in front of him on the table: a hat that had belonged to Evelyn McGavitt that we'd dug out of storage, its once jaunty black and white swan feathers now a bit dusty, bent, and bedraggled; a lilac glass perfume decanter just like the one Tabitha had shown me a picture of at the Historical Society; and a photograph of Evelyn holding Keith's grandmother, Sylvia.

It began to rain, and a bolt of lightning pierced the dark sky. A second later a crash of thunder ripped through the air, shaking the windows. The lights flickered, and Nigel looked up, impressed. Perhaps I wouldn't need to do anything to prove whether there were ghosts or not.

"Couldn't ask for better sound effects," I heard my mother whisper over her shoulder to Jesse.

Xavier shot my mom a look, and she wiggled in her chair.

"Spirits from the beyond," Hunter intoned, gathering his hands in front of him. He closed his eyes and dropped his voice an octave. "We're here to talk to you. Who are you? What do you want?" He joined hands again with the ghost hunters flanking him.

The crew waited patiently in the semidarkness. They must be used to this. The show did ghosthunting features in historical buildings, and editing probably heightened what passed for paranormal activity: shots of shadows moving, strange lights and orbs, and objects moved and knocked off of surfaces.

So when the sibilant whisper slithered through the air to reach our ears, the crew nearly jumped out of their skin.

"Evelyn . . . ," the disembodied voice sighed, just barely audible because of our intense concentration.

Xavier's eyebrows shot up, and I nodded to Jesse. The big man was surprisingly light on his feet and disappeared down the hall to the back stairs. No one noticed, as their heads were all trained in the direction the voice had emanated from.

Hunter's eyes nearly bugged out of their sockets. *This is real, or he's an exemplary actor.*

"Evelyn McGavitt, are you with us? What do you want? What has disturbed you?"

We all waited with bated breath, and I scooted forward in my chair.

The newly installed electric fireplace blazed to life, the orange and red crackling flames surprisingly lifelike.

"Arrgh!" Rachel jumped up and broke the séance circle. She moved away from the fireplace and rubbed her arms, which were now covered in goose bumps.

"What the . . ." My gaze strayed to the remote control that powered the fireplace, still and unused on the edge of the coffee table.

"Get . . . *out!*" A gust of wet air blew into the room as the door to the widow's walk blew open. The lights went out.

Rachel screamed, and there was a scuffle.

"Power's completely out," one of the cameramen lamented.

The lights blinked on in a flash, and Ezra ran through the room chasing someone.

"What's he doing here?" Rachel stood and pointed to Ezra, who turned around and shot her an exasperated look.

"She's getting away! Come *on!*"

"The ghost?" Hunter stood and bounded toward the hallway, in hot pursuit of his brother.

The two men jockeyed on the short flight of stairs, and we all crowded around them. While they pushed and shoved each other, we heard a scream and a sickening thud.

We all raced up the short flight of stairs to the roof and peered down from the widow's walk.

Charity Jones lay on the ground, three stories down. The full skirt of her antique gown billowed out around her like a fan. The rain pattered softly on her face, which was frozen forever in a look of utter surprise. Her still hands twined around a useless sisal rope, and she stared up with lifeless eyes at the empty fire escape.

Rachel began to cry. Truman strode through the slick leaves on the front yard around to the side of the house, his face a grim, closed mask.

"Everybody get back inside. *Now.*" His eyes flickered up to the cameras trained on Charity. "And turn off the damn cameras." He knelt to take her pulse.

"She's gone."

Chapter Eighteen

"She did special effects for Cirque du Soleil." Truman delivered the news the next day.

"She wasn't an acrobat?" Confusion registered on Rachel's face, and I shook my head. "I guess she never claimed she was. She just insinuated, and we believed her."

Jesse and his crew were busy removing the tiny microphones Charity had installed in the millimeter-wide gap the picture rails of the house provided. The subtle decoration feature allowed the former owners of the house to hook and hang wires from the gap, which looked like it sat flush against the ceiling but really provided just enough space for Charity's theatrics.

"We found walkie-talkies and transistors in her house." Truman looked as amazed as I'm sure I did. "All she had to do was wait to see your lights go on, or off, stand in the garden or at the side of the house, and turn on her ghostly effects. That night she huffed over here and gave us a talking to? It was all an act. She'd just locked everyone in their rooms, then slipped out." Truman shook his head. "She also had notes about the history of this house and its inhabitants. Tabitha remembered her spending some time with the files at the Historical Society."

"What about the smells?"

"Your olfactory hallucinations?" Truman leaned forward. "She had lilac water in spritz bottles and probably snuck in to spray them when you were sleeping. She was coming and going via a rope tied to the fire escape. That way she could avoid the security system on the first floor doors and windows. She must've dropped that handkerchief you found on the roof by accident and then snuck in to take it back from your bedside table. She wasn't a professional acrobat, but she was a yoga teacher and strong and limber. She climbed up the rope and shimmied down, and you were all none the wiser."

"She must've let the kitties out onto the roof the day they were locked out in the rain," I mused.

"And she already knew we were opening this place as a B and B when she moved in. It was always her intention to drive us out." I shuddered.

Truman shook his head in wonder. "She really wanted you out of here. Her whole house was soundproofed, with acoustical tiles on the ceiling, heavy drapes, and triple-paned windows. She truly was worried about noise. She called us a few times about it, actually, and wondered whether there was a noise ordinance to cite you with."

My heart ached for Charity, despite her antics and sabotage of the renovation. "I never meant to drive her crazy."

Truman shook his head. "It was all in her head, I'm afraid. We went over three times when she claimed she could hear construction noise, and each time we heard nothing when we were inside. She was worried about summertime weddings, but if you really were going to locate them in the far southwest corner of your property, I don't think she could have heard them with your acreage. She was obsessed."

It didn't make me feel better, but knowing we had no real ghosts in the house and exonerating Ezra did.

"You figured it out!" Rachel bounded up and threw her arms around Ezra. A blush spread from his cheeks to the tips of his ears.

Jesse had hired him back, and he had started this morning, just in time. It was Thursday, and the wedding was only two days away.

"No problem." Ezra sheepishly patted Rachel's back. "Is Hunter around?"

Rachel shook her head, and this time a scarlet bloom blossomed on her face. It hadn't been pretty when Xavier realized there were no ghosts. A shouting match ensued between Hunter and the crew, who packed up to leave. Xavier insinuated that Hunter was in cahoots with Charity, and I wondered the same thing.

"No, we believe Charity was acting alone," Truman assured me. "Hunter was tricked just like the rest of us."

He'd slunk off and not returned, and now that he wasn't getting her a spot on a reality show, Rachel's ardor for him had cooled considerably.

"I hate to admit it. I thought it was my brother." Ezra shook his head. "And he thought *I* was sabotaging this place. I'm just glad you ladies are alright." He cast a tender look at Rachel and left us in the breakfast room to return to painting.

"I feel awful about Charity." I couldn't get the image of her in the fallen leaves out of my head.

"She brought it upon herself," Truman said gently.

My cell trilled in my pocket, and I gingerly answered the call from an unknown number.

"Are you looking for a Westie? I may have found him."

"Thank goodness!" Things were looking up.

I picked up Whitney, and we drove the Butterscotch Monster to a little blue Cape Cod–style house on the northern outskirts of town. An older woman with fake cobwebs stretched across her lower windows met us at the door, and a matted, bedraggled but tail-wagging Bruce bounded out and into Whit's arms.

"Bruce! Don't ever run away again!"

The dog gave her a slurpy kiss.

"What a happy ending," the woman sighed and patted the Westie.

"And here's your reward." Whitney clasped a leash around Bruce's neck and took out her wallet.

"I can't possibly—"

"No, please." Whitney's firm voice allowed no exceptions, and we left the astounded woman on her porch. Whit gathered up the wriggling mass of dog and settled him on her lap.

"Lois would be so happy we found him." She glanced up as if she were addressing her aunt.

Bruce would have to agree. His stumpy tail

wagged so fast and hard it could have acted as a propeller and sent him skyward. I drove us straight to the vet, who gave Bruce an X-ray and a clean bill of health.

"The amethyst is gone." The vet raised his brows. "Maybe someone did take him to get their hands on it."

"That's awful!" Whitney grabbed up her Westie and clasped him close to her. "But who would have known? It was just my family at Bev's bridal salon."

The veterinarian threw back his head and laughed. "Bev as in Beverly Mitchell? Oh, Miss Scanlon, you really haven't been back in Port Quincy in a long time. If Bruce ate that amethyst in Bev's presence, there isn't a person on the eastern seaboard who doesn't know about it."

"He's right," I affirmed. "Bev is the biggest gossip in town. She'd have started spreading the story the minute we left the store."

I dropped Whit off at her father's apartment so she could give Bruce a bath and headed back to the house.

"Where is everyone?" I followed the uneasy silence to the parlor, where Jesse, Ezra, Rachel, and my mother stared sorrowfully up at the ceiling. The mural, which was still damaged but beautiful enough to stand until we found an artist to completely restore it, was riddled with a thick, black X. Beneath it in neat black letters a message was scrawled: "Get out." Black paint was splattered on every wall of the parlor, which we'd meticulously painted a pretty pistachio green, and the floor, which was awaiting a polish.

"We went to get pizza." Jesse's voice was small

and high. "Every single one of us. Who would've done this?"

A clamminess spread between my shoulder blades. "Not Charity. And I don't believe there are ghosts here."

A frisson of realization skittered across my brain. "Ingrid Phelan."

Jesse snorted. "That harridan? What's she got to do with this?"

I shook my head in wonder as the realization hit me. "She's hell-bent on being the only B and B in town, and now she's going to hold weddings at the Mountain Laurel Inn as direct competition. I bet she's been sabotaging our renovation in addition to Charity."

"Now that Charity's out of the picture, it would make sense." Jesse stared up at the X.

Rachel puzzled at the abomination. "I can't picture Ingrid scampering up the scaffolding to do it." Her eyes lit up with an idea. "What about Keith?"

I nodded at my sister. "Ingrid and Keith both come to mind."

"Hey! Where are you going?" Jesse's eyes snapped up as four painters from the Senator Hotel trooped out of the house.

"We're done."

"I'm not painting that room again."

"This place is cursed."

One by one, they streamed out the door.

"Oh no oh no oh no!" I ran after them with Jesse, and we begged and pleaded, but it was a no-go.

I willed myself to stay calm once we were back inside. "We still have tons of painting to do, and sanding floors, and putting down new tile, and the furniture isn't back. Not to mention covering up that X." I sank into the window seat and stared ahead, willing a solution to appear.

"There have to be contractors willing to work here," my mother soothed, taking a seat next to me.

"Word gets around." Rachel's voice was flat. "No one will want to work in this house of horrors."

A drop of black paint dripped from the ceiling and stained my sleeve.

"If we pull a couple all-nighters, maybe we can pull it off." Ezra's tinny voice betrayed him, and I shook my head.

"There is one person we can call." My voice was infinitesimally small.

"So do it!" Rachel jumped up and took my hands in hers.

I reached for my cell phone.

Chapter Nineteen

"Well, well, well. What brings me the pleasure of meeting with you?" Helene, my once mother-in-law-to-be, fingered the gumball-sized black pearls at her throat. A spray of diamonds and rubies littered her right hand. She was wearing one of her ancient but perfectly preserved tweed Chanel jackets, and her rings played off the red and gold threads running through the thick bouclé wool. She'd donned her panty hose and pinched mouth, completing her trademark look. She arched a gray eyebrow at me. She was enjoying watching me dine on crow.

"My contractors quit. I'm throwing a wedding on Saturday." I swallowed. "I need your help." *That wasn't so bad.*

Helene's smile tipped up even more at the corners.

"Oh?" Helene took a sip of white wine and left a shadow of coral lipstick on the glass.

"You must have some incredible contractors at your disposal."

Helene had whatever she wanted at her disposal.

She was the reigning queen bee of Port Quincy, and a request for people to jump left many in her wake clambering and repeating, "How high?"

"Who do you have now?"

"Flowers Historical Restorations."

"Jesse Flowers does exceptional work." Helene lifted her fork and took a tiny bite of her wedge salad. "But he isn't the fastest."

"He was going at a pretty good clip until the workers quit."

"So I heard." Helene's flinty eyes sparkled. "A little problem with some ghosties this October?"

This wasn't going as planned. I felt like a juicy fly writhing in a web, and Helene was the spider gearing up for the kill.

"Aren't there any secrets in town?" I bit into a crusty roll. Any pretense of begging Helene with grace and dignity flew out the window. "I drove by the lot you bought for me and Keith in late July, and there was just a bare-bones foundation. Now it's completely finished, and it couldn't have been an easy house to build." I pictured the cubist colossus and suppressed a smirk.

"It's an abomination of a house," she admitted. "But yes, it was built fast, per my specifications, if not my design."

So Whitney was right. Helene had decorated the inside, and Becca had designed the outside.

Helene cut a single leaf of iceberg with exquisite precision and dipped it in Thousand Island dressing. She delicately nibbled it like a rabbit. "I *could* make a call to my contractors, who would be most amenable to help if it were on my behalf."

"And there's something else." I twisted my napkin

into a ball in my lap and dared to look up at Helene. "It doesn't look like the Planning Commission will approve my rezoning application from residential to mixed use. If it doesn't go through, no wedding, and no B and B."

Helene nodded, as if this were old news. "I believe," she said carefully, patting at her lipstick with her napkin, "I *may* be able to help you."

My heart soared.

"But I would need something from you."

I had a flashback to Lois's shakedown, and my throat got tight.

"Helene, Mallory. I've sent over an appetizer for you ladies. It'll be out shortly." Angela materialized at my elbow, and I gave her a grateful look.

"Everything ready for my niece's big day?"

"We've had a few setbacks," I cautiously began. "But things are looking up." *Thanks to the deal I'm about to make.*

"Let me know if you need anything. And keep up the good work." Angela parceled out a rare and genuine smile, and I was invigorated.

Helene couldn't want something too extravagant. "Name your price." I boldly picked up another buttered roll.

"You will put on the Dunlap Women's Academy's Winter Ball in February. Free of charge, of course, in exchange for my . . . help."

I dropped the roll back on its plate. I knew Helene was on the board of her alma mater, a swanky boarding school. "How many guests?" I squeaked out.

"Fifty."

That's not too bad.

"Fifty debutantes," Helene clarified. "And their dates."

I winced. A debutante ball for one hundred, at no charge? "No way, José."

"That's my final offer." Helene sat back and crossed her legs.

Check and mate.

Whitney was getting married in two days, and the house had hours of work left. A modern-day cotillion for one hundred would eat into my profits and tie up the B and B for a whole weekend in prep work, not to mention the actual ball. But desperate times called for desperate measures.

"Deal," I croaked.

"Here you are, compliments of Mrs. Pellegrino." The waitress arrived with our appetizer, a plate of old-fashioned chilled shrimp surrounding a bowl of cocktail sauce. Helene's favorite. Angela knew her customers. "Would you like anything else?"

"A glass of white wine, please. A big one."

Helene extracted her cell phone from her tiny quilted purse and gave a few clipped orders.

"Regis Contracting will be at Thistle Park within the hour. They will be at your disposal between now and Saturday afternoon, when I presume Whitney Scanlon's nuptials begin. They will do all that you and Jesse Flowers ask, but their price will be triple their usual rate." Helene quoted a number that made my head spin, and I did some quick calculations in my head.

"I can swing that," I whispered. *But I'll have nothing left.*

We ate in silence. Well, Helene ate, and I picked

at my linguine puttanesca and studied my copious goblet of wine. Finally, I lifted my head.

"Why are you doing this for me?" *Besides the crazy high price you just exacted.*

Helene weaved her fingers together and set them before her. "I was somewhat impressed that you agreed to house Keith and"—she shuddered—"his fiancée after they were attacked. You consented to take them in, and you didn't have to do that." Her mouth screwed up in an approximation of a smile. "So thank you."

Helene finished her meal and motioned for the check. "I can guarantee the contractors." Her mouth twitched, making the deep lines around her mouth dance up and down. "But I make no promises regarding the Planning Commission. Good luck, Mallory." She gave me her enigmatic Mona Lisa smile and wafted out of the room, a whiff of Calèche trailing after her.

I sat for a moment and pondered my fate. I hoped I wouldn't regret making a deal with Helene Pierce.

Regis Contracting trucks were already in the drive when I pulled in, and Jesse gave me a thumbs-up as I walked past.

"You sure do have friends in high places." He stared in awe at the army of men tiling, buffing, and painting.

I considered his statement. "I'm not sure if she's a friend, but time will tell."

A knock on the door startled me, and my mother breezed past us.

"The furniture is here! I'm going to start my transformation." She clapped her hands together with glee and bustled to let the movers in.

I braced myself for tropical splendor and opened my eyes to see a tasteful, high-backed couch done in yellow and maroon stripes. It looked stately and comfy.

"Shoo!" My mother clasped her hands over my eyes and shuffled me toward the stairs. "I still have some surprises up my sleeve. I don't want you to see until every piece is in place."

I obeyed my mom and scampered upstairs to paint the last two bathrooms, my mind suddenly at ease.

"Um, Mallory?" Jesse appeared in the doorway. "Can I come in?"

"Sure." I sat on the edge of the claw-foot tub, bending down to coat the baseboard with rose paint.

"I need your help." He dithered in the doorway, an edgy, hulking ball of nerves. He unconsciously buttoned and unbuttoned the top of his shirt.

"There's a special woman in my life—," he began and gripped the black pedestal sink.

"Oh, God—"

"Who I'd like to ask to be my wife."

"Jesse? Where are you?" Delilah's sixth sense must've kicked in, and she'd realized her son was about to cut the cord. She had spent the whole day marauding around the second floor after the contractors carried her and her scooter up. She wheeled into the big bathroom. "Where have you been?" Her voice echoed through the tile room, bouncing off the walls and sounding doubly accusing. Her eyes swept over her son. She took in his nervousness. "Why aren't you downstairs with the new contractors?"

"I need Mallory's opinion about something. For the house," he added lamely.

Delilah scooted off, her countenance full of disbelief.

"That was close." Jesse shut the door firmly behind him. "Like I said—"

"This mystery lady," I interrupted. "It's not anyone I know, is it?"

Jesse bristled. "You'll just have to wait until I propose." He rubbed his hands over the stubble that had cropped up on his cheeks this week in the mad rush to finish the house, scattering silver whiskers over his usually smooth face. "So, will you help me find a ring?" He blinked at me, his eyelashes a nervous flutter.

"Sure thing, captain."

As soon as Jesse left the bathroom, I whipped out my cell phone.

"Red alert." I texted my stepfather Doug. "Jesse is buying an engagement ring."

A second later, Doug's face filled the screen. I accepted the prompt to have a face-to-face call.

"That lily-livered momma's boy lumberjack. I swear, if he has designs on your mom, he'll have hell to pay!" Doug's usual cheerful, calm face was filled with anguish.

Just then the bathroom door burst open again. It was Jesse and my mom.

"You ought to see what your mother put together for you, Mallory. She's a decorating phantom." Jesse's face was florid and flushed with admiration and excitement.

"Don't you mean phenom, Jesse?" I tried to hide my phone, but it fell out of my hands and onto the black tile with a clatter.

"Thank you, Jesse dear!" My mother gazed at Jesse, and the pair left the room.

I inhaled sharply and chanced a glance at my phone.

"How much of that did you see?" I asked Doug.

"I saw it all," he replied grimly. "I'm on my way."

I was done painting hours later and itching to see Mom's decorating. She'd made me promise to wait until every last piece was in place. I stood from an interminable squat in the corner of the now bright pink bathroom.

"You have to see this." Rachel grabbed my arm and pulled me out the door.

"Wait!" I yelped. My foot was asleep. I tottered after my sister as she pulled me down the hallway, my feeling-less left foot catching on the carpet.

"Rach!" I limped after my sister as she dragged me down the stairs.

"Whoa—when did you . . ." I stared up and up and up. A new chandelier winked merrily from the top of the great hall ceiling. It was massive yet delicate, with ever larger rings of sparkly brown, blush, and yellow sparrows in flight, chasing each other around and around in concentric circles.

"Is that made with McGavitt glass?" I recognized the birds. There had been hundreds of them scattered in the curios around the house. My mother stood beaming below. "I had it made since the original chandelier was destroyed."

I hopped around on my right foot and marveled at the light. It was historical and fresh, at the same time, and utterly beautiful. It embodied everything I'd wanted for the B and B renovation.

"Mom, it's amazing." I followed her around from room to room, where she showed me the treasures she'd scrounged up at flea markets and in the house's storage. The furniture was at once plush and comfortable, with lots of chocolate velvet, navy twill, yellow silk, cream cotton, and sage-green chintz. The palette she chose was colorful enough to provide interest, with a riot of patterns and textures, and it would hold up well to years of use as a B and B and wedding venue.

The old scarred and faded lacquer furniture was renewed with slick finishes and bold paint. She'd decorated with glass and paintings that had already been in the house, but the modern creature comforts like the flat screen in the library were tastefully displayed, and there were new poufy ottomans that doubled as storage. The downstairs was a masterpiece.

"Thank you, Mom. I'm sorry I ever doubted you."

"Nonsense, Mallory. This was the most fun I've had in years." Her eyes twinkled merrily. "You and Tabitha didn't even need to craft that fake contest. And there's one more surprise, but you'll just have to wait until after the wedding."

I grinned and gave her a crushing hug. I just hoped the surprise wasn't a proposal from Jesse.

* * *

That night I settled into bed with a full heart. Whitney's wedding was in less than forty-eight hours, and we might just pull off the renovation. My excitement dampened as my mind strayed to Lois's murder. It seemed like Truman was no closer to finding the killer. I reached for my laptop and idly perused the Senator Hotel website, trying to imagine Lois's enemies there. The photos were old and out of date.

The Senator seemed to cater to gas industry muckety-mucks, and the online comments were the usual mixed bag of praise and complaints. I took mental notes and used the reviews as a hint to what I might deal with at the B and B. Customers protested about water pressure, lackluster breakfasts, and noise.

"The Senator was once the grand dame of hotels in Port Quincy, but she's past her prime," Jeff from Cincinnati wrote.

"Enjoyed the Virginia spots at dinner, but my asparagus was overcooked." Judith from Clarksburg, West Virginia, opined.

"MY CREDIT CARD HAS SHOWN HINKY CHARGES EVER SINCE I STAYED HERE," Luther Bayliss's review screamed out in all caps. Out of several dozen reviews, two more people complained of phantom charges. Below each review was a rebuttal, posted by a Senator employee.

"We're sorry to hear that, but we take the security and comfort of our guests very seriously. We are certain the charges you are experiencing are not due to your stay at the Senator. H. H."

Was H. H. Hunter Heyward? His responses didn't do much to allay visitors' fears, and I made a note to never argue back with customers when the B and B had reviews online. I drifted off to sleep with my laptop open next to me, trying to prepare for the Planning Commission hearing the next day. Helene's contractors had almost saved the day, and I hoped for one more miracle.

Chapter Twenty

Halloween dawned cool and gray. The sun barely showed its face behind somber clouds, and a mist blew in from the west. Almost all of the leaves had fallen from the trees, and the wind clicked bare branches against the window. I threw back my comforter and strained to hear the floor buffer in the hall downstairs. It was music to my ears, the last key to the renovation before we could turn to preparing for Whitney's wedding tomorrow. I quickly showered in the newly painted bathroom and suited up for battle. Today was my hearing before the Planning Commission. If they didn't approve my application for rezoning, I wouldn't be able to hold weddings at Thistle Park or run it as a B and B. My bequest from Sylvia, Keith's grandmother, would turn into the ultimate white elephant gift.

"You'll be approved," I admonished my reflection and smeared on some tinted lip gloss. "You have to be."

But even Helene hadn't been confident about swaying the Planning Commission to my side, and she was the reigning dowager empress of all Port Quincy.

I donned a black suit from my days as an attorney and added an orange scarf at my neck in a nod to the holiday.

Rachel knocked, then peeked her head into the bathroom.

"How do I look?"

"Like you can kick ass and take names." Rachel straightened my scarf and untangled a curl from a hoop earring. "Knock 'em dead."

We both winced at her choice of words. I knew she was thinking about Charity too.

I drove the Butterscotch Monster into town, with shaking hands on the big steering wheel. Rachel rode in the back, and Mom rode shotgun, there for support. I nodded to the silly statue of the town founder, Ebenezer Quincy, on my way into the municipal building. I sent a little prayer skyward.

The hearing took place in a medium-sized meeting room in the basement, across from the Planning Commission office. The board sat arrayed before me: Troy Phelan in a black turtleneck, Keith in a double-breasted suit, and three other people I didn't recognize: an older woman, a man in his mid-forties, and a gentleman who had to be over eighty. Ingrid Phelan was seated in the back and blew a kiss to her husband.

"This meeting is now called to order." Troy pummeled a small mallet and gestured for me to stand with a flick of his hand.

"Mallory Shepard has petitioned this board to rezone her property at one twenty-seven Sycamore

Street from strictly residential to mixed use so she can reside there and also run a bed-and-breakfast and wedding venue."

The older man at the end of the row began to snore, his hairy chin rising and falling gently with each breath he took.

"State your case, Ms. Shepard." Troy shuffled papers in front of him with practiced, self-important movements.

"My property consists of several acres and adequate space for parking and tents. The house itself, along with the greenhouse, can safely accommodate parties of two hundred per the fire code. The grounds are large enough to host weddings quietly, without disturbing other residents." I thought of Charity and stifled a shiver. "The traffic study concluded Sycamore Street can handle the occasional traffic that a wedding or large event will bring. All of the renovations and construction permits were approved. I successfully completed online coursework to become a hotel operator, and you've found all of my papers to be in order." I took a deep breath and stepped around the table to approach the board. "My request to have Thistle Park rezoned as mixed use, allowing me to operate my bed-and-breakfast and wedding-planning business should be approved and granted. Thank you." I carefully paced back to the small table in front of them and gingerly sat down. The chair was extra low, and the small table was dwarfed by the high semicircle of the bench in front on me. The effect was to force the petitioner to stare up at the board in a beseeching manner.

"Be that as it may, there might not be enough business in this town to support two B and Bs. Especially," Troy smiled, "now that the Mountain Laurel will be hosting weddings."

"The subject at hand for this hearing is my property, I believe, not speculation about business at another venue." I tried to steer the conversation back to Thistle Park and approving my request for rezoning.

"He's right." Keith stared down his nose at me. "This town doesn't need two B and Bs."

"Ahem." All of the board members turned left in surprise. The older gentleman on the end cleared his throat again and let out a phlegmy cough. He hadn't been sleeping after all.

"It seems to me," he leaned forward, "that there is a need for another B and B. The gas company execs have told me there's often no vacancy at the hotels here in Port Quincy, and that they have to board people in Pittsburgh and make the drive."

"And there aren't many places around here to hold big weddings," the middle-aged man mused, rubbing his chin. "Your B and B is awfully small, isn't it, Ingrid? And it's not like you're currently hosting weddings." He stared at Ingrid in the back of the room.

Ingrid bristled and opened her mouth when the older woman piped up. "This isn't really the matter at hand, as Ms. Shepard stated. Her concern is rezoning her property, and she seems to have put in the proper paperwork and proof." She patted the nearly foot-high stack in front of her.

"All in favor of rezoning one twenty-seven Sycamore Street as mixed use, to allow Ms. Shepard to run it as a B and B and hold weddings?"

"Nay." Keith and Troy bellowed their answers.

"Aye." The older man and woman and the middle-aged man were more measured in their assent, but it was clear. Three to two in favor of rezoning.

"Whoo-hoo!" I jumped up in a very unladylike manner and did a mini fist pump in the air.

A chorus of cheers sounded behind me. Mom, Rachel, and Garrett stood at the back of the room, clapping and grinning. Garrett winked, and my heart fluttered.

"You may hold the wedding as planned tomorrow, Ms. Shepard. We'll issue you a temporary emergency variance. Pick up your rezoning paperwork on Monday. This hearing is adjourned." The older woman reached over Keith to grab Troy's mallet and hit it with a resounding clang.

"You did it! You did it!" Rachel hopped over the bannister and enveloped me in a hug.

Keith frowned at us and stormed out of the room. He was closely followed by Ingrid and Troy Phelan, muttering about fixed votes.

"I had a little help," I admitted, thinking of Helene.

I finally recognized the older woman. She was a member of the board at Dunlap Women's Academy, just like Helene. She was regularly featured in the newspaper's society page. Had I bought her vote by promising to throw the Winter Ball? A haze of regret clouded my head, and I began to think of all the strings attached to our deal, some ethical, some not. But I didn't have time to stew over it.

Thank you, Helene. I looked up for the pigs I was sure would be aloft, flapping their wings in V formation like autumn geese. I wouldn't make a habit of being in Helene's debt.

"C'mon, sis." I linked arms with Rachel, and we walked back to my mom and Garrett. "We have a wedding to put on."

My phone rang and rang as I left the municipal building. Garrett kissed my cheek and glanced at his watch.

"I've got to go, but I'll see you later tonight with Summer?" His eyes twinkled in anticipation of Halloween.

I grinned in return. "I wouldn't miss it for the world." I watched him amble away, with moony eyes. Rachel rolled hers.

She glanced at my cell phone as I pulled it out of my purse. "Just let them leave a message. You don't have time for calls."

I glanced at the screen and shook my head. "I've got to take this. It's Jesse, and it must be pretty important if he can't just wait until I get home."

"Mallory, we need to talk. I know you're good for it, but, um, your last check? It bounced." Panic seized my heart then dissipated. It had to be a mistake. I'd just checked the account I used to pay for construction this morning.

"There must be some misunderstanding. Paying Helene's contractors and the furniture restoration nearly wiped me out, but I have enough. Tell you what. I'll check my account, and if there's a problem, I'll make it right with the bank," I said.

"That didn't sound good." Rachel gestured to my phone. "Are we having money problems?"

"It'll be super tight this month, and we have no wiggle room, and I really need Whit's wedding to go off. But Jesse's check couldn't have bounced." I punched in the numbers for my online banking account and felt the blood drain from my face and hit my stomach.

"Money doesn't just walk out of bank accounts all on its own."

Rachel, my mom, and I sat in supplication before the bank manager at the Port Quincy Savings and Trust.

"It didn't walk out, Ms. Shepard." Charlene Rigsby, bank manager, turned her monitor around and slid her finger down a line of transactions.

"There. Three days ago, you logged in and transferred twenty-five thousand dollars to this account in Zurich."

"But I don't know anyone in Switzerland!"

Charlene shook her head. "You can fill out these forms, and we'll get to the bottom of this. It could be identity theft."

"It could be? We need to call the police."

"We'll be doing that, Ms. Shepard," Charlene sniffed. "Are you positive you didn't transfer these funds yourself? The bank can't just reimburse you at your word."

My mother stared, incredulous. "If my daughter said she didn't transfer these funds, she didn't. There must be some explanation and a way to get the funds transferred back."

"We'll leave that up to the authorities and assign our fraud team to this matter immediately."

"But when will the funds be returned?"

Charlene gave me a level look. "I'm not sure. That depends on the results of the investigation."

The three of us left the bank swathed in a cloud of dread.

"What am I going to do?" I wailed.

"Jesse will believe you," Rachel soothed.

"I know he will. But he has a business to run, and he can't wait months to get paid. Thank goodness all of the vendors are paid for Whitney's wedding, and the food and drinks are purchased."

"Who could have broken into your account?" My mother fingered the mother of pearl buttons on today's sweater set ensemble, black with a haunted house and Casper-like ghosts embroidered on the front.

"No one! I change all of my passwords every few months. And this was an account that wasn't tied to a debit card. I created it strictly for the renovations, and I meant it to be a slush fund, untouched. The checking account I wrote Jesse's payments out of was tied to this account. There should be plenty left."

Rachel bit her lip. "We don't have time to figure this out right now, Mall. We need to get Summer ready for trick or treating."

I willed my heart to stop beating like a hummingbird. We climbed into the Butterscotch Monster and dropped Mom off to work on Whitney's decorations. Rachel and I headed over to quickly transform Summer into the prettiest, most horrific zombie princess Port Quincy had ever seen.

Summer paced nervously in her room, and I stood back in awe.

"You've got to stop moving around, sweetie."

Rachel stood before Summer with blood-red lipstick and a fine makeup brush. "More gore on your left cheek?"

"Yes!" Summer stared in the mirror as Rachel expertly painted on another dribble of red.

"There. Whaddya think?" She spun Summer around, and I stared for a minute then burst out laughing.

"It's brilliant."

The Glinda the Good Witch dress, an airy, floaty, gauzy pink cupcake of a gown, was slashed and drenched in red paint. Summer's arms were awash in ichor, and her face was a study in dark zombie eyes and bloodstains, thanks to my makeup-artist sister. Her short blond pixie was concealed under a ratty brown wig. She affected a zombie's herky-jerky gait, her arms stretched out before her.

"Wait, I have one more thing." Rachel reached into her bag and extracted a tiara she'd artfully painted with something that resembled blood. Half of the pink rhinestones were painted rusty red, and bits of leaves and twigs had been glued onto the crown.

"Where did you get that?"

"I was Miss Pensacola Spring Break last year. I took first in the swimsuit contest." Rachel beamed proudly and affixed her trophy to Summer's wig. "Perfect."

"Let's go show Dad and Grandma!" Summer tore open her bedroom door.

"I don't know how Lorraine is going to take our execution of this zombie princess idea."

"She'll love it," Rachel flicked her hand in dismissal. "Everybody wins. Lorraine gets a princess, Summer gets to be a zombie like her friends, and

we get to destroy Natalie's dress. Speak of the devil."
She nodded her head to the window, where I saw a
yellow VW Bug pull into the drive.

"I didn't think Natalie would actually care what
Summer did to her costume, since she said she
didn't want it back."

"Summer, you look awesome!" Garrett laughed
and picked up his daughter's hands. He stepped
back to take in the full effect of her zombie-princess
glory. "You're the prettiest, scariest zombie in the
history of Halloween." He gave his daughter a hug
and came away with fake blood on his cheek.

"Thanks, Dad." Summer grinned and did a twirl
in her Glinda dress.

"Let's see this costume." Lorraine bustled into
the room carrying a plate of Halloween goodies:
candied apples, black and orange thumbprints with
sprinkles, and a pitcher of apple cider. She took in
Summer and stopped in her tracks, then let out a
wail like a banshee.

"What have you done to my grandbaby!" She
dropped the tray. The pitcher glanced off the coffee
table, drenching her carpet in sticky sweet liquid.

"Mom, it's alright." Garrett steadied his mother
and sopped up the cider with a pile of leaf-pattern
napkins.

"I just thought I'd snap a few pics of Summer
in my costume . . . you ruined my Glinda dress!"
Natalie raced into the room and made a grab for
Summer.

I jumped in front of her and pushed Summer
back into her father's arms.

"You gave her the dress, remember? You even
specified she could use it for her zombie costume."

Her face turned as orange as an Oompa-Loompa. "I wouldn't have done so if I knew she'd *ruin* it!"

"Natalie, I won't have you talking to my daughter that way." Garrett stepped out in front of Summer and joined me by my side. "Perhaps I should have run Summer's plan for the dress by you, but really, if you gave the dress to her as a gift, you can't place restrictions on its use."

"That little brat!" Natalie took a step back. Her saccharine shell dissolved as if she'd been left out in the rain. In her place was no longer Glinda, but a very bad, very mean witch.

Lorraine found her strength. "Don't talk to Summer like that!" All her misgivings about the costume melted away, and Lorraine morphed into Grandma Bear.

"Summer is my daughter, Natalie." Garrett placed his arm around her. "Anything that went wrong was between the two of us and had nothing to do with her. Now. Get. Out."

Natalie turned on the heel of her little white Keds and motored out of the room, into her Beetle, and reversed hard down the driveway, with a squeal of tire rubber on the pavement.

Summer hugged her father, and Rachel and I helped Lorraine sit down.

"She never liked me, Dad." Summer sat on the couch and picked up the lone thumbprint that had remained on the tray.

"She's crazy, sweetheart." Rachel sat on one side of her, and I sat on the other.

"We're a package deal, kiddo." Garrett smiled at his daughter, and she smiled shyly back.

Phoebe showed up as a zombie scuba diver, and

Jocelyn had borrowed her mother's white coat and stethoscope to become a zombie doctor. The girls oohed and aahed over each other's costumes. They kidded around in the living room and took shambling steps with their arms outstretched. We took pictures of the three girls with their cell phones and sent them out into the night with Garrett as chaperone.

"Thanks for working on Summer's costume with her." Lorraine walked Rachel and me to the door.

"I'm sorry it was such a shock." Maybe we should have warned Lorraine what a zombie princess costume would entail.

She bit her lip as if trying to decide whether to say something. Finally she wiped her hands on her candy-corn apron. "I loved Natalie like a daughter. I appreciated her cheerfulness and positive attitude. But I never for a million years thought she wasn't going to be anything but kind to my Summer." She paused and gave me an impetuous hug. "I know you love my granddaughter, and I thank you for that."

I left with tears in my eyes. Rachel and I hightailed it out of there for Whitney's rehearsal.

"I now pronounce you man and wife. You may now kiss the bride." The Reverend Marcus Callender, clad in jeans, grinned as big as he would tomorrow during Whitney and Ian's real ceremony.

Ian swept Whitney up in a dramatic dip on the grand staircase landing and kissed her.

"Woot-woot!" Rachel and I cheered from the hall below. The rehearsal was going off without a hitch.

Whitney and Ian walked down the stairs hand in hand.

"It's all coming together." Whitney took in the delicate bird chandelier and turned around in a slow circle. "The house looks fabulous. I just knew you could pull it off."

She and Ian left to talk to her father, who was looking on fondly at his daughter.

"We were able to pull it off, thanks to you." I hugged my mom, and she pulled Rachel into her embrace. I lowered my voice. "Now all I have to do is find the missing money and everything will be resolved." *Except for Lois's murder, and the identity of Vanessa's real killer.*

"How did Jesse take the news?" Mom murmured, trying to look nonchalant.

Doug couldn't arrive fast enough.

"He believes me, thank goodness. After all we've been through, he knows I wouldn't stiff him. I wrote him an IOU. And he'll be able to manage until we resolve this with the bank." Jesse had been tense, but ultimately understanding.

Marcus Callender sidled up to me. "I hear the prosecutor has started exploring whether to free Eugene Newton." His soft brown eyes were filled with hope. I didn't want to dash them.

"The prosecutor could file a motion to vacate the conviction and claim the case against Eugene is without merit. But it would be even better if they could find the real killer. He's not out of the woods yet."

Marcus's face fell. "I thought the diary would be enough."

"Garrett thinks if he presses the issue, Eugene could be out by Thanksgiving. We'll have to wait and see. But at least he has a shot, thanks to you."

Marcus blushed. "I never put two and two together

before. Thank you for asking the questions to jog my memory."

Whitney, Ian, and Porter gathered their coats to head over to Pellegrino's for the rehearsal dinner. There was a knock at the door that shook it like a battering ram.

"Police! Open up!" I hurried over and threw it open. There stood Truman and Faith, their faces grim.

"We have a warrant for the arrest of Whitney Suzanne Scanlon for the murder of Lois Scanlon. Whitney, you have the right to remain silent. Anything you say—"

"Is this a joke? It isn't very funny." Ian took a step toward Truman and blocked him from approaching Whitney. A vein throbbed and pulsed on his forehead.

"I'm sorry. Please step aside." Truman glared at Ian, and he finally acquiesced. Ian's hands balled into fists and his knuckles turned white.

"Whitney, don't say *anything*. I'm calling a lawyer."

Faith cuffed Whitney and led her away, sobbing. We stared out the front door as Faith gently sat her in the back of the police car and drove down the drive.

Ian talked animatedly into the phone, then swiped it off. "We'll get my fiancée out of jail."

"I'm not so sure if it's a murder charge," I began.

"Mark my words. Whitney and I are getting married tomorrow, no matter what I have to do."

Chapter Twenty-one

The dog groomer's was about to close. Even though Whitney and Ian's wedding was in limbo and the doggies probably wouldn't serve as ring bearers, I still needed to pick them up. I pulled in front of Peggy's Pooch Palace, a combination doggie hotel and pet salon. A chime made of silver dog bones clinked softly in the blustery wind. I swung open the door, and a barking noise announced my arrival. It was canine heaven, with dog drinking fountains, an activity course, and grooming stations.

"I'm sorry I'm here so close to closing time," I apologized.

The mêlée that had ensued after Whitney's arrest delayed me about half an hour. I wanted to get back home and brainstorm a way to spring Whit from jail, but the dogs needed to be picked up.

"You're fine, dear," the heavyset woman with soft copper curls smiled from behind the counter. "I bet these guys will be happy to see you." She led Fiona, Bruce, and Maisie around from behind the counter.

"They look adorable!"

Bruce was restored to his former shiny glory, his hair trimmed and dematted. He sported a new tartan collar and sat on his haunches, waiting for a treat. The woman rewarded him with a small bone cookie. He trotted over to me and pawed at my knees. His nails had been trimmed and his doggie teeth brushed. Fiona looked happy to dote on her son. She wore a red sash around her neck. Maisie had small pink bows along her collar, and her white fur was gleaming and soft.

"Hi, babies." I was going to miss them when Whitney went back to Baltimore. It hit me, if Whitney couldn't shake the murder charge, she might not be leaving Port Quincy anytime soon.

"Big day for these three tomorrow, right? It's not every doggy that gets to be a part of a wedding ceremony." The woman knelt in front of the pups and presented them with more treats.

I didn't bother to correct her and spread the news of Whitney's arrest.

"C'mon, sweeties. You need a good night's sleep," I counseled the dogs. "I don't have your beds, but you're staying the night with me."

The woman frowned and hustled back behind the front desk. "That reminds me. I still have a key for Lois's house. Will you give it to Whitney? I was going to give it to her tonight. I'm sure you can get the dogs' things over there if you need to. To tell you the truth, they're a bit stressed. Bruce, especially."

I didn't doubt it after his ordeal roaming the streets for a week.

"I know Lois sometimes gave him doggie Prozac.

You could get it for him at her house. It'll keep him from chewing your things."

I thought of the damage Bruce had done to Rachel's Jimmy Choos and wished we'd known about his meds before.

She presented me with a small house key clearly labeled with Lois's name.

I gave her an incredulous stare. "Are you sure you don't want to give this to Whitney yourself?"

The woman shrugged. "Give it to her tomorrow. And you can go get the dogs' beds and get them settled for the night. Wish her a happy wedding for me!" She gaily sent me off with an enthusiastic wave and a pat for each dog.

I left with the key and directions to Lois's house, and the dogs trotted obediently beside me. I settled them in the backseat and stared at the key.

Truman will kill me.

I shrugged and headed for Lois's house. It was a pretty, Tudor-style cottage on the eastern side of Port Quincy. Har.ly fall weeds had started to encroach on the orderly but shriveled beds of petunias edging up to the house, long dead from the first frost. Brown leaves were piled up in the yard. Still, you could tell Lois had meticulously maintained it.

The trio of Westies sniffed each blade of grass and rock as I approached the front door. I glanced around at the neighboring houses and decided to enter from the back, in case anyone called Truman. I was sure my trespassing couldn't hurt anyone, since the police had probably already looked through the house in the course of investigating Lois's murder. I inserted the key and jiggled it for a minute before it caught. The back door opened with a whine. Bruce and Maisie excitedly yipped and hurried past me, pulling me in after them on their leashes. Fiona gazed up at me as if to question my decision to enter the house. Then she gave an eager bark and followed her children.

"Whoa, you guys sure are excited to be home!"

I stood in a neat, pale blue kitchen, decorated with photographs of what looked like Scotland. There were fields dotted with flocks of sheep and tumbledown castles, craggy oceanside cliffs, and meadows of heather. It appeared that the pictures were all amateur shots, but skilled ones. I wondered if Lois had taken them on her travels.

The house smelled musty and unlived in. The dogs had a field day sniffing and pawing through their old abode. I followed them to the living room, where three plaid dog beds sat before the fireplace. The walls were covered with extremely lifelike portraits of Westies. The painter had captured their personalities, and it was easy to see which canvases featured Fiona, Maisie, and Bruce among the host of other pups Lois must have cared for over the years. The hair at the nape of my neck prickled as the dogs seemed to watch me. I didn't want to believe in ghosts and was glad they'd been debunked at Thistle Park. But the portraits were giving me the willies, as if guard dogs from beyond the grave were keeping watch over the house.

"Let's go, pups."

They trotted after me but whined at the pantry, and inside I found a bag of fancy gourmet dog food.

"Might as well take this." I picked up the heavy

bag, and it split open from the bottom, scattering kibble all over the kitchen floor.

"Oh, no," I groaned and looked for a broom. "Don't eat too much." The dogs tucked in to the spilled food, when something caught my eye. I reached down and pulled out something enclosed in a plastic freezer bag amidst the dog food.

"What the . . ." I slid a small notebook embossed with the Scottish flag out of the plastic baggie while the terriers noshed. The first page contained a list:

PQPS
Wi-Fi
$$$

The rest of the pages were blank. A prickle of recognition raced up my spine, and I drew in a sharp breath.

"Doggies, we have to go." I knew who killed Lois, and if I played my cards right, we could spring Whitney and the wedding would go on.

I sent a text message and gunned the engine of the Butterscotch Monster on the way over to Pellegrino's. The dogs barked and slid around in the backseat, sensing my tension. I hoped Truman and Faith could meet me, but they might have been trying to question Whitney. I wanted a public place when it all went down.

I power walked into the restaurant and ran straight into Angela. The dogs barked and twined their leashes around my ankles. I stepped out of the tangle and apologized.

"Mallory! I'm so glad to see you." She looked distraught. "I just got the call from Whitney's lawyer, and then Ian. I was wondering why no one showed up for the rehearsal dinner." She gestured behind her to the private dining room, where servers were dismantling an elaborate buffet. She was dressed in a pretty green velvet dress, even fancier than her usual restaurant attire, probably anticipating joining her niece and family for the rehearsal dinner rather than working.

"I'm sending all of this food over to the soup kitchen. I can't believe this is happening, and that Whitney has been accused of this awful thing." Her hands shook, and she blinked her eyes in agitation. "That dear girl would never do this to her aunt."

"Do you know why they think Whitney did it?" I knew that, unlike Rusty, Truman played by the books. If he'd arrested Whitney, he had a good, if not erroneous, reason for doing so.

"They found a small vial of Bloody Mary mix in her luggage, according to Ian. Someone called it in anonymously to the police." She wiped a tear from the edge of her eye, completely rattled. "Obviously it was planted. There's no way Whitney would've murdered her aunt Lois." Angela was near hysterics.

I grabbed her shoulders to calm her down. "It'll be alright. I think I know who killed your sister."

Angela stared at me as if I'd gone mad. "How did you figure it out? And who is it?"

I felt a buzz in my pocket and ripped my cell phone out.

I'll be right there.

"I don't have much time. He'll be here soon. I went to Lois's house."

"You what?" Angela bristled. "How did you get in?"

"The dog groomer, Peggy, gave me the key to get the dogs' things since I thought they'd be staying with me indefinitely. A note fell out of their food."

I held up the notebook, encased in plastic once again.

"Don't you see? The ghost hunters are using Wi-Fi at the hotel and in other inns they're inspecting to access guests' financial information from their laptops and tablets. They hack into their computers through the wireless connection, use keystroke software or find passwords typed into files, and steal from the guests."

Angela frowned. "But what does this have to do with my sister, Lois?"

"Lois was known as the Senator Hotel Stasi."

Angela blanched at the moniker.

"She spied on her employees in her role as head of HR. She blackmailed Hunter, and he killed her in retaliation. He works security at the Senator and could have easily doused her Altoids with Bloody Mary mix." I was nearly breathless after my cursory explanation of motive, means, and opportunity.

"Very good, Mallory. Too bad no one will get to hear your theory play out."

A cold, hard object pressed into my back.

I stifled a cry.

"Come with me. Both of you. And don't make any sudden movements."

Hunter led Angela and me out Pellegrino's back door into a wide, dark alley. It stank of rotten garbage and gasoline. The only light was from a gorgeous half moon hanging diagonally in the sky. A large dumpster blocked my view of the exit to the alley. I gulped cold air and tried to think fast. I said a prayer that I wouldn't lose them for good this time and let go of the leashes holding the Westies. They scampered off into the night, and Hunter removed the gun from my shoulder blades for one second to point it at the retreating dogs.

"You killed my sister?" Angela moaned, and her cries got louder as Hunter trained his gun on her.

"Shut *up*. I need to think. Both of you, against that wall, and keep your hands up where I can see them."

Angela and I shimmied against the cold brick and stared at Hunter, pacing and pointing his gun at us.

"So Lois was blackmailing you," I ventured.

Hunter gave me a barely perceptible nod.

"She tried to get me to pay her a bribe," I offered.

Angela stifled a little gasp next to me.

"It made me feel awful. I can't imagine what it would have been like to work with her looking over my shoulder."

Hunter shook his head, and the gun wobbled. "You have no idea. She brought those mutts with her and let them roam the halls, like watchdogs. She was in all of my business, personal and professional, and tried to get me fired for updating the paranormal group website just once during work hours. All I had to do was remove her EpiPen from her purse and swap in the doctored mints."

"And she found out about the theft with the Wi-Fi."

Hunter's eyes grew wide, then reduced to icy slits. "You're the second one to figure that out, and the first one is dead. Yes, I used the Paranormal Society as cover to steal from guests through the Wi-Fi."

"So how did you transfer my funds to Switzerland?"

"It's easy. I installed keystroke-recording software in your laptop. The bank will find that *you* logged in and transferred the funds. I answered all of your challenge questions correctly. Not that you'll live to dispel that notion. I needed to get out of here, and I hoped *Haunted Histories* would come through for me, but you managed to ruin that for me, too!"

I didn't remind him that it was actually his brother, Ezra, who had exposed Charity Jones as a fake ghost. I'd just had Jesse cut the power.

A bit of spit flicked off his lips and hit me in the face.

"I'd be out of here if Xavier had decided to make me a regular feature on the show. I lucked out with Charity's pranks. She even had me fooled at first. I thought for once there were real, live ghosts. I only had to set up one haunting, the black X on the ceiling. I thought I'd have one more shot to get back in the show's good graces, but Xavier was already done with me."

"You painted over the mural?" So it wasn't Ingrid Phelan or Keith trying to sabotage the B and B.

"Charity started the hauntings, and I finished them. Too bad she found out about me pilfering financial info from you."

A sickening new realization washed over me like a tidal wave.

"You killed Charity. It wasn't an accident!"

"Very good, Mallory." Hunter whirled around to

stare at me. "I knew Charity was climbing up a rope attached to the fire escape, so I loosened it for her." A sinister smile marred his boyish good looks.

A soft whine emanated down the alley. I prayed the dogs had fetched help, like good little reincarnations of Lassie. Hunter didn't seem to notice. He continued to pace back and forth, almost ignoring Angela and me.

"Charity was going to turn me in for stealing using the Wi-Fi until I threatened to turn her in for the pranks. I had to get rid of her."

A loud bark ricocheted down the alley.

"Those dogs!" Brandishing his gun, Hunter ran down the brick wall and straight into Truman.

"Oof!" They fell into a tangle of whirling arms and legs, and a gun went off.

"No!" I ran down the alley and scooped the howling dogs into my arms.

"Arrgh!" Truman kneeled on top of Hunter's back. All of the air came out of his lungs in a stifled wheeze.

"Get that gun, Mallory!"

Angela stood rooted to the spot against the wall where Hunter had left us and slowly slid down to the pavement, as if her legs were made of jelly. I picked up the gun and trained it on Hunter with shaking hands.

Chapter Twenty-two

We headed to the police station, Hunter locked in the back of Truman's car and Angela and me in the Butterscotch Monster. Whitney ran down the stairs in front of the station and into Ian's arms as Hunter was led, cursing and straining his handcuffs, up the stairs.

"I knew it would work out." Whitney flung herself into her fiancé's arms. He embraced her in a bear hug and swung her around, laughing.

"I need to get home and get some beauty sleep. I'll see you later today for our wedding!"

Ian and Whitney joined hands and half ran to his car.

"All's well that ends well." I turned to Angela with a smile.

"Thank goodness Truman heard Hunter confess." Angela was still shaking from our encounter with Hunter's pistol.

I dropped a weary Angela off at Pellegrino's and headed home.

* * *

"I'm never dating again." A glum Rachel put down her pastry bag and burst into tears.

My mother and I raced to her side, and I held her at arm's length.

"He fooled me too, Rach. He was charming and charismatic and a grade-A con artist."

She sniffed and wiped away a tear. "Well, the show has to go on. Help me with these cakes, would you?" Rachel's hand shook, and her piping bag followed suit. The rose she was making wobbled and collapsed.

I gave my sister another hug, and my mother and I helped her ice the remaining two cakes for Whitney's wedding.

Whit and Ian's wedding day dawned cold and clear. The sun shone like a golden wafer in a deep cerulean-blue sky. Pale rays hit the frost on the grass, each blade glittering with translucent white sparkles. The sharp air felt good in my lungs. I shuffled off to the car with a hazy smile lifting the corners of my tired mouth. It was going to be a beautiful day. A day I wasn't sure was going to happen, but now it was here.

"Are you ready to go to the jewelry store?" I turned to Jesse with a nervous glance. I still wasn't sure if he was purchasing some type of ring for my mother.

He nodded wordlessly. He was jumpy and moved his long limbs with jerky little movements. He settled into the station wagon passenger seat and blinked enough times to dry out his eyes.

I texted Doug

Where are you?

He returned his answer a few seconds later

Just landed at airport. Taxiing in.

"Are you sure you're ready to get engaged?"

Jesse crossed his beefy arms. "Yes. It's now or no time. I need to make an honest woman out of her."

I gunned the engine, and minutes later we pulled up to Fournier's Jewelry Store. Mr. Fournier was carefully removing the tasteful Halloween decorations of gossamer cobwebs and pumpkin brooches from the display window and installing items more befitting for December than November; he was clearly a subscriber to Christmas creep. He swapped chunky enamel fall-leaf pins for delicate diamond snowflake earrings, and amber and citrine necklaces for ruby rings and emerald bracelets.

He left his window display to greet me and take up his station behind the glass counter. "Hello, Mallory."

"Mr. Fournier. I couldn't help but wonder what happened with the emerald and diamond band Whitney brought in."

"Confirmed stolen," Mr. Fournier said crisply, folding his hands with a satisfied motion. "I've been informed it was reunited with its original owner in Tuscaloosa, Alabama."

"And how did it get stolen?" I was afraid I knew the answer.

Lois and Charity's murders might be solved, but Vanessa Scanlon's murder was no closer to resolution.

"The owner was here in Port Quincy in nineteen ninety-four for a funeral. She dined in the Senator dining room and checked her coat and believed the ring slipped off in her glove, which remained in her pocket. Or she thought maybe she left it on the hotel dresser. Because she couldn't be sure, the Senator was off the hook. But she filed a police report anyway."

Vanessa had been in charge of managing housekeeping. Her position gave her ample opportunities to steal jewelry from guests.

Jesse dithered next to me, turning his poor hat around and around in his hand. I snapped myself back from my thoughts.

"Mr. Fournier, my friend Jesse here is looking for an engagement ring."

Jesse blushed red and nodded, suddenly struck mute.

Mr. Fournier smiled and rubbed his hands together. He was eager to help Jesse find the right piece.

"And what do you think she would like? Something elegant, like a solitaire?" He bent down to remove a display of simple, sparkly rings, but Jesse found his voice.

"Oh, no, those are much too plain for her. She has a lot of pizzazz. She's bold and original and creative." His eyes took on a dreamy cast, and his wide mouth lilted up in a small smile.

Mom was bold and original and creative, especially with her designs. I felt a sickening clench in my stomach. He wouldn't really try to woo Mom right out from under Doug's nose, would he?

"These have a lot of flair." Fournier selected a different tray, with antique rings arrayed on a bed of gray velvet. "All from the art deco era, estate pieces. They're one of a kind. Can you picture her in any of these? They're very daring, and nontraditional."

Jesse swept his designer's eye over the display and pointed decisively to a large cluster ring of rubies and pearls. "That one. She looks killer in red."

The ring was gorgeous, heavy, and vibrant, but it wasn't anything my mom would ever wear. My spirits lifted marginally.

Mr. Fournier rang Jesse up, and I waited a minute in the store as he headed to the station wagon.

"One more thing, Mr. Fournier. Did you ever sell an amethyst and diamond necklace, one that presents as an iris touched by snow?"

Fournier's face lit up. "No, but I know the piece exactly. Angela had one just like it, and she'd wear it for big events. It was striking, especially on her. You know she loves to travel," he gushed. "I believe she got it in Thailand. Amethyst is her birthstone, for February. She's an Aquarius."

A niggling thought tickled my brain, but I pushed it away.

"Are you sure *Angela* wore the necklace, not Vanessa? Could Porter Scanlon have gotten her something similar?"

"Oh, no." Fournier shook his head. "I'd bet my life on it. That necklace is Angela's. You don't forget a piece like that. It's one of a kind. Though, come to think of it, she hasn't worn it in years." I left the store pondering what it all meant and hightailed it home. I had a wedding to put on in six hours, and I'd need every minute from now until then.

Jesse was a jangling ball of nerves as we pulled into the driveway.

"When are you going to propose to your mystery lady?"

He glanced at his large nautical watch. "Hopefully within the next hour."

My heart sank. It was just me, Rachel, Mom, three culinary students from our class this fall who we'd hired to help us cook for the wedding, and the wait staff. Was Jesse's mystery woman among them, or was it Mom?

And where in the heck is Doug?

There was no sign of a rental car, and I feared he hadn't arrived.

"Good luck," I muttered to Jesse as we parted ways in the hall.

He disappeared into the library, and when I peeked in a few minutes later, he was pacing around and practicing a speech.

Delilah wheeled up the hallway and dogged my steps.

"Um, what brings you here today?" I tried to sound polite.

"My son is here," she bristled. "I'm not sure why, as it's Saturday, and his contract with you is complete. But he said he had to do something important, and as soon as he's done, we'll be out of your hair."

The doorbell chimed, and I hurried down the hall to open the door.

"It's ready, just in the nick of time." Bev bustled into the foyer with Whitney's voluminous dress in tow, battened down within its garment bag.

"It's great you were able to pull this off," I gushed to the seamstress. "I'll just hang this upstairs." I turned to go just as my mother and Rachel hustled down the hall from the kitchen to see who had arrived.

Jesse burst out of the library and made a beeline for my mother. She hadn't seen him yet and moved to chat with Bev and Rachel.

"Oh no, oh no, oh no," I muttered as he reached into his pocket for the ring.

The doorbell rang again, but the newest guest didn't wait.

Jesse bent one long leg and touched his knee to the ground. My mother's face formed a tiny o.

"Get away from my wife!" Doug burst in the front door and made a run for Jesse. My stepfather isn't tall, but he managed to tackle all six-foot-eight inches of Jesse with a loud oomph.

"Get off of me. Are you crazy?" Jesse stood and jumped back from Doug. The velvet jewelry box bounced out of his hand and down the hall.

"You were about to abscond with *my* wife. Unhand her."

Rachel started to laugh at Doug's chivalrous speech, but I wasn't laughing. Neither was Delilah, who zipped down the hall on her scooter toward the commotion.

"Jesse! What are you doing?" She leaned her

cane over and used the claw attachment to snatch up the ring box.

"Give that back, Mother." Jesse seized the ring out of his mother's extended grasp and, panting, ran back to my mother.

Doug moaned on the ground after being tackled, and my mother moved over to tend to him.

"That was so brave. You're the love of my life, Douglas Shepard."

"Help me up, please. I think I popped my back out."

Jesse resumed his kneeling stance and whipped the top of the box off and presented it to a blushing, gushing Bev.

"Beverly, darling, you are the sun to my moon. The yin to my yang. Would you do me the honor of becoming my wife?"

"Yes!" The seamstress squealed as Jesse stood and clasped her tight, and Delilah's screams could be heard echoing around Thistle Park.

"No! You can't get married! What about me?" Her hoop earrings shook and her bandana slid down over her eyes. She clawed at the cloth with her fingers and wailed in a maudlin caterwaul louder than Whiskey and Soda when they heard me open a can of tuna.

"Mother," Jesse puffed out his chest and placed his arm protectively around Bev, "I'm moving out. It's high time I got my own life." His eyes flickered sideways to my mother, who was settling Doug onto the bottom stair. "This is something I should have done a long time ago."

Rachel and I left them in the hall and hurried up the stairs to hang up Whitney's dress.

* * *

For the next four hours, we worked at Mach speed to transform the newly completed B and B into a scene of autumn splendor for Whitney and Ian. We spread dark espresso tablecloths on the long banquet tables in the back hall and topped them with plum and milk-chocolate overlays. Lucy's team arrived with the flowers, and we helped them create wavy lines of lush mums in copper, dark wicker, and brass pots marching down each table. Nestled among the blooms were fat and squat pillar candles in varied shades of brown. We positioned Penelope's savory chocolates in their gold boxes at each place setting among the brown toile china and Fiestaware.

Whitney's wedding decorations looked lovely against the furniture and décor my mother had chosen. She had done a masterful, if expensive, job. It was cozy and mostly historically accurate, but also warm, rich, inviting, and livable. It was a home for fancy weddings, and a place where guests could cozy up with a book.

Our three friends from our cooking class put the final touches on the meal we'd envisioned back at the beginning of October, and Rachel and I bustled around the kitchen, making sure the lamb was done just right.

Helene's contractors finished painting over the black X on the mural in the parlor just in time. Jesse painted fluffy white clouds on a periwinkle-blue background and the contractors moved quickly to break down their scaffolding.

"She's all finished." A tear beaded up in Jesse's eye. "This was a helluva job, but we pulled it off."

I grinned. "And now that Hunter has been apprehended, I'll actually get my money back to pay you."

Rachel carefully applied makeup to Whitney's face, concealing the red the roller coaster of emotions had brought out. She had performed the same careful ritual this morning, blending and wiping away the blotches and puffiness due to stress and tears over Hunter. My sister was a true artist, whether the medium was icing or makeup.

"How do I look?" Whitney twirled around in front of the full-length mirror in the purple bedroom. The deep-satin gown had been transformed by Bev into a full yet sleek dream of a dress, the champagne satin rich and mellow against Whitney's skin. The brown sash tied it all together with the chocolate theme, and she had replaced the amethyst necklace with a pretty coffee-colored quartz pendant. I left her with her father in the hallway, as they enjoyed a moment together.

I found my mother, Rachel, and Doug gathered at the other end of the hall.

"We did it!" my mother whispered.

We smushed in a group hug, and I thought about how much I loved my family. We'd made order out of chaos, and it all came together at the end. I beamed and thought of Whitney, Porter, and Angela as I looked over my shoulder. They were getting pictures before Whitney walked down the staircase to meet Ian on the landing.

Whitney broke away from her father right before she descended.

"Thank you," she whispered.

"Go get 'em."

She linked arms with a frail but buoyant Porter and started her march as the accompanist struck up. She clasped a bouquet of mums and rust-colored freesia, tiger lilies, and maroon foxgloves. Angela's eyes swept over her niece's bridal splendor, and she clasped a hand over her mouth, overcome with emotion.

"Sweetie, you look just radiant."

The ceremony went off without a hitch. Becca descended the stairs on the arm of Keith, a little unsteady but resplendent in her café-au-lait satin gown.

She sent me a little smile, which I found myself returning.

Fiona, Maisie, and Bruce appeared at the top of the stairs, a small champagne satin pillow tied between them like a yoke. Rachel lifted a slender silver dog whistle to her lips to summon the dogs down the stairs and to the landing. The doggie's ears pricked up, and they bounded down with exuberant barks, past the couple on the landing, and headed for the guests, yipping and cavorting.

"Oh no!" Whitney's hands flew to her mouth in horror as the pillow between the dogs came untied and skittered under a guest's chair.

"Somebody get the rings!" Ian started to make his way from the landing.

Bruce emerged from beneath the chair with the

pillow in his mouth. Maisie grabbed a corner, and the two executed a short game of puppy tug-of-war as guests lunged for the scamps. Fiona gamboled around them in a blurry, furry circle.

"Bruce, no!" I moved toward the little white Westie as he tore the rings from the pillow and made a run for it.

"Here, Bruce, here, sweetie!" Whitney crouched down in her billowing gown on the landing and pulled a tiny dog treat from her pocket. Bruce scampered up the stairs and dropped the rings, still tied in their chocolate satin ribbon, at his mistress' feet and accepted the treat.

"Thank goodness," I muttered under my breath, as the ceremony proceeded.

Marcus Callender led Ian and Whitney through their vows, and in no time, they were pronounced man and wife. The party began in earnest, and Whitney's guests danced the night away in the front hall.

Rachel, my mother, and I scurried around in the background, putting out small fires and making sure the first wedding at Thistle Park ran smoothly. I finally caught a break near ten and checked out the guest book. Next to it was an iPad playing a slideshow of Ian and Whitney's childhood photos on a continuous loop. There were silly photos of Whitney dressed up for Halloween with her friends when she was about Summer's age, and several Christmas gatherings around a tree. My eyes caught on one photo, and I swiped my finger to reverse the slideshow.

There was Angela, standing with Whitney in a professional kitchen. Whitney couldn't have been more than three. She was perched on a stool to reach the height of the stainless-steel counter. She was grinning at her aunt and stirring something in a bowl. Angela wore white chef's garb, including a poufy, mushroom-top cap. I drew in my breath and glanced around to make sure no one had viewed my reaction.

I let the slideshow commence and stopped it again at the last picture. It was of Whitney's christening, when she was a tiny, bouncing baby. Her mother, Vanessa, and her father, Porter, cradled their daughter in their arms at the front of the Presbyterian Church. The little nuclear family was flanked on either side by aunts Lois and Angela. A bit of purple and white gleamed at Angela's throat, peeking out from behind her red blouse like a little plum hummingbird. It was the amethyst pendant.

My veins turned to ice, and I swiveled around, looking for the restaurant owner. I spotted her in the hallway, conversing with an exhausted Porter, her hand on her brother's shoulder.

He hasn't realized it. Vanessa had so much jewelry, Porter hadn't known. *Beware the Aquarian.* Purple was Vanessa's signature color, and she loved amethyst. But it was also Angela's birthstone.

"Son of a gun."

Chapter Twenty-three

"What a magnificent reception. I knew I made the right decision recommending Whitney marry here rather than at the Senator Hotel." Angela clasped my hand in hers and gazed into my eyes intently.

"It's been a long day." I took a step back from her and pasted on a nervous smile. "But a fantastic one. I'm so happy for Whitney."

A horn honked in front of the house, and the last few guests rushed out onto the porch to watch Whitney and Ian depart. Angela and I moved to the flung-open front doors in time to see Ian give Whitney a dramatic kiss on the front walkway.

"Whoop!" The guests clapped and cheered, and Whitney threw her bouquet jubilantly behind her. Becca, no doubt still feeling out of sorts from her attack, made a feeble attempt to catch it and missed, but my sister executed a graceful dive and popped up standing, holding the bouquet triumphantly.

Ian held the door open for his bride in the old-fashioned limousine, and she climbed in, laughing as she tried to squeeze the yards of champagne satin into the small bucket seat. Ian took his place behind the wheel, and they jaunted off into the crisp November night, to the chorus and call of the guests.

People began leaving, and I retreated to the hall with Angela, rubbing the goose bumps on my arms. Rachel stood outside, talking to my mom.

"It's a shame the amethyst seems to have, er, passed from Bruce by the time he was found." I carefully studied Angela, and her hawkish eyes flinched.

"It is a shame. If you'll excuse me." *I'm running out of time.* She wheeled around, and I caught her wrist.

"I saw the picture of you wearing the amethyst. It was yours, not Vanessa's."

"So? That is irrelevant." But a flicker of concern danced across her eyes and furrowed her brow.

"I read the police report from Garrett. It was found in Vanessa's pocket, with the chain broken. As if she'd pulled it off in a struggle." *A struggle overheard by five-year-old Whitney.*

"Vanessa Scanlon was a dirty jewel thief." Angela drew herself up to her full, prodigious height. "She must have stolen it from me. I don't have to stay here and listen to this."

Garrett spotted me from across the room. His eyes went wide, and he gave me the barest of nods.

"I think you should hear what I have to say. Some of the jewels and money stolen from the Senator were taken from the dining room. That was your purview, as head cook, not Vanessa's in housekeeping. You worked together, didn't you?"

Angela edged closer to the copse of trees flanking the house, as if measuring the distance and calculating whether to break out in a run.

"Vanessa was a flake and a child," Angela stammered. "She wanted to run off with that silly painter Eugene, and she wouldn't give me my cut from our final heist. I threatened to tell my brother, Porter, about the affair, but Vanessa didn't care. Lois was already going to inform Porter and had tried to blackmail her. I needed that money to get out from under my family's thumb at the hotel and open my own restaurant." Her eyes were narrow slits, and her neck muscles twanged. "How did you figure it out?"

"You stopped wearing white the day you murdered Vanessa. You never cooked in your chef garb again, right? You're always so exquisitely dressed, even when you taught our cooking class. But Whitney saw you that day. You wore white."

She laughed, and a chill slid down my vertebrae. "I stopped cooking in white because it was impractical. It shows every stain. Besides, no one will ever believe you." She pulled a tiny pistol out of her purse and ground the tip between my ribs.

I gasped and tried to pull away, but she was taller and stronger and wrapped her arm around my middle.

"Keep walking." We were edging closer and closer to the woods.

"You stole Bruce, didn't you?"

"Yes. I had to pick through that mutt's excrement for three days until I found the amethyst, which I should have looked for a lot more thoroughly when I murdered Vanessa. It's at the bottom of the

Monongahela now. A pity. I did love it. And I had to knock out Becca. I didn't expect anyone to be home. It's a shame she woke up. I took her ring to make it look like a robbery. I took the letters as well, to try to figure out what ridiculous person was claiming Eugene didn't kill Vanessa."

I gasped. "You broke into Garrett's office to see what kind of a defense he'd built all those years ago for Eugene! They thought a professional picked the locks, and you were a professional thief."

Angela nodded, and the moon glinted off her silver watch. "I tore up Whitney's room as well." She winced at this admission. "I didn't want to hurt my niece, but I couldn't have her poking around in Port Quincy, looking into her mother's death. I hoped she'd cancel the wedding and go back to Baltimore. And now you're next."

A snap sounded in the woods behind me, and I bit Angela's wrist as hard as I could.

"Arrgh!" Angela threw me off of her and booked it for her car, shucking her high heels along the way. Her long legs covered the ground quickly. She pressed her key fob and threw herself behind the wheel of her Audi. It sprang to life, and she peeled out of the driveway.

"She's getting away!" I gasped for breath and motioned for Garrett to follow me. He caught up to me and grabbed my hand, pulling me along. I ran so hard I tasted blood at the back of my throat.

"Arf! Arf!" Maisie ran after us, yapping and barking, thinking it was a game.

We jumped into the Butterscotch Monster, and Garrett turned around. "Oh no, Maisie, we don't have time."

I ignored him and pulled out with the dog barking her head off in the backseat and caught up with Angela at a breakneck speed. She turned down side roads with a squeal of her tires, trying to shake me, and I followed, the old Volvo gamely keeping up.

Finally we reached the water. Angela pulled her car up next to the dock astride the Monongahela and hesitated beside her door.

"Just give it up," Garrett counseled out the window. He slowly approached her and spoke in a calm voice. "It's no use, Angela."

"I'm not sticking around to be hauled in after all these years." A crazy light danced in Angela's eyes, and she stood on the dock, panting in her panty hose.

A horn sounded, and a disembodied voice echoed over the water.

"All aboard!" The last ferry crossing the river was pulling away. Angela raised the small silver pistol as she backed up the ramp.

"No!" Garrett hid me behind him, and her shot went wide.

"Perfect timing!" Angela sneered and leaped onto the boat as they pulled up the gangplank.

"She's getting away," I moaned, as Garrett pulled me to my feet.

A blur of blinding white leaped from the dock and attached itself to Angela's heel.

"Maisie!"

The little Westie hung onto Angela with the ferocity of a wolf.

"Stop! You're hurting me!" Angela looked at her leg and the dog attached and fervently kicked her heel. A spot of blood appeared on her ankle, like a burst maraschino cherry, and trickled down her foot. Angela yelped and fell into the drink.

The wail of a police car pierced the air. Faith jumped out of the passenger side and ran to the edge of the dock. She leaned over and fished out the Westie, but let Angela stew in the water for a bit.

"Help me! I can't swim!" She bobbed up and down for a moment until Truman hauled her out. She kneeled in a wet, bleeding, howling mess on the dock while passengers on the ferry snapped photos of the mêlée with their smartphones.

"All's well that ends well."

Chapter Twenty-four

Three weeks later, I met Whitney at the Senator Hotel for brunch. She had returned from her honeymoon in Mexico and appeared sun-kissed and relaxed.

"I'm still shaken up about Aunt Angela." She set down her spoon and peered out the window at the Monongahela, only a few blocks from where it all went down. "I've learned that my mother was no saint, but Angela had no right to take her from me."

"But at least now you'll have your father's health."

Porter was making a quick recovery, now that the arsenic Angela had been poisoning him with had been found in her house. Her poor husband had mysteriously died after a long, unsolvable illness much like Porter's and was going to be exhumed to find out if she'd poisoned him as well.

"I'll miss the Westies." I wouldn't have minded fostering the pooches indefinitely, and I'd enjoyed keeping them while Whit and Ian were on their honeymoon. Soda the kitten had delighted in their stay as well, although Whiskey the calico was glad to see them go.

"I have a surprise for you." Whit's eyes twinkled. "Ian and I are moving to Port Quincy! Life is too short, and we want to be around Dad. Ian is going to take over Hunter's position at the Senator managing security, and I'll be taking over Lois's tasks in HR."

I beamed at my friend. "I'm glad you're coming home, Whit." And I was glad to be home, too. I'd just returned from a three-day wedding venue conference and hadn't been back to Thistle Park. I'd received a text while at lunch with Whitney that my mother's final surprise was ready. I hurried back and met Rachel in the hall, and we waited for my mother.

"Surprise!" Mom led Rachel and me up to the third floor and dramatically threw open the door. The space had been transformed to the beautiful, warm, tropical design she'd first presented for the first floor.

"How did you do this?" I threw my arms around my mother, and Rachel ran from room to room, exclaiming over the repurposed space. It was a gorgeous apartment, cozy and airy and bright and relaxing. Whimsically patterned furniture in a rainbow of sherbet colors was scattered about. The walls were awash in soft shades of yellow and cheerful hues of turquoise. Lush, verdant flowers and plants filled the windowsills. Antique glass ornaments from around Thistle Park sparkled on shelves. Thoughtful pictures of my trips to visit my family in Florida nestled among vintage framed postcards from the Gulf of Mexico and the Caribbean. It would be a welcome haven, separate from the business part of the house. My mother had listened and taken to heart my exclamation that her original design would be the perfect thing for the third floor.

"I did this while you went to the wedding expo. I just want you girls to be happy, honey."

We walked from room to room in awe.

"I have another announcement." She cleared her throat and crossed the room to clasp Doug's hand. The two wore matching electric-blue ensembles today with Mom in her sweater set and Doug in his polo shirt.

"We're moving back to Pennsylvania! We've decided to unretire and claim Port Quincy as our home."

Rachel and I looked at each other and beamed.

"We knew it. We knew you'd caught the decorating bug again and wanted to stay." The four of us spent the day together in the newly refurbished apartment and counted our good fortunes. It was wonderful to be surrounded by my family.

The next day Garrett and I pulled up in front of the Presbyterian Church right before our official first date. We parked behind an old beat-up white pickup truck and swung open the heavy doors to the church. The smell of fresh paint wafted down the aisle.

Eugene put down his paintbrush and gave me a bone-crushing hug, then one for Garrett.

"My sister saved my pickup for me for ten years. Can you believe it?" His eyes crinkled at the corners, and we all stepped back from the mural. He was painting the scene with the lambs anew, but it looked different from before. In this mural there was a stormy sky on the left, and the lambs were led to safety and the sunshine and peace that filled the other end of the frame.

"I can't wait for you to come to Thistle Park and finish the mural there," I smiled.

"Me too." Eugene touched up the golden rays of the sun in the mural. "It feels good to let the light shine."

Recipes

CHINESE FIVE-SPICE APPLE TARTS

Crust

  1½ cups flour
  2 teaspoons sugar
  1 teaspoon salt
  1½ sticks butter cut into small pieces
  ⅛ cup ice water

Preheat oven to 450 degrees. Combine flour, salt, and sugar in a bowl. Mix in butter pieces with your fingers until the mixture resembles coarse sand. Add ice water. Form dough into a ball. Wrap in plastic and refrigerate for half an hour. Roll the dough out on a floured surface, adding flour if necessary. Use a small plate to cut out 12 tart circles. Place each circle in an individual section of a greased muffin tin and trim edges.

Filling

　　5 apples, peeled, cored, and diced
　　1 cup brown sugar
　　4 tablespoons flour
　　1 tablespoon Chinese five-spice powder
　　1 stick of butter, cut into 12 small pats

Mix brown sugar, flour, and Chinese five-spice powder together in a bowl. Mix in apple pieces. Spoon mixture into tart shells in muffin tin. Dot each tart with a pat of butter.

Bake for 25 minutes or until tart shells are golden and apples are soft.

PUMPKIN RUM CAKE

　　1½ cups granulated sugar
　　1 cup brown sugar
　　2 sticks butter
　　3 eggs
　　2 cups pumpkin
　　3 cups flour
　　2 teaspoons baking soda
　　1½ teaspoons cinnamon
　　1 teaspoon nutmeg
　　1 teaspoon ginger
　　¾ teaspoon salt
　　½ teaspoon ground cloves
　　½ teaspoon allspice

Preheat oven to 350 degrees. Beat granulated sugar, brown sugar, and butter in a bowl. Add eggs and beat well. Add pumpkin and beat well. Combine flour, baking soda, cinnamon, nutmeg, ginger, salt, cloves, and allspice in a separate bowl. Slowly add flour mixture to pumpkin mixture, mixing well. Bake mixture in greased Bundt pan for approximately 65 to 70 minutes, or until a toothpick inserted into the cake comes out clean. Cool for 10 minutes and invert cake.

Rum Glaze
   1 stick butter
   ¾ cup sugar
   3 tablespoons water
   ¼ cup rum

Combine butter, sugar, and water in a small pan. Bring to a boil. Remove from heat. Stir in rum. Poke holes in top of cake. Pour rum glaze on top of cake.

FLOURLESS RED VELVET TORTE

   Cocoa for dusting
   24 ounces semisweet chocolate chips
   3 sticks butter
   12 eggs
   1 cup sugar
   1 tablespoon red food coloring
   1 teaspoon vanilla extract
   ½ teaspoon salt
   Raspberries to decorate

Preheat oven to 350 degrees. Grease 2 round cake pans. Dust pans with cocoa powder. Melt chocolate chips and butter together in a double boiler and stir until smooth. Beat eggs, sugar, vanilla, food coloring, and salt together until mixture is frothy, for approximately 5 to 10 minutes. Fold chocolate mixture into egg mixture. Pour batter into cake pans. Bake for approximately 50 to 60 minutes or until a knife or toothpick inserted in the middle comes out almost clean. Cool completely on a rack. Remove from pan, and spread cream-cheese frosting between each layer. Spread a layer of frosting on top, and top with raspberries.

Cream-Cheese Frosting
    1 stick butter, softened
    8 ounces cream cheese
    3 cups confectioner's sugar
    2 teaspoons vanilla extract

Beat butter and cream cheese together. Add confectioner's sugar and vanilla, and beat until smooth.

MELLOW COCOA CAYENNE TRUFFLES

    ¾ cup heavy cream
    1½ teaspoons cinnamon
    ½ teaspoon cayenne pepper
    12 ounces semisweet chocolate chips
    1 teaspoon almond extract
    Cocoa and red pepper flakes for rolling

Heat the cream, cinnamon, and cayenne pepper in a saucepan until simmering. Remove from heat. Add chocolate chips and almond extract to cream mixture, and stir until melted and combined. Chill for at least an hour. Scoop out truffle balls with a teaspoon or a melon baller. Roll into balls and coat with cocoa and red pepper flakes. Makes approximately 30 truffles.

SALTED CARAMEL MARTINI

2 ounces caramel vodka
1 ounce Irish cream
1 ounce half and half
Sea salt for martini glass
Cocoa for dusting

Dip martini glass in water, then a plate of sea salt to salt the rim. Combine vodka, Irish cream, and half and half. Shake. Pour into a martini glass over ice. Dust with cocoa.

Please turn the page for an exciting sneak peek of
Stephanie Blackmoore's next
Wedding Planner mystery

MURDER BORROWED, MURDER BLUE

coming soon wherever print and e-books are sold!

Chapter One

"The groundhog didn't see his shadow!" My sister, Rachel, turned from the television with a look of anguish marring her good looks. I would've expected her to be upset if the furry little guy *had* seen his shadow.

"What's the problem? I could do with an early spring." We were deep into the snowy season, and I was ready to take a break from burrowing under blankets each night and donning winter boots each day. I loved an excuse to curl up next to the fire with a good book and a cup of hot cocoa, but I'd be thrilled when warmer weather arrived.

"Dakota wants a winter-themed wedding. We need the snow to stick around." Rachel pulled back the heavy gray velvet drapes and peered outside, her eyes anxiously sweeping the grounds.

"I don't think we have anything to worry about," I soothed, joining her at the window. "Everyone knows that groundhog stuff isn't reliable."

Outside was a veritable winter wonderland. A

lacy lattice of intricate, icy crystals spread across the library window like a delicate doily. Beyond the glass, the evergreen trees seemed to groan with the weight of a thick blanket of snow straining each branch. Tracks from deer and raccoons were the only patterns etched upon the smooth expanse of white ground. The newly risen sun reflected off the snow with slicing, blinding rays. It was a beautiful, cold, clear February day.

"I just want it to be perfect." My sister spun around and aimed the remote at the television. She turned off the footage of Punxsutawney Phil and paced the room. I was as anxious as her, but didn't want to show it. The crew for the celebrity wedding reality show *I Do* was going to arrive in minutes, and I wanted to show off my B and B, Thistle Park, at its very best.

We were hosting the wedding of actress Dakota Craig, recently anointed America's newest sweetheart. Dakota had fallen on hard times after starring in a teen soap opera, and had risen, phoenix-from-the-ashes style this past year with a string of acclaimed film roles. Everyone loved a comeback kid, and Dakota was it. She was also a humble, generous woman, if the emails and phone calls we'd been exchanging these last few months to plan her wedding from afar were any indication.

Her fiancé, Beau Wright, was the reigning king of country music. I'd always thought of him as something of a lothario, and there had been a lot of speculation about his hurried engagement to Dakota. But he'd been gracious and polite in the few dealings we'd had planning his nuptials. I couldn't say the same for Dakota's mother Roxanne, who behaved like a stage mother on steroids.

My cell phone buzzed in my pocket.

"Is it the crew? They're officially late." Rachel crowded next to me to peer at the screen. I stifled a groan.

"It's Helene again." Helene Pierce was once almost my mother-in-law, until I'd called off the wedding to her son. I counted my lucky stars nearly every day for that decision.

"How many times has she texted this morning?" Rachel arched a perfectly plucked brow.

"This is the fifth. Not counting the three phone calls and two emails from her. All before the sun came up. I haven't even had my second cup of coffee." I typed back a hasty but professional reply to her query and hit send. I jammed my cell back into my dress pocket. I promised myself to take a sterner line with my former arch-nemesis turned client. "She knows the crew of *I Do* is arriving today. She's trying to rattle me."

And it was working.

I wondered for the thousandth time what I'd been thinking when I agreed to throw a modern day debutante ball, free of charge, for the posh Dunlap Women's Academy, at the behest of Hurricane Helene. The Winter Ball was to go off on the eve of Dakota's Valentine's Day wedding. It would be an almost impossibly tight turnaround, not one I'd ever agree to in saner moments. But I had needed a mammoth favor, and Helene had granted my wish as the worst incarnation of a fairy godmother a girl could have. And now she'd called in her chips. I was at her constant beck and call.

"Did we take on too much?" I turned to Rachel in a moment of panic. The start of a headache began to spread between my eyes. "How will we finish planning Dakota's wedding, film for *I Do*, and pull off the Winter Ball, all with Helene underfoot?"

Rachel waved her hand and dismissed my worries, but her keen green eyes told a different story. "You pulled off Whitney and Ian's wedding in a month, all while renovating the house. We've held half a dozen weddings since. You could do this in your sleep."

I took a steadying breath and slowly let it out. "I'd just feel better if the Winter Ball plans were finalized. Helene is purposely making things difficult. I wish there were a little more time between each event."

Rachel snorted. "You didn't really have a choice. Let's just make lemon slushies out of the crummy lemons we've been given."

My sister was right. And being featured on a popular reality show was just what we needed to advertise our B and B and wedding planning business. Rachel and I had spent the last two weeks with a bowl of popcorn between us, watching every previous episode of *I Do*. We were nervous about appearing on television and wanted everything to go off without a hitch. The show was edited to highlight drama between the wedding planners, venue owners, celebrity couples, and the host of the show, Adrienne Larson. But I was determined for the Thistle Park

B and B to come across in a good light, with minimal shenanigans.

"Besides," Rachel continued, bringing me back to the present, "We have an unlimited budget for this wedding. It's going to be spectacular." Her eyes gleamed with Gatsby-esque plans for Dakota and Beau's big day.

"We have to take into account their personal style, Rach," I reminded my sister. "Dakota isn't a fan of bling and razzle-dazzle, as far as I can tell." The bride's selections had been tasteful, restrained, and seemed to value sentimentality over opulence. Dakota's measured choices hadn't stopped Rachel from living vicariously through her, and she'd suggested some over-the-top details that Dakota had politely declined. Roxanne, Dakota's mother, was all too willing to advocate for a flashy wedding. I'd logged some tense time already during conference calls with the bride and her mother. I'd deftly deferred to Dakota, and Roxanne had eventually come around.

"Ooh!" Rachel whipped around from the window, her wavy, honey-kissed tresses fanning out behind her. "I see a van coming down the driveway."

The two of us raced from the library to the front hall and stationed ourselves expectantly at the front door. I smoothed down the wine-colored merino dress I'd donned for the occasion and tucked an errant curl behind my ear. Rachel shimmied the skirt of her spangly navy shift down a few inches and fluffed out her hair.

"This is it," I whispered to my sister.

"Our chance to put the B and B on the map!" We practically wriggled with excitement and barely contained ourselves from flinging open the heavy front door until the merry peal of the bell sounded.

"Mallory and Rachel, wonderful to finally meet you." The woman perched before us on the front porch was dressed in icy blue finery. She wore an exquisitely tailored Alexander McQueen coatdress in a vivid periwinkle. It probably cost more than my whole wardrobe put together. Lozenge-sized aquamarines graced her earlobes. Her tiny feet were ensconced in creamy suede, high-heeled boots. I stared at them with incredulous eyes. I couldn't figure out how she'd made it from the production team's van and up the front walk without a single drop of moisture falling on the buttery leather. Her shining, perfect cap of flaxen hair was protected under a jaunty fawn-colored cloche hat. She swept into the hallway and removed white angora gloves. She gave my hand a firm shake, with cold hands.

"You must be Adrienne. Welcome to Thistle Park." I ushered the host of *I Do* into the front hall, where Rachel stared at her designer outfit with eyes agog. Adrienne Larson had impeccable taste, an artist's eye, and a will of steel. She'd earned the moniker of Ice Queen through subtly vicious battles with wedding planners and celebrity brides on *I Do*. She was a formidable figure, and not one I wanted to tangle with anytime soon. I'd vowed to outmaneuver her overbearing suggestions about Dakota's wedding.

The rest of the crew filed in, and introductions were exchanged. The producer and cameramen didn't seem ruffled by Adrienne's presence, and after a few minutes, I relaxed. We gathered in the parlor before a roaring fire and chatted with the crew over croissants, fruit, and coffee. We were about to start a tour of the house when a familiar black Accord advanced up the driveway.

"Garrett's here," I mused to Rachel. "I wonder what's up?" I eagerly threw open the door before Garrett had a chance to ring the bell.

"What a lovely surprise." I tilted my head back to receive a brief kiss and grinned up at my boyfriend.

"I can't stay long. I'm dropping Summer off at school." Garrett's usually warm voice was tense and distant. I took a step back but held onto the lapel of his black wool overcoat.

"Is everything all right?" I tried to tamp down the edge in my voice.

"I just realized something. Last night, I watched an episode of *I Do*." His eyes were pained.

I laughed and let go of his coat, the tension broken. "Totally not your style, but I appreciate you checking in to see what I'm up against this month."

A wave of panic seemed to wash over Garrett. My laughter died in my throat.

"I should have watched it sooner. Mallory—"

"The TV crew is here. I saw their van." Garrett's thirteen-year-old daughter Summer peeked her head around the massive front door. Her heart shaped face was surrounded by a cheery red ski hat. Her hazel eyes were eager and bright.

"Summer, I told you to stay in the car." Garrett's voice was clipped and strange. I stared between him and his daughter, confused. She scooted around the open door and stood in the front hall, seeming to search for someone.

A plate crashed in the parlor.

Summer ran to Adrienne and almost knocked her over from the force of her embrace. Adrienne hugged Summer back with impossible fierceness and slowly raised her tear-stained eyes. They were heavy with a mixture of sadness and elation.

"Mom! You came back!"